PERFEKT BALANCE

THE ÆRE SAGA: BOOK THREE

S.T. BENDE

To my three boys—may your kind hearts continue to brighten every realm you touch. Jeg elsker deg.

"Awake, dear heart, awake. Thou hast slept well.
Awake."

-Prospero, *The Tempest*

"I'LL SHOW YOU MINE if you show me yours." Forse Styrke lifted one corner of his mouth in a lazy smile. My heart thudded before tumbling headfirst into a familiar abyss.

"It doesn't work like that, and you know it," I reminded him.

Forse shrugged. "Fair's fair."

"And if the God of Justice says it, it must be true."

Forse just winked.

"Are you going to let me do this or not? Odin knows I need the practice." I planted my hands on my hips and blinked at my longtime crush and longer-time friend. It didn't take him long to break.

"All right, all right." Forse held up his hands. "The big, blue deal-closers win."

I batted my eyelashes with a smile.

Forse reached up and brushed my temple with the

back of one finger. A wave of goose bumps broke out across my neck as I leaned into the touch. Seconds after his knuckles grazed my cheek, Forse pulled his hand back and took a step to the side. "All right, Miss Unifier, give me your best shot."

I pressed my lips together and extinguished the feeling of disappointment. Forse and I had danced this dance for a few months—longer, if I counted the time before I was stuck in the coma. Forse liked me…or I thought he did, but he pulled back every time we started to get close. And even though Odin had gifted me with the ability to read feelings, auras, and the occasional mind, I couldn't get a grasp on *why* Forse wouldn't let himself fall for me. My normally intuitive brain picked up on an inkling of fear flashing from somewhere in Forse's emotional center, but I couldn't for the life of me determine its source.

The God of Justice was proving to be one irritating wall of hard-headedness. And my supposed *gift* was completely letting me down.

"Elsa?" Forse waved his hand, and I snapped back to the present.

"Mmm?" A gust of wind pulled my attention to the redwood grove outside the window of my tiny house. Another storm was blowing in—the second one this month, and the sixth since December. A March shower in Northern California wasn't unusual…but a winter of snowfalls this close to the ocean sure was. *Better keep an eye on that.*

Forse furrowed his brow in concern. "I lost you. Do you still want to practice your energy analysis, or do you need to lie down for a while?"

"I'm good. Let's get started."

"It's only been a few months since you came out of the coma, and you know there can be residual effects. Maybe we should—"

"I'm fine, Forse, I swear. I just got distracted. There's a lot riding on me getting this right, so pretty please stand there and let me practice."

"I would, but—"

"But nothing. You and I both know that if I don't get a grip on this ability soon, the realms will be in serious trouble. Asgard needs a proper Unifier. My mom held the light realms in balance so well, they've kept it together since she died. But that can't last much longer, and I don't even want to think of how powerful the dark worlds will become if I don't make this work."

Forse shook his head. "I still think it's too soon. Fenrir nearly killed you. You—"

I placed my hand on his arm and kept my voice soft. "I've got this."

Forse and I stared at each other for a seemingly endless beat. He was the first to blink. "You'll let me know if you need a break?"

I ran my fingers along the throw that rested on my tan sofa. The soft blue fibers matched my new curtains perfectly. "You have my word. Now let's go over what we've learned since the Norns named me interim

Unifier. Maybe we can avoid repeating some of our earlier, uh, mistakes."

"Like the time you accidentally filled my energy with so much love I very nearly kissed Brynn?" Forse raised one eyebrow, and my cheeks grew hot. That hadn't been an accident. Right after my parents' deaths, the Norns had named me my mom's replacement, and Forse had volunteered to help me practice unifying—bringing opposing factions together. On my first attempt, I'd pushed an overwhelming amount of adoring energy into Forse's love center, thinking it would make him own up to his feelings for me. Brynn had walked in at just the wrong moment and almost reaped the benefit of my misguided work. *Right place, wrong goddess. Lesson learned.*

"Um, yes. Like that." I stared at the recessed lights in my living room, willing the blood to drain from my cheeks. "So we won't try that one again. Just like we won't try to override your consciousness—sorry I ended up making you think you were a fairy."

Forse glared at me.

"And we won't try to mute your sense of self-preservation—seriously, I did not see the whole 'handing over your broadsword and kneeling before my brother' thing coming." I giggled.

Forse glared harder.

"Right." I covered my mouth. "And we definitely won't invoke the guardian spirits from Valhalla. That did not end well."

"Thanks for pulling me out before the inebriated ones tried to decapitate me. Remember, they train during the *daytime*. Off hours, it's one giant mead-fest." Forse folded his arms across his perfectly sculpted chest. His grey T-shirt strained against a set of flexed biceps, and his profile was backlit by the lamp beside the three-quarter-length window, giving him an almost ethereal glow. *Oh dear gods, he is beautiful. So beautiful. It's completely unfair that Odin would—*

"Are you sticking your tongue out at me?" Forse asked.

Oops! I hadn't realized I was licking my lips. Thank Odin Forse was as dense as a forest. "Erm, just giving you a hard time. I promise I won't make those mistakes again. But you'd think with all the research we've done, all the books we've read and the subjects we've interviewed, we'd be closer to understanding *how* my mom did what she did. She made it look so easy. And it's just…not."

"That's the thing about this particular job." Forse shrugged. "Unifying's an intuitive skill. It's not like Tyr's job, where he can look at old war strategies to assess an enemy's weakness, or my job, where I can study the legal systems of the realms to get a handle on how they operate. What you're trying to do is a mystery. All of the subjects we interviewed had no idea how your mom helped them; they just knew that she did. We really don't have much of a choice—it's trial and error or bust here."

"Fair enough. So today we're going to..." I blew air out of my lips in a frustrated stream. "Odin's beard, what haven't we tried? We've been at this for ages."

Forse smiled, pale pink lips curving up to reveal a glimpse at two rows of blinding white teeth. Everything about him was *perfekt*. "Why don't we stick with what you know? You're an epic High Healer; try scanning my energy centers for blocks like you would with a regular healing, and if you find something pull it out. A removed block should make me more open to befriending thine enemy, *ja*?"

"Something like that." I smiled back, trying not to get lost in the beautiful green vortexes of his eyes. "And if that doesn't work, I'll just bang my head against your chest and cry."

Ooh, if I cry, maybe he'll comfort me. Wrap his arms around me and pull me close so I can—

Not helping!

Forse chuckled, oblivious to my inner turmoil. "My chest can take the head-butt," he pointed out. "You crying, on the other hand, might just break me."

My cheeks flamed again. "Okay, here we go. Unifying 101, take nine hundred." I was going to learn how to bring spirits together if it was the last thing I did. Not only was it my Odin-given destiny, at least until I could pass the torch to my brother's mortal girlfriend, Mia, but it was a key function of Asgardian security, therefore vital to the survival of our race and the realms as we knew them. Plus, there was a smidgeon of a chance my using Forse as a practice buddy might just open his heart to the possibility of *finally* dating me. Which, of course, would just be a pleasant side effect of my education, and not at all the reason I was working so hard.

I wasn't *totally* selfish, after all.

"Let's do this," Forse said. He closed his eyes, and I followed suit, drawing a deep breath. I exhaled and pressed my palms toward the ground, expelling all foreign energy from my body. Calling my energy back to me was second nature, and as I expanded my energetic bubble to nudge against Forse's space, I sent a prayer of thanks to my mom for passing on this extremely useful, albeit highly confusing, gift.

"You're in now, aren't you?" Forse sounded uncomfortable.

"What's the matter, Justice? Don't trust me?"

"I trust you. It's just…"

"It's okay; I know it's weird. You can push me out at any time. You know the drill, just intend to eject my energy from your space. Your energy will follow your intention."

"I'm not going to push you out," Forse said. "We've got to be getting close to cracking this."

"It would have been a lot easier if we'd known I got Mom's unifying gene," I whispered. "She could have explained everything to me before Fenrir…well, before."

Forse's energy flickered, and an air of remorse passed through his aura, dimming it a notch. "I'm so sorry we lost your parents."

"It's not your fault. You didn't sic Fenrir on them." I sent a wave of love at him—just enough to be the equivalent of an energetic hug, definitely *not* enough to send him off trying to kiss the first girl who walked by. Again. *Lucky Brynn.*

"Yeah, but—"

"But nothing. They're gone; it's nobody's fault but Fenrir's…well, Fenrir's and *hers*." I forced the image of Fenrir's accomplice out of my head. "And that devil woman fled Asgard the day of the attack, so let's move forward and give Mom a legacy to be proud of."

Forse nodded. I knew it was hard for him to put his worry aside, but he stayed very still and his energy started to calm. "I'm all yours."

Gods, I wish.

"I'm going back in," I declared. "Let's see if I can get it right this time."

Forse nodded again. With the path to his energy centers clear, I began my assessment. *Analyze each location. Identify any blocks. Isolate and remove the barrier.* It seemed simple enough. Odin willing, this approach worked. Between Fenrir's attacks, Hel's abduction of our love goddess, Freya, and this bizarre cold spell in a realm plagued by global warming, I sensed the *perfekt* balance of our realms was starting to tip toward the dark side. If I could just hold it together until my brother got around to marrying his girlfriend, Mia, then under Asgardian law she'd assume the role of Unifier. I had every confidence she'd be brilliant at the job. She had an innate knack for smoothing out emotionally charged situations, and she somehow managed to make my normally uptight brother calm enough to see the big picture. Once Mia could take over as Asgard's Unifier, I'd get to go back to my *other* full-time job, High Healer—a calling I was considerably less bad at.

For all our sakes, I hoped Tyr proposed soon. Like, yesterday, soon.

"Elsa? Are we still doing this?" Forse interrupted my derailed train of thought.

"Yes. Sorry. I'm really distracted today."

Forse chuckled. "Am I that boring on the inside?"

"Quite the opposite. You're positively brilliant on the inside." He was. His entire being was filled with a striking golden light. It was a testament to a life lived with *ære*—honor.

"You flatter me, *hjärtat*. Now get to work."

"Yes, sir." I zeroed in on the glowing light at the base of Forse's spine. Mortals called the pulsing markers along the spine chakras, but Asgardians knew them as energy centers. These tiny orbs contained a blueprint of Forse's past, and predicted the choices of his future. Each represented a different function—for example, Forse's first center, the one at the base of his spine, permeated a clear white light. It made sense that the center reflecting his family of origin would be so pure —Forse's dad, Balder, was the God of Light, and his mom, Nanna, was the Goddess of Warmth—the immortal embodiment of maternal love. Forse's childhood had been uncharacteristically secure for an

Asgardian, and he'd maintained a close relationship with his parents and his brother once he took his own title.

"Your first center's clear—no blocks there. How are your parents?" I asked.

"They're good. Mom wants you to come for dinner the next time we're in Asgard. She looked at those pictures I sent her of you with Mia—she's convinced you're not eating enough, and she wants to fatten you up." I could hear Forse's smile, even with my eyes closed.

"I love your mom." I grinned back, then furrowed my brow as I analyzed the next two orbs. "Your second center's clear, and your third center is gorgeous—you really know where you fit in the world, don't you?"

Forse sighed. "It's the blessing and the curse of being of Asgard—when Odin gifts you a title, you kind of have to stick with it."

"Tell me about it," I murmured. "Fourth center is…hmm."

"What?" Forse asked.

"There's something in your love center—a little speck that's popping against the gold. Would you mind if I went in deeper?" Asking permission was a requisite of healing; I assumed the rules were the same for unifying. A god's spirit was uniquely theirs, after all.

"You do what you have to do," Forse agreed. But the speck grew bigger as he spoke. *Interesting.*

"Okay." I took a breath and pushed my energy against Forse's, making my way through the waves of gold surrounding his heart until I neared the speck. This close to the core of the love center, the energy was a muddied brown. *That's strange.* I pressed closer, and for the first time I felt a resistance. With another breath, I ploughed forward. Forse's energy pushed back, rejecting my advances. I squared my shoulders and tried again, and this time the energy parted to let me though. The moment I caught sight of the iron wall surrounding the center's core, the brown energy closed ranks and pushed me back, forcibly ejecting me from the justice god's energy field.

"Elsa? Are you all right?" Forse's hand reached out to steady me. My eyes flew open. The sudden transition had thrown me off balance. Forse's fingers squeezed my shoulder, and I fixated on the way the thick muscles of his forearms flexed as he pulled me back up. "Why don't you lie down for a bit?"

"I'm fine." I tore my eyes away from Forse's arms and studied his face. "What happened? You pushed me out."

"I...uh..."

Forse's body language spoke volumes. His shoulders were tense, his fists clenched. Everything about him screamed *run*.

"Hey." I reached up and placed my hand over his heart. It pounded against my palm in a frenetic rhythm, its anxious beat a stark contrast to the soothing snowfall outside the window. "I'm sorry. I shouldn't have pressured you. You don't have to talk about it, whatever it is."

"I want to help, Elsa, it's just—"

A whirl of violet-blue eyes and vanilla perfume interrupted Forse's explanation. My brother's girlfriend threw open the front door and burst into my living room, her normally sleek hair frizzing beneath a light layer of snowflakes.

"*Hei*, Mia. Is everything okay?" My hand fell from Forse's heart as I moved to her side.

"Not exactly." She finger-combed her hair into submission.

"What's going on?" Forse asked.

"Well, first of all, it's snowing again. We live in Arcata, for Pete's sake. If I'd wanted to walk to class in the snow, I would have stayed on the East Coast for college." Mia shook her head. "But more importantly, Tyr wants to see Forse back at his place right away. I figured I'd find him here."

"Am I that predictable?" Forse asked.

"Yes." Mia nodded. "Elsa, you'd better come, too. Tyr was doing the jaw-clench thing. Whatever it is that's got his boxer-briefs in a twist, it's probably not good."

Forse raised an eyebrow at me, and I shrugged. We'd had a string of calm months since we got Freya back from Helheim. We were about due for a crisis.

"Let's go." Forse crossed to the hooks by the entry and helped me into my jacket. He tugged his sweater over his head and opened the front door. Mia filed through, and I followed suit. As we walked across the forest to my brother's house, I snuck a glance at the god clenching his fists beside me.

Something told me it wasn't Tyr's summons that had him on edge. What was Forse Styrke hiding behind that iron wall?

CHAPTER 2

"TYR'S IN THE MAN cave. He told me to send you up." Mia closed the front door of my brother's cabin and hung her keys on the hook. Back in Asgard we left our houses unlocked, but Midgard was so crazy these days, we'd agreed the extra security was necessary.

"Elsa, will you be okay if I go upstairs?" Forse turned to Mia before I could answer. "She was working with me back at her place, and I think it took a lot out of her."

Mia wrung her hands. "Are you all right, Elsa? I made lasagna for dinner, and my lasagna usually makes people feel better. Do you want to stick around?"

I shook my head. "I told you, Forse, I'm *fine*. Wait, did you say lasagna?"

"I did indeed." Mia nodded.

"We wouldn't want to impose…" Mia's lasagna was amazing. But she and my brother hadn't had a lot of alone time lately, and I did *not* want to incur the wrath of the crankiest god in the cosmos. Maybe Forse and I could take dinner to go…

"Hush your mouth, you're not imposing. Brynn and Henrik will be home any minute, and you know how much they eat. I made enough to feed a small army."

"Well, if you insist." I grinned. "Can I help you make a salad?"

"All done." Mia took my hand and pulled me toward the kitchen. "You can keep me company while we wait for the guys."

I felt Forse's concerned gaze as I followed Mia down the hall. Before I got to the doorway, I released Mia's hand. "I'll be right there," I said. Mia nodded, heading into the kitchen as I turned to study Forse. He stood at the foot of the stairs, a deep *V* between his brows.

"Are you sure you're all right?" he asked.

"I'm fine. You know you're never going to get anything done if you spend this much time worrying about me."

"I know, but you almost fell back at your place. You're pushing yourself too hard." Forse kept his voice soft. He tucked his thumbs through the belt loops of his fitted jeans. Concern emanated from his grass green eyes.

The whole effect kind of made me melt.

"I don't really have a choice. Asgard needs a Unifier. Besides"—I turned the tables—"you've barely slept since we got Freya back. Between your regular work as

Justice and whatever it is you and Henrik are doing with that locationizer—"

"The locator. It's going to be a useful tracker if, Odin forbid, there's another abduction. If it had been operational when Hel took Freya, we could have found her in under a day." Forse raked his hand through his light brown waves. They were streaked with gold highlights that complemented his tanned skin beautifully.

"Really?" I asked.

"Pretty sure." Forse raised his voice so he could be heard in the kitchen. "Mia, you sketched the initial design. If we'd had the locator in December, it could have tracked Freya within twenty-four hours, right?"

"Sure, if she'd been in one of the light realms. But given her coordinates, the answer is no." Mia poked her head around the corner. "The locator's infrastructure incorporates *älva* dust, which is a light magic-based compound. The surplus of dark magic in Hel's sanctum would have rendered the dust, and therefore the locator, useless. The device will perform in dark realms like Jotunheim, Svartalfheim, and even the outlands of Helheim, but dead spots neutralize the *älva* dust. And by dead spots, I mean spots heavily riddled with an excessive dosage of dark magic. Not spots covered in dead people…like where Hel was keeping Freya." Mia shuddered before ducking back into the kitchen.

"That's a major design flaw," Forse admitted. "Henrik and I need to get on that."

"Maybe you do," I agreed. "But you don't have to do it tonight. Between the locator and catching up on your sentencings, you've been working nonstop lately. You need a break."

"Mmm." Forse's brow relaxed and one corner of his mouth turned up just a fraction. "How about we make a deal? I'll slow down for a night if you will."

"Meaning?"

"Meaning it's Friday. After dinner, we go back to your place, pop in a movie, and forget about our to-do lists."

"Okay," I said, my outward calm a stark contrast to the joy pinging around my heart. I knew Forse well enough to know I needed to let him take this at his own pace, but the thought of snuggling up against him in my darkened living room, sharing a bowl of popcorn in front of the fireplace...well, it made me feel positively euphoric.

Thank Odin I was the only one in the room who could read energy. Mine was absolutely bouncing off the walls.

"Say *hei* to Tyr for me," I said casually.

Forse nodded, then jogged up the stairs to find his friend. His dark jeans hugged the *perfekt* muscles of his backside, and when I finally turned around and walked into the kitchen, Mia gave me a rueful smile.

"Sorry I interrupted you guys back at your place." She handed me a cup of tea and tilted her head toward the hallway. "It looked like I walked in on a moment."

I took the mug and crossed to the island countertop. Then I pulled out a stool and sat down. "You didn't. Forse is…well, he's Forse. You know how guys are."

"Overprotective? Overbearing? Bossy? Stubborn? Impossibly concerned with your wellbeing to the point they assign you a full-time bodyguard?" Mia came to sit beside me, carrying her own cup of tea.

"You must be talking about my brother." I took a sip. *Mmm. Spearmint.*

"One and the same. I love Brynn, and I love spending time with her, but you and I both know she'd rather spend time with Henrik, instead of following me to midterms and hovering over my shoulder in the library. At some point, Tyr's going to have to understand that I can take care of myself." Mia tapped her French-tipped fingers against her cup.

"True," I agreed. "But that 'some point' isn't going to be a few months after a homicidal wolf tried to kill you."

Mia let out a delicate harrumph.

"Face it, Mia, when you signed on to date Tyr, you signed on to a lifetime of weird. And part of that weird comes with a security detail. If you don't like it, you can always get a mortal boyfriend." I bit back my smile, knowing full well what was coming next.

"You hush your mouth, Elsa Fredriksen. I love your brother, and that's that. But sometimes I wonder if he's ever going to see me as his teammate, instead of as someone else he has to protect."

"He's Tyr the Protector. It's literally in his job description." I took another sip of tea.

"I know, but…"

"Hey." I reached over to cover Mia's hand with mine. "I get it. He treats me the same way, and I'm a Key." Keys were gods who played integral functions in the Asgardian infrastructure—Seers, Procurers, Transporters, and me—the quirky High Healer/Unifier hybrid. "But you're a mortal. And he's in love with you. It's going to take him a while to stop helicopter boyfriending you."

"Helicopter boyfriending?" Mia giggled.

"You know what I mean." I squeezed her hand. "Someday you'll stand at Tyr's side and protect our realm with a strength that matches his. You're just going to do it in your own way. And until then…" I shrugged.

"Helicopter boyfriend."

"Exactly."

We exchanged a smile. Mia brought her mug to her lips and took a sip. After a minute, she turned back to me. "So when do I start training?"

"Training?" I tilted my head.

"To be a Unifier. The sooner I get up to speed, the sooner I can help you guys protect Asgard and Earth. And the sooner Tyr will drop the whole bodyguard thing, right? God knows Brynn needs to be focusing on her *own* life right now, not mine."

Adrenaline surged through me as Mia's question ran across my brain. *Train Mia?* I barely understood what unifying was, how was I supposed to teach the most important person in my brother's life to use it to protect the realms…and herself? I stilled an involuntary shiver and pasted on a smile to deflect the question. "Brynn's a pretty formidable valkyrie. She's got things under control."

"Yeah, but she needs to be spending time with Henrik. They've waited *forever* to get to be together." Mia nodded.

"True. But they're making time for each other when they can." I willed my heartbeat to settle. "They're not here right now, are they?"

"No. They're out for a run. Wait." Mia's brows shot up and I permitted myself an inward sigh of relief. *Mortal diverted. Mission accomplished.* She'd dropped the Unifying question for now, but I knew my reprieve was only temporary. Mia was as tenacious as she was smart, and she desperately wanted—and deserved—to use her natural gift of bringing people together to help our team. My resolve to learn the elusive unifying skill strengthened. Mia needed me. The realms needed both of us. I wouldn't let everyone down. *Figure it out, Elsa. Fast.*

"Wait what?" I grounded my energy to the kitchen and centered myself in present time. I could worry another day.

"Wait, Henrik never runs." Mia connected the dots. "He lifts weights and boxes and does that suspension training thing, but he hates jogging. There's no way he'd…"

"Exactly." I nodded. "They're good. Now how about

you? We haven't gotten to catch up since you finished midterms. Are you doing all right?"

I did a quick scan of Mia's energy. As always, her love center emitted a radiant, pinkish-gold hue. She was one of the most refreshingly open mortals I'd met. But her visualization center was muddied. She was understandably anxious about the future and what it meant for her, especially since Tyr's nightmares kept coming true—the gods close to him were under siege, and so far we hadn't done the best job of protecting ourselves.

"I'm a little uncomfortable," Mia admitted. "I'll feel a lot better once I know I can help keep the peace around here. Maybe then we'll stop being attacked by people. Or, by dogs. Or by demons. Or whatever."

The poor girl didn't yet understand that we would *always* be under attack. It was the nature of being of Asgard. You didn't get to rule the realms without making a *lot* of enemies. Loss was just the name of the game.

I miss them so much.

"Elsa? Are you okay? You're gripping your mug really hard." Mia gently pried my fingers away from my cup.

"Sorry. I was supposed to be checking in on *you*." I shook the memories from my head. There was little point to dwelling on the past. It wouldn't bring my parents back, and it sure wouldn't help Mia's peace of mind. I grounded myself in the present. Again. "Okay. What were you saying?"

Mia squeezed my fingers. "I'm asking you to train me. I'm tired of feeling like the helpless human—I want to do something to actually help y'all out. Midterms are over, and I've got two weeks off for spring break. My parents and Jason are coming out for the first week, but then they're going back to the East Coast, so I've got free time. If you're up to it?"

I bit my bottom lip. My reprieve hadn't lasted a full two minutes. But how could I train Mia to be a Unifier when I hadn't mastered the allegedly inherited skill set myself? Unifying was supposed to be in my blood. Under my mom's dominion, we'd lost fewer lives than at any point in our history.

And here I couldn't even break through the blocker on the crush-of-my-existence's heart.

"About that," I hedged. I owed Mia an explanation for my foot-dragging. "I'm not exactly the best Unifier just yet."

"Too bad." My brother burst into the kitchen like a bull in a china shop. He stopped in front of the sink, crossed his arms over his chest, and eyed me levelly. "At the moment, you're the only Unifier we've got. Time to goddess-up and get in the field."

"What are you talking about?" I tucked one blond wave behind my ear as Forse stalked into the kitchen behind Tyr. His jaw was clenched, his shoulders pulled back to military attention, and the wrinkle between his brows was so deep, it could have held a pencil. "What's going on?"

"Ask him." Forse jutted his chin at Tyr and stood

behind me. He put his hands on the back of my chair as he stared my brother down. "For the record, I do not agree with this."

"I know you don't." Tyr met his glare. "But we don't have a choice."

"There's always a choice." Forse's voice was even, but his hands clenched my chair so hard, I heard a knuckle crack. The tension in the room was palpable; the kitchen was draped in the thick, red fog of anger.

The emotions were overwhelming. I shut down my abilities so I could focus. "What. Is. Going. On?"

Before I got my answer, the front door slammed and Brynn and Henrik's footsteps pounded in the hallway. When they skidded to a stop in the kitchen, I noticed Brynn's T-shirt was on backwards. I bit back a smile.

"How was your 'run?'" Mia teased, using her fingers to make air quotes.

Brynn flushed before tucking her head into Henrik's chest. "Good," she muttered.

"We got your text, *kille*. Everything okay?" Henrik rested his hand on Brynn's lower back. She stuck her tongue out at Mia, who giggled in response.

"Everything is great. We have a twenty on one of our top-ten fugitives." Tyr didn't take his eyes off Forse.

I turned around. "That's a good thing. Right, Forse?"

"That's not why I'm upset." Forse held Tyr's stare. I'd turned off my extra sense, but anyone could see the equivalent of energetic fire shooting from his eyes. *Yikes.*

"What's Forse upset about?" Mia asked.

"He's upset because I'm bringing Elsa into the field with us to retrieve the perp." The vein in Tyr's neck pulsed. Oh, great. He was *really* mad, though whether it was at Forse, me, or this yet-to-be-identified perp, I hadn't yet assessed.

"She's not ready. And you know it's probably a trap." Forse spoke through gritted teeth.

"Maybe. Which is why Brynn and I are going with you." Tyr nodded.

"What? Who's going to watch Mia? Or is she coming with us to…wait, where are we going?" Brynn asked.

"I can take care of myself," Mia objected.

Tyr glanced at Mia out of the corner of his eye. It didn't take a High Healer to see how irritated she was, and my normally thick-headed brother crossed to her side to soothe her in an uncharacteristic display of sensitivity. He wrapped his arms around her shoulders and spoke to Brynn. "You and your boyfriend can swap jobs for a few days. Henrik, I want you to stay here with Mia. You can call Freya back from Asgard if you need help getting anything ready for Mia's family's visit. Mia, you've been adding to that 'Must Bake For Jason Cookie List' in your backpack for weeks, and Henrik is Asgard's resident baker's man. I know he'd love to help."

"If this is your way of making me forget how

annoyed I am that you don't trust me to take care of myself, then you aren't as bright as I thought you were, Tyr Fredriksen." Mia huffed. Then she turned to Henrik. "But he's not wrong, I have a laundry list of things to do to get ready for my family's visit. Including bake."

"Hold up." Henrik held out one hand. "Where are you going? And why is Forse about to kill someone?"

We all turned to look at Forse. Sure enough, his eyes were slits, his breathing was sharp, and he had a pulsing forehead vein that rivaled Tyr's neck one. He positively seethed anger.

"We are going to Svartalfheim," Tyr answered coolly. The four gods in the room drew a collective gasp.

The mortal took in our reactions with practiced calm. "Which one's Svartalfheim again?" she asked lightly.

"The worst one after Helheim," Brynn muttered.

"It's the realm of the dark elves," I explained. "When the cosmos was born, the blackest souls were sent to a wasteland—a realm of isolation and soot. Svartalfheim."

"And you're all going there?" Mia squeaked.

"Forse, Brynn, Elsa, and I are going there." Tyr spoke with his chin on Mia's head. "You're staying here with Henrik."

"Elsa doesn't need to go," Forse argued.

"You of all people know how delicate this retrieval is. The perp has been a fugitive since...well, it's been a long time. She's being harbored by dark elves who demanded Fenrir in her place, and I have no intention of unleashing that beast again. The elves agreed to accept one of the Svartish treasures from the vault instead of the wolf, but they could very well turn on us once we get there. We need a Unifier to make sure this exchange goes peacefully. Right now, Elsa's all we've got," Tyr finished.

"Um, thanks?" I said.

"You know what I mean." Tyr turned his gaze to me. "I don't want to drag you into Svartalfheim any more than Forse does. I know you're not up to speed on the peacekeeping function, and I don't like putting you in danger. Not only are you my baby sister, but you're a Key—you're one of the gods we train to protect. I hate everything about this. Unfortunately, I don't have another option."

"I could go," Mia offered. Her voice was shaky, but she held her head high.

"No." Five voices sounded as one. A combination of relief and disappointment flickered across Mia's features.

"If I'm not ready, you're definitely not ready," I reminded her. "I'll get this one, and once I have a handle on this bizarre skill set I'll pass the torch to you. I promise."

"I'll hold down the fort from here this time." Mia stared me down. "But I don't want to be on baking duty with Henrik forever."

I swallowed. *Figure this out, Elsa.*

"Hey, there are worse things than baking with me."
Henrik raised an eyebrow. "I never did teach you to
make my mom's chocolate mousse cake, did I?"

Mia looked up with a small smile. "Does she use
Mexican vanilla?"

"Tahitian," Henrik countered. "And I've got a stash
in my secret cabinet."

"Now that that's settled, does anyone want to tell
me the name of the perp we're retrieving from that
Odin-forsaken realm?" Brynn chimed in.

I turned to my brother and waited for his answer.
When he spoke, his voice was clipped.

"Runa."

The name fell like a lead balloon at a birthday party.
Brynn's mouth dropped open, and Henrik sucked in a
breath. I couldn't see Forse's face, but the sound of
knuckles cracking behind me let me know he wasn't
happy. I could relate.

Oh dear gods. We're going after Runa.

The room swirled in a violent vortex, and Forse
gripped my arms to steady me. As he righted me in my
chair, the world slowed to a standstill. Runa was more
than just Forse's psychotic ex-girlfriend. She was the
monster who committed *the* crime—the one that
changed everything.

When I finally found my voice, it came out dry and
scratchy. "We're going after Runa."

"Yes." Forse watched me carefully.

"And you're charging her with high treason."

"Yes," Forse repeated.

"Good."

Forse kept his hands on my arms as I breathed through my rage. "Elsa, if you don't want to go with us we can—"

"We can what?" Tyr interrupted. "We can't let the dark elves keep her—her crime was against Asgard, and she needs to answer to *our* realm for what she's done. Not Svartalfheim. You of all gods know that."

"*Förbaskat*, Tyr, I'm not letting her hurt Elsa!" Forse exploded. The words echoed off the marble countertops, piercing the normally calm kitchen.

"I'm not letting her hurt anyone!" Tyr yelled back. "And the only way I can ensure that is if I bring her to Odin!"

"Enough!" I interjected. With my emotions under control, I re-opened my abilities and sent waves of calm at Forse and Tyr. Their chests continued to rise and fall with angry breaths, but their auras reflected a slight decrease in rage. It was the best I could do. "Forse, I understand where you're coming from. But Tyr's right. Runa needs to be brought to justice. And since that's you"—I tapped the justice god with my pointer finger—"and since I've got your back whether you like it or not, I'm going with you. Tyr's spot on; we don't want this exchange going bad. We can't let her hurt anyone else. I need you to have that faith in me you promised you would."

"I believe in you, Elsa. I've always known you have what it takes to master this job, even before you believed it yourself. You're incredibly powerful, and you can do anything you set your mind to. But there are so many forces working against us these days. If anything happened to you, I'd never forgive myself." Forse pressed his forehead to mine. His concern was sweet, and normally I'd have melted into a giggling mess at the contact, but right now I just couldn't go there.

"Let's make sure we're all safe then. We'll bring Runa in so she can be prosecuted to the fullest extent of Asgardian law." I shot Forse a look brimming with confidence I didn't actually possess. Since the energetic fireballs shooting between him and Tyr suggested they still operated at a six on the anger scale, it was clear I was a woefully ineffective Unifier.

And I had the job of my life ahead of me.

"When do we leave?" Brynn placed her hands on the island countertop.

"First thing in the morning. I've got to head to Asgard after dinner to retrieve that weird-shaped crystal from the treasure room." Tyr ran a finger along Mia's arm. She shivered.

"Odin's willing to part with that?" Henrik sounded surprised. "The research team hasn't figured out what it does yet."

Tyr shrugged. "Whatever it takes to get Runa in custody."

"Well then, it sounds like you're going to need your energy." Mia jumped up and put on her oven mitts. As she bent over the stove, she called out orders of her own. "Henrik, get the drinks. Forse, add two more place settings to the table. This lasagna's not going to serve itself."

"Yes, ma'am." Henrik saluted. He swatted Brynn on the behind and gave a rakish grin as she giggled.

"Henrik!"

"Brynn, you can get the salad out of the fridge." Mia carried the lasagna to the table and set it on hotplates. "Tyr, make sure we've got enough ice cream. If not, please bring some in from the garage fridge."

"Aye aye." Brynn set to task.

Tyr checked the contents of the freezer and closed the door. "We're fully stocked. *Prinsessa*, this looks amazing. Come and sit down. Oh, and Brynn?"

"Yes?" Brynn set the salad on the table and turned around.

"The next time you and Henrik get dressed in a hurry, try to wear your shirt the right way." Tyr winked as he took his seat.

Brynn glanced at her T-shirt and her hands flew to her mouth. "Oh my gods!" she squealed, before running out of the room. She returned half a minute later, with a righted shirt and a mortified expression. She picked a dish towel off the counter and threw it at Tyr, who wiped tears of laughter from his eyes. To my right, Forse chuckled quietly, and even Henrik sported an enormous grin.

"I'm going to remember this moment when you're crying for your bodyguard to save your life in Svartalfheim," Brynn warned.

"You do that," Tyr guffawed.

Mia sat beside him, muffling her laughter behind one delicate hand. "Sit," she giggled. "Eat. You've all got a long day coming up tomorrow."

Forse held out my chair and I shot him a grateful grin. The smile he returned me looked forced, but I'd take it.

Mia only knew the half of it. Long day didn't begin to cover what it would take to retrieve Runa. But we'd get it done. And if that monster was the reason Forse kept that wall around his heart, then maybe I could do more than just keep the peace on this recovery mission.

Maybe I could give Forse—and myself—a real chance at happiness.

CHAPTER 3

"**E**LSA, YOU'RE WAY TOO** good to me. You made my favorite." Forse tossed a kernel of popcorn in his mouth, and I tried my hardest not to stare at his lips while he chewed.

I failed.

"Light sugar, extra butter." I forced my eyes upward. "The *perfekt* balance of sweet and savory."

"Thanks. I have a surprise for you, too." Forse set the bowl on the end table and walked to the kitchen. He returned carrying two glass containers and an easy grin.

"Coke in a bottle! Where'd you find that?" I bounced on my knees.

"A market in Eureka just started carrying it, so I ordered you a case. I popped a few in your fridge and left the rest in your garage."

I clapped my hands together. "Forse Styrke, you are

too much. How did you remember how much I like this?"

Forse raised one eyebrow. "I don't remember you *liking* it as much as I remember you *trying to kiss me* because of it."

My face went from zero to blazing in half a second. "*You* spun that bottle and it landed on *me*, thank you very much."

"True." Forse opened both bottles and handed me one, then reclaimed his spot on the couch and took a long drink. "But *you* were the one who jumped across the circle and tried to attack me. If Tyr hadn't pulled you back, who knows how far you would have tried to go."

That was my brother. Interfering with my love life since early adolescence.

"Whatever." I took a delicate sip. The bubbles tickled my nose as the sweet liquid slid down my throat, bringing on a delightful wave of nostalgia. "Oh my gods, this is so good."

Forse raised his beverage. "Thanks for the popcorn."

"Thanks for the Coke." I clinked my bottle against his, and picked up the remote. I pressed "play" as we finished our beverages in companionable silence. Forse set our empty bottles on the end table and settled the popcorn in his lap, then threw his arm across the back of the sofa and shot me his easy smile.

"Get over here, *hjärtat*." Forse tilted his head. My heart raced at the endearment as I scooted into the nook he'd made just for me. I nuzzled my cheek against Forse's chest, and tucked my feet underneath me. It was a calculated position—just enough contact to evoke that warm feeling of safety I got whenever Forse touched me, but not so much as to signal his emotional red flags. Despite our comfortable exchange, I knew Forse was one awkward hand-brush away from bolting out my door faster than he had at Freya's spin-the-bottle party. I didn't know if it was a guy thing or a *me* thing, but boys hadn't exactly lined up to date the God of War's little sister. Tyr's overprotective streak and propensity to blow up when anyone looked at me twice were massive turn-offs to would-be suitors. But Forse had always been the exception; Tyr never minded my spending time alone with his friend. Maybe it was because they'd known each other for hundreds of years, or maybe it was because Forse's title bound him to a certain honor code that eluded lesser gods. Either way, it made things infinitely easier for me to spend time with him.

I shifted my weight so my knees brushed against Forse's thigh. The additional contact sparked a wave of warmth that ebbed up my legs, through my stomach, and settled around my heart. With a contented sigh, I increased the pressure of my cheek on Forse's chest. Smooth muscle muffled the heartbeat, but I heard its tempo increase. *Yes!* An elated grin broke out across my face at the sound. It might take him years to figure out how *perfekt* we'd be together—if he ever put it together—but at least I had physical confirmation that I had some kind of effect on him.

Forse cleared his throat and leaned slightly away. My mouth twitched as I tried not to frown. *One step forward, two steps back. Every. Single. Time.* With great reluctance, and the long-suffering patience only an immortal could summon, I lifted my head and met Forse's eyes. I wanted to ask why he felt the need to pull away from me, but I knew having *the talk* would freak him out. So I settled for the first thought that came into my mind. "Are you nervous about tomorrow?"

"Elsa," he started. Then he pressed his lips together so they made a fine line. He'd closed off. *Dang it.*

"We're just watching a movie," I reminded him. "That's it. We're two friends who've known each other for centuries, watching *The Tempest*."

"That's it, huh?" Forse withdrew his arm from the back of the couch and set the popcorn on the end table. When he turned around, he rested his palms on his thighs.

I mirrored his posture, hoping to put him at ease. "It can be. Unless you want to talk? About…anything?"

Please, please, let Forse want to talk about us. After years of not asking me out, please let today be the day he tells me he's secretly loved me all along and he wants to spend an eternity making up for lost time by—

Be quiet, brain! Stop getting my hopes up.

"We can't do this tonight *hjärtat*." Forse shook his head. "In the morning we're going to see Runa. We can't afford to lose focus, even for a minute. The last time we saw her, she…she…"

"I know," I said softly. "If she hadn't released Fenrir, my parents would be alive."

Forse's skin paled and a thin sheen broke out across his forehead. "She's a monster. Tyr doesn't see that we're walking you straight into a trap."

"Oh, Tyr sees it." I tapped my temple, reminding Forse of my link to the sometimes disturbing inner workings of Tyr's mind. "Odin gave us freaky sibling powers, remember? I know Tyr's taking care of things on his end. He had you drop off the locator before we started the movie, right?"

"*Ja,*" Forse answered.

"Then you *know* Henrik's upping the tech on that tonight. Probably trying to decrease the search time, increase the radius, maybe even plug in that app Mia and I are working on to identify mind signatures. Trust me, Tyr's making sure we're going into this mission with every tool in our arsenal fully prepped." I paused. "Have you trained Brynn on how to use the locator? Somebody other than you should know how to operate it."

"Thanks for the vote of confidence in my ability to not get captured." The corners of Forse's eyes crinkled with his smile.

"You know what I mean. Having an alternate is just good sense."

"True. And it's why I trained both Brynn and Henrik on how to use it." Forse rubbed the back of his neck.

"Hey, we've got this. We'll be back before you know

it, and then you can go back to *not* touching me on movie night." I elbowed Forse in the ribs.

"Else, I—"

"I'm kidding. I'm trying to make you laugh."

Forse pressed two fingers between his brows. "We're dragging you into the middle of an obvious setup. Nobody's even trained you to defend yourself."

"I took combat in school," I argued.

Forse looked up. "You knew you were a Key so you followed the *protected* god curriculum—not the *protector* god curriculum. The two terms of basic swords your program required aren't enough. Not when you're dealing with Runa."

"Okay, then you teach me." I sat up. "We've got tonight—teach me whatever tools you think I need to take her on."

"That'll take more than one night."

"Well, one night's what we've got," I pointed out as I paused the movie. "It's not how I was hoping we'd spend the evening, but I'll make you a deal. I let you teach me whatever would make you feel better about my going with you—offense, defense, swordsmanship, gun safety, those stupid Three Stooges routines Henrik finds so amusing—whatever. You get two hours to prep me as you see fit. And after, you curl up on this couch with me, and we watch a movie or talk or just stare at the fire—*anything* but think about what we're doing tomorrow. Because you and I both know what a giant bucket of stress you are right now, and that's no way to go into a hostile zone. We both need to relax."

If the rigidity in Forse's shoulders was any indication, relaxation was going to be a tall order.

"Do we have a deal?" I asked him.

Forse drew a slow breath. "Your brother's going to kill me."

"For the self-defense class? Or the relaxing on the couch?" I teased.

Forse didn't crack a smile. "Both."

"Well, he can just deal. Keeping me in a bubble didn't help us when Fenrir came knocking, did it? I'm long overdue for a combat refresher. High school was forever ago."

"Actually, you *just* graduated." Forse rested his head against the back of the couch. I wanted to reach up and touch his light brown waves *so very much*, but my intuition told me that would send him running faster than a frost giant fleeing Muspelheim.

"Details." I waved my hand as I stood. "Come on. Let's do this behind the cabin in case Captain Overprotective is using his super senses. It'll be harder for him to see us from there."

Forse pushed himself off the couch and walked to the weapon closet. Tyr had installed one in each of our residences, but since I came into Midgard unconscious, and harbored a general aversion to tools used to hurt living things, I hadn't bothered checking out the contents of mine. I drew a calming breath as Forse came out carrying a dagger, a rapier, one of Brynn and Henrik's implosion guns, and two sticks on a chain. *Using weapons for self-defense is totally different than using them to attack. I will only use these tools to protect myself and my friends. I will not cause unnecessary harm.*

I tried not to shiver as Forse shifted his cargo to one arm.

"Okay, little fighter. If I've only got two hours, I'm going to use every minute. One hour on weapons, one hour on creative combat."

"Creative combat?" I asked.

"You don't always have the luxury of having an actual weapon. Sometimes you need to improvise. Use what you can find wherever you are—sticks, boulders…if you're lucky, in Svartalfheim you can find a hot lava rock. They're the ones with a slightly purple-ish glow. They'll singe the Hel out of any being they come into contact with. They can even cut through iron, so be careful with those."

"Good to know," I said with a smile.

Forse pointed to the hooks by the door. "Put on a jacket. The snow's stopped, but it's still cold outside."

I shrugged my coat on. "Do you want me to hold those swords while you put on your coat?"

Forse gestured to his tight sweater. "I'm fine like this, *takk*."

Gods, yes he is.

"Okay." I feigned nonchalance.

Forse held out his hand. "Come on. We've got a lot to cover."

"And then it's couch time. Complete with more Cokes in a bottle."

Forse raised an eyebrow. "Have I ever gone back on a deal?"

"Nope." Thinking about a night curled up on the couch with my favorite god and my favorite beverage brought on a grin that made my cheeks tingle. I felt almost giddy as I placed my hand in Forse's, and followed him outside. "Let's do this."

"Elsa." The low rumble of Forse's voice pulled me out of my dream. It had been a *really* good one—Forse and I walked hand in hand in the forest behind my cabin, and as we passed a moss-covered redwood, he spun me behind the tree. He leaned against me, pressing his chest to mine, brought his lips to my neck and—

"Elsa," Forse murmured again, pulling me fully into the present. *Dang it.* I dragged my eyelids open, only to realize my reality was *so very much better* than my dream.

Apparently we'd fallen asleep on the couch watching *The Tempest*. Our bodies were twined together in a way Forse would *never* allow if he were awake. He rested on his back, one hand behind his head and the other tucked securely around my waist. I nestled against him, my torso draped comfortably across his, and my cheek pressed against his heart. Its steady beat pounded in time with mine, confirming my long-held belief that we were really two souls destined to come together in a glorious—

"No, *hjärtat*." Forse interrupted me again. "The broadsword is too heavy for you…use the rapier…" My mouth turned down at Forse's mumbling. The poor god couldn't dream about walking on the beach or skiing in the Alps like the rest of us; even in sleep he worried about me, recounting his instructions from last night's lesson. *Identify two plausible escape routes in any scenario. Assess an opponent's weakness, then exploit it. Use the most lethal weapon at your disposal, or barring that, the first one you can reach. Strike to kill.*

A chill ran through my torso. My healer's instinct wouldn't allow me to kill; the concept went against the very purpose of my gift. If we went to Svartalfheim today and I had to end someone's life to save my own, would I be able to do it?

Dear Odin, please don't let it come to that.

Forse stirred underneath me, bringing my attention back to the present. I rested my chin on his chest and ran the tips of my fingers along his collarbone as he woke. Long, dark lashes fluttered, revealing emerald-green eyes clouded with sleep. One corner of his lips pulled up in a lazy smile, and when he spoke, his voice sounded deep and gravelly. "Morning, *hjärtat*."

Please let this happen again. Please, please *dear Odin, don't let this be a one-time deal.*

"Morning," I murmured. "Did you sleep well?"

"Better than I have in years." Forse lifted his head. He took in the way my body was nestled against his, my arms folded over his chest. The arm he held around my lower back flexed, pressing me closer to his side.

His eyes twinkled as he brought a hand to my cheek. "We fell asleep like this?"

"Kind of." My neck grew hot.

"Mmm." Forse tucked an errant strand behind my ear. My pulse skyrocketed as I leaned into the touch.

"Is that a good *mmm* or a bad *mmm*? You're kind of hard to get a read on."

Forse ran his thumb along my jaw and closed his eyes. "It's just *mmm*."

I had no idea what that meant, but the fact that he hadn't leapt off the couch and run out of my cabin was definitely a good sign. Last night, I'd enjoyed the most peaceful sleep I'd had since Fenrir's attack—no night sweats, no bad dreams, and not even the standard-issue ache from teeth-grinding. At the moment, I inhabited the Zen-like state I'd enjoyed before all Helheim broke loose for the Fredriksen family.

Forget meditation. The key to inner peace was a night in Forse's arms.

"I can't believe I forgot." Forse shifted to reach into his jeans pocket, and his hips pressed against mine in a movement that sent my pulse to the stratosphere. *Breathe, Elsa. Breathe.* He shifted back, and I buried my disappointment. "I was going to give this to you last night, but you distracted me with your scary dagger skills."

"Ha ha." I propped myself so my forearms rested on Forse's chest. There was no way I was moving any farther away from him than necessary.

Forse pulled his fist from his pocket and held it above my hands. "I got you this."

"You got me a present?" My cheeks flushed. We exchanged gifts on Christmas and our birthdays, but that was it.

"It's just something little. I saw it and I thought… well, it made me think of you." He opened his fist and a necklace fell into my palm. It was exquisite, a pale-blue crystal with green swirls that appeared to glow from within, held by a delicate silver chain.

Time stood still as I held the stone between my fingers. "This is a larimar crystal. I've wanted one of these forever. Where did you find it?"

"I was walking by the jewelry store in Arcata, and I saw it in the window. Something about it made me think of you, and I knew I had to get it." Forse brought his hand to my lower back and rubbed softly. I tried not to melt into the touch, but considering I was holding a stone that originated in mythological Atlantis, the purpose of which was to heal a wounded heart while guiding it to its soul mate, I was finding not melting inordinately difficult.

"This is…I can't even…" I blinked up at Forse's eyes, the exact same shade as the green in the crystal. I didn't have to check a mirror to know that mine matched its silvery blue. "Thank you."

"I'm glad you like it," Forse said simply. Then he held out his hand. "May I?"

"Of course." I dropped the crystal into his palm and tugged my hair to the side. He fastened the clasp behind my neck, and the larimar fell, resting calmly against the hollow of my neck. My entire body warmed as the crystal's subtle vibration pulled on the energy of my heart, and Forse's. He raised an eyebrow at my knowing smile.

"Do I want to know?" he asked. "Or is the fact that I suddenly feel warm and fuzzy one of those mysterious High Healer things?"

"All you need to know is that I'm *very* happy you gave this to me. *Takk.*" I pushed myself up so I could kiss his cheek, pulling back before I could scare him off. But Forse still didn't look afraid—either the larimar was having its desired effect, or we were *finally* making progress.

Either way, I was feeling pretty darned optimistic.

"Any time." Force's eyes turned a deeper green as an intensity consumed his gaze. It moved slowly from my face down my torso, then came to an abrupt stop at the pale pink mark on my forearm. His eyes narrowed as he ran a finger lightly over the wound. "You cut yourself pretty badly with that dagger last night. This one's nearly healed over, but is anything else hurting?"

"My muscles are a little sore," I admitted. "But I'm a lot more confident than I was yesterday. You gave me a solid foundation to fight the dark elves, or trolls, or mountain giants, or whatever questionably guided being we come across."

"True, but remember, most fights are avoidable. And I don't want you engaging unless it's absolutely necessary. Self-defense is one thing, but the second you're in a position to get yourself to safety—"

"I know," I interrupted. "You want me to run away from conflict—not into it."

"Exactly."

I lay my cheek on Forse's chest and let the rise and fall of his breathing ebb my anxiety. I could have stayed right there all day.

Unfortunately for me, Justice was swift this morning.

"Much as I hate to move, I'm sure Tyr's ready to catch the Bifrost." Forse gently lifted me off him, and guided me to my feet as he rose. I stared wistfully at the couch, committing the feel of our bodies nestled together to memory. The way things went with us, it could be months before Forse dropped his guard enough to let us get that close again. Why did boys have to make everything so complicated?

"You can take the first shower," I offered. "I'll whip up a batch of Henrik's Swedish pancakes, and we can be at my brother's within an hour."

Forse bent to kiss the top of my head. "You sure you're up to this?"

"I'm Asgard's only Unifier," I reminded him. "Nobody can do this for me. If I stay behind, it increases the likelihood one of you will get hurt. And I can't let that happen."

"If you feel like any of this is too much—"

I covered Forse's lips with one finger. It took every-thing I had to ignore the electricity that sparked beneath my digit. "Get in the shower. I'll try not to eat all the pancakes before you come out."

Forse stared at me for a long moment. I let my hand fall as I pushed calm into the energy center trying to leap from my chest. When my heart rate was respectable, I sent a wave of peace at Forse. His fear dimmed considerably. I held his gaze as he came to a decision.

"You're honestly okay with all of this," he assessed.

"I have to get my feet wet sometime." I shrugged. "It might as well be today."

Forse nodded. "I'll be with you every step of the way."

"I know you will. Now get in the shower, Justice." I shoved him toward the bathroom. "I've got pancakes to cook."

Without looking back, I moved cheerfully toward the kitchen and pulled out eggs, flour, sugar and milk, whipping the ingredients together. It wasn't until I heard the sound of running water that I permitted myself one short burst of nerves. I braced my palms on the counter, and dropped my chin to my chest. Anxiety tore through me, spiking my heart rate and sending prickles of sweat along my brow.

What the Hel have I gotten myself into?

CHAPTER 4

"**I DON'T CARE HOW** immortal metabolisms work. I know you, Tyr Fredriksen, and you're going to get hungry. Just take the sandwiches already!" Mia stood in the clearing in front of the Arcata cabin, one hand on her hip, the other staunchly yielding a brown paper bag. Her chin was raised in a characteristic display of stubbornness. If I wasn't so in-tune to energy, I'd have believed she was annoyed. But behind Mia's insistence was vulnerability. She worried for Tyr's safety, and she was frustrated at her inability to fix things. Making food was her way of being a part of this mission.

"Thank you, Mia." I gently removed the bag from her hands. "Your sandwiches are always the best. And you're right, we're going to be starving in a few hours, and Svartalfheim isn't the most hospitable realm. These will come in handy."

Mia's shoulders relaxed. "If you want, I can go back

and make a few extras. I only packed one batch of brownies, but I could whip up another in forty minutes."

Tyr grabbed her arm as she backed toward the house, his black T-shirt pulling taut at the movement. "*Prinsessa*," he rumbled. "We'll be back before you know it. Have I ever lied to you?"

Mia stared up at him. "'*Mia, I'm an exchange student from Sweden, not an immortal war god with a whole heap of monsters trying to kill me.*' Sound familiar?"

"You'll never let that go, will you?"

"Nope."

Tyr used the pad of his thumb to free Mia's bottom lip from between her teeth. "Listen, baby, when we get home, we're going to be *really* hungry. I'll bet your famous pot roast would make a lot of gods happy. What do you say?"

Mia's eyes lit up. "I say get ready to be amazed. I've got a new marinade that's going to knock your socks off."

"That's my girl." Tyr wrapped one arm around her waist and pulled her into him. She closed her eyes as he lifted her so her face was level with his, then gave her a kiss that left more than just the mortal blushing.

"Enough already," Henrik groaned. "You're showing the rest of us up."

"Speak for yourself." Brynn threw her arms around Henrik's neck and planted an enthusiastic kiss square on his mouth. He groaned in approval, then dipped her low, resting one hand on the back of her black tank top, and wrapping the other around her blond waves.

I raised an eyebrow at Forse. "It looks like it's just you and me."

Forse didn't crack a smile.

I sighed. Everything had been so easy back on the couch, but that might as well have been a century ago. Now, Forse's shoulders were drawn against his black V-neck shirt, and his voice cracked with stress. "Let's just get this job over with."

My fingers grazed Forse's thick biceps as I pushed confident energy at him. "We've got this."

"Maybe." Forse's eyes narrowed. He was *so* not receptive to the optimism I sent his way. "This whole mission feels like a trap."

I pushed out a more forceful wave of confidence. "If it is, we've got a strong team to thwart it."

Forse's brow didn't smooth one bit, but he did give a slight nod. And when Tyr set Mia on her feet and grabbed the brown paper bag from my hands, Forse took my hand and pulled me after him.

"Henrik, enough already. You'll see Brynn in a few hours; a day, tops," Tyr barked.

Henrik reluctantly released our valkyrie, and Brynn skipped to Tyr's side. "Miss you," she said breathily.

"Take care, *sötnos*. Tell the dark elves we said *hei*." Henrik grinned.

"Henrik, give us the breakdown on the tech you're sending with us," Tyr ordered.

"Brynn's got the brighteners, the extractors, and

Elsa's emergency healing kit in her backpack," Henrik responded.

"Oh, give me the healing kit. There's one more thing I need to add." I held out my hand and Henrik passed over the bag. While he and Forse spoke quietly about another piece of technology they were working on, I removed my new necklace. I couldn't risk losing something so precious on the wild ride that was the Bifrost, but I couldn't bear to leave it behind, either. With a breath, I held the larimar in my hand, infusing it with extra love and healing before placing the crystal in the emergency bag, where it could energize the other stones. It might have been overkill, but we needed all the help we could get.

When I'd tucked the necklace into the healing kit, Henrik held out his hand and waggled his fingers. I handed over the backpack.

"*Takk*. So our newest piece of tech is something Forse and I have been developing off one of Mia's sketches." Henrik pulled a palm-sized tablet out of the bag, then handed it to Forse. "Keep this on you. It's the modified locator."

"Were you able to decrease the track time and up the search radius like we talked about?" Forse asked.

Henrik shook his head. "I'm sorry, *kille*. I gave it my best, but I haven't been able to conform the *älva* dust to the specs we wanted. I've adjusted the device so it remains functional under twice the amount of dark magic it could handle before—so now it should be able to track subjects in even the blackest regions of Svartalfheim. But if the dark elves do the impossible and find a way to throw out Helheim-level dark energy, the locator's not going to be able to trace the subject."

"No trace at all?" Forse asked.

"No," Henrik confirmed. "But honestly, that level of bad juju is rarely conjured outside of Hel's inner sanctum. On their own, the dark elves can't produce anywhere close to the amount of dark magic this baby can handle now. And I've altered it so it's got a few-hour track time—it should take two to four hours, hopefully less, to locate a subject."

"That's longer than it took before." Forse frowned.

Henrik shrugged. "Adjusting the *älva* dust had a price. We had to compromise speed for strength."

The rumble in Forse's throat let me know he was *not* happy.

"Mia and I will keep working on the blueprints from this end. In the meantime, everybody, take one of these." Henrik pulled four thin plastic strips out of the backpack, each labeled with one of our names. Henrik removed the identification tags and handed them out. "They're your new communication devices. Let's give the human a hand for her innovative design."

Five pairs of eyes turned to our mortal, who took a bow amidst our applause. "I hate that y'all need a backup com device in case the dark elves confiscate your phones," she grumbled.

"Luck favors the prepared. Remember?" Tyr winked. "How do these work?"

"Remove the wrapping and place them sticky-side

down on the inside of your forearm." We all did as Mia instructed. In seconds, the clear device adapted its texture to be a *perfekt* match to our skin.

"The ultimate camouflage—well done, *flicka*," Brynn praised.

"Thanks," Mia said. "To turn them on, you'll need to press your pointer finger to the vein that runs in the center of your wrist, then speak the name of the person you want to call—the coms are coded to recognize your fingerprint and your voice, so nobody else can activate them. Worst-case scenario, if your phones are taken and you're separated from the group, you can use these to call each other for help. They can also send and receive electronic transmissions like e-mails, but we've designed them so there's no digital trace."

"Meaning?" I asked.

"Meaning, if one of you is captured and your abductor somehow figures out you have a communication device on your arm, we don't want said abductor to be able to force you to activate the com, then trace the other three devices. These communicators make it impossible to track their user's location through an IP address or whatever magic passes for internet service in Svartalfheim. And since there's no fairy dust involved, these devices will work anywhere—even, God forbid, in Hel's dark magic-laced inner sanctum." Mia crossed her arms.

Tyr frowned. "Let's not go back there. Brynn, what's our weapon count?"

Brynn held out her hand, and Henrik passed the

backpack. She shouldered it and tightened the straps, before turning back to Tyr. "Forse has a broadsword, a nanomolecular particle accelerator, and a pistol. Anything else?"

"The locator." Forse tucked the Asgardian GPS tablet in the pocket of his cargos.

"And the locator." Brynn nodded. "I've got my rapier, dagger, and my killer right hook. Tyr, you've got your broadsword, a handgun, and…anything else?"

Tyr held up his palms. "I don't need anything else. I've got these."

"Excellent. And Elsa, here." Brynn held out a small blade. I tried to wave it away, but she pressed it into my hands. "Take it. I know you don't want to hurt anyone, but use this dagger if you need to. It's better to be safe than sorry."

"Okay," I whispered, tucking the weapon through the belt loop of my black skinny jeans. Since my role on this mission was a peacekeeping one, I'd passed on wearing the regulation cargos donned by my friends. I'd also broken with the all-black vibe, choosing a long sleeveless shirt in pale blue. The soothing color was a known mood relaxer, something I intended to use to my every advantage.

"So that's the weapon count." Brynn turned to my brother. "Tyr, what's the strategy once we touch down?"

Tyr crossed his arms, his biceps flexing with the movement. "Strategy's simple—we drop in, meet the dark elves at a mountain range near the drop site, exchange the crystal for the fugitive, and Bifrost out. Anyone who gets separated should find their way back to the drop site, call for Heimdall, and return to Arcata. But if, Odin forbid, you're captured, do not try to escape. Dark elves aren't smart enough to strategize, and they'll kill you before they ransom you. Just sit tight, gather as much intel as you can, and scream my name in your head. I'll hear you and track you down."

"Unless there's a dark magic block. You can't read minds through thick fields of the black stuff. If you find yourself in one of those, or if Tyr gets captured, call for me." I looked at each of my friends. "So far as I know, Tyr's is the only head I can press my thoughts into, but I can hear anyone who consciously opens their mind to mine. If you do that, it'll be a one-way communication, but at least you'll have a way to reach someone."

Brynn turned to Tyr. "So we're clear on strategy?"

"Yes," Tyr confirmed. "Forse, keep physical contact with Elsa until it's time for you to make the exchange. At that time, Elsa, stick close to me and Brynn, and do your calming thing on the dark elves. If everything goes well, we'll be home in time for dinner."

"Promise?" Mia turned to Tyr. With her head buried in his chest, I couldn't see her face, but fear radiated off her back, filling the air around her with a quivering energy.

"I wish I could." Tyr rubbed his thumbs just above Mia's hips. "But I *can* promise to return as soon as I can. I love you, *prinsessa*. Henrik, take care of my girl."

"I will," Henrik vowed. "And don't worry, War. My girl will take care of you."

When Tyr rolled his eyes, Henrik winked at Brynn, and motioned for Mia to follow him to the porch. They stood together, waving with a calm I knew neither of them felt, while Tyr glanced at Forse, Brynn, and me.

"Are you ready?" he asked.

"As we can be," I said honestly.

Tyr nodded, and I knew he understood. As much as I wished I had more time to practice, being of Asgard meant you learned a lot of things on the job. Trial by fire was a way of life. And retrieving the perp who'd committed *the* crime, from the realm populated by the darkest souls in the cosmos, with only a partially trained Unifier to keep things from going downhill... we were definitely walking headfirst into the flames.

My brother raised his head to the sky and let out a yell. "Heimdall! Open the Bifrost!"

The next moment, a brilliant rainbow shot down from the sky, engulfing us in its luminescence. The colors bounced off each other, the vibrations of each shade emitting a different level of energy. I stepped into the golden hue and pulled Forse close to me, knowing the color would soothe his anxiety. He wrapped his arms around me and tucked me to his chest, shielding me from the fierce wind that howled while the Bifrost sucked us upward. I clung to the corded muscles of Forse's back and willed away the nausea that coursed through me. We shot through Midgard's atmosphere, past its moon, and through the cosmos, en route to the black realm. Having my bones nearly sucked through my skin in an intergalactic rainbow vacuum made me inordinately queasy, though I'd take the Bifrost every day if it meant Forse would hold me like this.

As I pressed my cheek to Forse's chest and committed the sensation to memory for *extremely frequent* future use, the Bifrost shifted. We started our descent. I bent my knees and prepared for the impact, but before I felt the familiar jolt, there was a pressure at the back of my legs. Instead of stumbling across an unfamiliar field when we touched down, I found myself cradled safely in Forse's arms, my hands around his neck and my forehead pressed against his. He rose slowly from his landing crouch, but he didn't let me go.

"Well, *hei* there, you." I smiled up at him.

"*Hei.*" Forse lifted his head just enough to scan the area, then turned his attention back on me. "I thought, you know, in case it was an ambush, I should hold on to you so I could port us out of here."

Porting was Forse's gift—he could instantaneously transport himself and two passengers to any location within a realm. It came in handy when moving perpetrators, since Asgard's enemies were often tailed by bounty hunters, rival criminals, or co-conspirators hoping to take out the justice god.

"You're sweet." I reached up to touch his cheek with one finger. Then I turned my head to study our landing area. Black soot covered the field where we'd touched down, and stretched clear to a horizon peppered with plants that looked an awful lot like cactus. A jagged mountain range stood on our other side, easily two kilometers high, and circled by a crimson ribbon. I narrowed my eyes. "Is that a river? Why is it red?"

"Because it's made of lava." Forse nodded. "The mountains are dormant volcanoes."

"But if they're dormant, how is the lava—"

"That's the million-dollar question. Welcome to Svartalfheim." Brynn took her time righting herself. When she stood, her face was tinted grey. The poor thing got horrible Bifrost sickness. She preferred to travel by pegasus, but she'd sent her mare, Fang, back to Asgard to guard Freya. She swayed back and forth, and I wondered if she regretted her act of altruism.

Tyr completed his surveillance, and sheathed his broadsword. "We're clear. But there could be scouts in the mountains. Let's move." With that, Tyr stalked ahead, his sights set on the mysterious red river traversing the landscape.

Forse set me on my feet with a lingering look, and took my hand in one of his. With the other, he held the nanomolecular particle accelerator at eye level. We moved together for five minutes, following Tyr in silence until we reached the base of the mountain. When Tyr held up a hand, we circled around. He examined the rocky overhang, and motioned for us to step underneath it. We gathered in the makeshift shelter. Neither Forse nor Brynn lowered their weapons.

"Brynn, test the coms." Tyr didn't take his eyes off the horizon.

"Yes, sir." Brynn tucked her rapier into her belt and adjusted her backpack. Between the extra ammunition and Mia's bagged lunch, it was stuffed full. Brynn giggled. "You want a sandwich?"

"Just test the coms." Tyr bit back a smile.

Brynn held her arm up, pressing her pointer finger to the center of her wrist. "Call Tyr," she ordered. And just like that, Brynn's forearm fogged, then glassed over to form a screen bearing her reflection.

When Tyr's forearm emitted a soft hum, he pressed his finger against it. The color ebbed, and Brynn's face appeared in its surface.

"Sandwich?" Brynn grinned at her arm.

"Stuff it, Aksel." Tyr tapped his wrist again, and Brynn's screen went dark.

"I can't believe you hung up on me." Brynn feigned indignation. "Whatever. Let's test yours." She pointed to Forse and me. "Call Elsa," she commanded her arm. "And Forse."

Our arms hummed, and when we touched our wrists, Brynn's face filled the surface of mine.

"Mine works," I confirmed.

"Mine too," Forse seconded.

"Awesome. These should help us stay in contact." Brynn tapped her screen off.

Tyr cracked his neck. "Let's just not get separated."

"Deal," Brynn chirped. She drew her rapier again and stared at the landscape. "Is this where they're supposed to meet us?"

"My source told me to stand under the innermost

overhang near the Kopfler mountains at forty degrees latitude." Tyr checked the mountain range before glancing at the sky. "We're at the correct latitude, and unless Heimdall altered the coordinates on the Bifrost, this should be the Kopfler range."

As Tyr spoke, Brynn kept watch on the horizon. In the distance, a cluster of dark figures led a hooded one across the soot. "We've got company," Brynn said. She gripped the hilt of her rapier.

"We sure do. Game on." Forse narrowed his eyes and positioned himself so he stood in front of me. Tyr moved beside him, so they stood shoulder to shoulder. I shifted my heels so my feet were planted firmly in the soot, and grounded myself to the black earth. I opened the energy centers in my feet, drawing strength from the depths of Svartalfheim's core. When I was securely anchored to the realm, I pushed my aura out so it pressed against my friends, and sent waves of calming energy throughout the protective bubble. They pulsed along the perimeter, bathing our party in a slightly-less-anxious glow. The energy coming back at me dimmed as Tyr and Brynn's energies relaxed infinitesi-mally. *Not my best work, but it's better than nothing.*

I'd only managed to soothe two-thirds of our party. Forse clung to his tension as he reached back to lace his fingers through mine. He put his other hand on his holstered pistol and spoke in a low voice.

"Here comes trouble."

CHAPTER 5

"**S** *NOKART*, **TYR.**" **THE TALLEST** of the dark elves raised a hand in greeting. The rogue team leader stood half a head taller than his comrades, and he wore a patch that seemed to designate some kind of rank. *Curious.* I'd been unaware there was order among dark elf outlaws.

"*Snokart*, Tosk," Tyr said in response. He and Forse held their positions slightly in front of me, while Brynn stood at my side. My friends feigned calm, but each stood with their shoulders pulled back, their knees slightly bent, and their hands on their weapons. They didn't trust the dark elves any further than they could throw them.

Judging from the malicious energy vibrating off the elves, my friends were spot on with this assessment.

Work harder, Elsa. I drew a slow breath through my nose, and expanded my aura so it slid around our group to bump against the approaching dark elf party.

On my exhale, I pushed another wave of calm to the perimeter of the bubble. It nudged my friends, bringing Brynn and Tyr's energy down another notch, but Forse, Tosk, and the rest of the foreigners remained unaffected. *What am I doing wrong?*

"Brynn," I whispered as our visitors drew closer. "What's the thing on Tosk's jacket mean?"

"It's a colonel's badge." She barely moved her lips as she spoke.

"If these are outlaws, why is he still wearing his military insignia?"

Brynn shrugged. "Maybe he doesn't have a lot of clothes?" She stepped closer to me, and held her rapier tight.

"*Hverte skille vas min keptlevko?*" Tyr gestured to the woman at the back of the group. The dark elves parted, revealing the hooded figure of a herculean woman. She was tall, easily more than six feet. Skin tight leather pants clung to her toned legs, and she wore a matching black vest that left her muscular arms exposed. Although her wrists were bound, and a bag covered her head, I had no doubt she'd be able to overpower her captors with the flick of one enormous man-hand.

So why doesn't she?

"Yes. This is the captive you requested." Tosk slipped into English, which was a *huge* relief, since my Svartish skills were remedial, at best.

"Where's our payment?" The female to Tosk's right stepped forward. A fierce wind whipped across the plane, lifting her long white hair to expose high, pointed ears, not unlike those of my beloved Alfheim meadow elves. The dark elves and the light ones shared certain physical traits, but their souls were polar opposites. Even without calling on my abilities, I knew this group had evil intentions. I pushed the thought into my brother's head. He registered my voice and opened his mind to mine.

This is wrong, I communicated silently. *I'm giving them my best dose of cooperative energy, and all they're sending back is malicious intent.*

I feel it, too. Tyr's words sounded in my head, though he continued to face the elves with an impassive expression. *We'll grab Runa and go. If the exchange turns south, let Forse port you out of here. Brynn and I will hold them off until he can come back for us.*

Runa's already done her worst, I sent back. *Let's just leave now while we—*

"Did you not hear me, *Asgardian?*" The white-haired girl spat the name like it was a dirty word. "I said, where's our payment?"

"Bagatha." Tosk silenced the female elf with a look.

Tyr eyed Bagatha levelly before pulling a coin-sized stone from his pocket. "The prisoner?"

"Fair enough. Let's allow your justice god to make the exchange. I presume that's why he is here." Tosk took the ropes binding Runa and jerked them forward. Runa stumbled, landing on her knees as she fell. Tosk hissed, "Get up."

Runa pushed herself to her feet, the bag still covering her head, and Tosk gripped her elbow in his hand. He guided her forward, standing halfway between his party and ours.

"Forseti? The exchange?" Tosk stared at Forse, who bristled at his full name. I sent a ripple of calm across the perimeter of my aura, but it brushed right past him. He wasn't receptive to my influence at all. That wasn't good.

Let's just go. I pushed my thought into Tyr's head again. *I'm failing—Forse isn't open to my unifying. Tosk's energy is so dark it's almost nonexistent, and he's got so many blockers up, I can't see his next choice—I think it's deliberate. And we don't know what that stone does, but I'm sure it's more than we think if it's worth as much to him as Fenrir. Don't do this.*

You want me to just let Runa go? After everything she did? A flash of darkness swept across Tyr's mind. *Think of the evil she's capable of now that she's spent time in the dark realm. She could do irreparable harm, not only to Asgard, but to Alfheim...Vanaheim...*His thoughts broke and an overwhelming feeling of sorrow came from his love center. *Think about what she might do to Midgard.*

I loved my brother, I really did. But for an immortal war god, he had a dangerously soft spot for the weaker realms.

I sighed. *I understand you have to do this. Make the swap, but do it quickly. You and Brynn are the only ones my unifying seems to be working on, and I don't want anyone getting hurt.*

I closed my mind and focused on sending cooperative energy to the edge of my bubble.

Tyr nodded his thanks, and handed the stone to Forse. "Forse, make the exchange."

Forse squeezed my hand before passing me off to Brynn. With the stone clenched in his palm, he marched toward Runa. Although both of his guns were holstered, Forse held his free hand over the non-implosive pistol's handle. When he reached Tosk, he exchanged the stone for Runa's ropes. He pulled hand-cuffs out of his back pocket, slapped them around her wrists, and lifted the bag high enough to catch a glimpse of her angular jaw, full lips, and strong nose. "It's her," he spat, before forcefully lowering the bag and leading Runa back to our party. Disgust was etched all the way from his narrowed eyes to his downturned mouth. His expression mirrored my feelings. Being this close to Runa for the first time since the incident left an unsettling feeling in my gut. Images from the last time I'd seen her flooded my brain, and as an acidic liquid rose against the lump in my throat, I swallowed it back down and refocused on my grounding. I wouldn't give her the satisfaction of making me ill.

You've got this, Elsa, I assured myself. *Just keep everyone calm enough to get through this exchange. You've got Brynn and Tyr at manageable anger levels—if you can just keep Forse from going berserker, and hold Tosk and his minions at bay for a few more minutes, we'll be back home and this will all be over.* I sent another shot of coopera-tive energy along the perimeter of my aura, praying some part of it would be absorbed by the dark elves, but it all returned to me, untouched. *Dang it.*

"If that's settled, we'll be on our way. Clear out before the Bifrost—"

Tyr's warning was cut off by a guttural growl. I froze as Tosk launched the crystal at the cliff directly behind us. The stone shattered against the black surface, raining down shards in a gravity-defying arc. Tyr, Forse, and Brynn quickly closed ranks around me, but their focus was misdirected. As one of the shards flew over Runa, she leapt off the ground and ripped off her hood. Red curls tumbled free, cascading down the back of her leather vest and stopping at her waist. As she leapt, Runa opened her mouth. The shard landed on her tongue, and when her feet touched the ground, her skin sparkled for a moment, as if the crystal had infused her with its brilliance. She pulled her wrists away from each other, tearing free of her handcuffs and twisting out of Forse's grasp in one quick movement.

"Skit." Forse turned toward me and dove, his arms outstretched to pull me close. I released my grounding and leapt toward him. As I did, I sent another calming pulse through my aura in a futile attempt to soothe his panic and help him make the most level-headed choices. But before he could port us out of danger, Runa held up a hand. A beam of light shot from her palm. It struck me in the chest and wrenched me away from my protectors.

"Arugh!" I cried out as the beam seared my flesh, pressed between two rib bones, and squeezed my heart in a vise-like grip. The organ thudded in protest as the beam drew me forward, pulling me with unfathomable force. I reached for my dagger to cut myself loose, but the beam shot through my arms, immobilizing them, as I was dragged toward the only goddess in the realms I truly feared.

It must have been my absence of love for Runa that enabled her to take me. I'd felt that same fear for the only other creature who'd ever managed to hurt me —Fenrir.

The mortals were right. Hate wasn't the enemy —fear was.

"Elsa!" Forse dropped low in a crouch as the beam ripped me farther from his reach. He launched off his toes at the same time as my brother ducked his head and barreled toward Runa. The closer they got to the beam, the faster it vibrated, sending me flying at Runa. It only took a second to reach her side, and once I was there she dug into my arms with her awful man-hands. I was barely able to cry out for Forse before Runa ported us out of the field, and into an abyss so dark, it looked like a black hole.

For all I knew, it was.

"*Hei?*" THE DARKNESS SWALLOWED my voice, before shooting it back. From the amount of time it took to echo around, I deduced I was in a small room—maybe three-by-three meters, if it was square. I was curled in a ball on a hard floor, my arms cradling my torso. My ribs were still tender from Runa's blue beam assault.

Tyr! Can you hear me? I shouted for my brother inside my head, and waited. *Tyr!* After a beat, I pushed myself to a seated position, ignoring the residual pain in my chest. *Tyr?* My spirits sank as I realized he wasn't going to answer. Wherever I was, the location must have held enough dark magic to block his telepathy… or maybe he was busy dealing with the evil elves Runa left behind. Either way, things were not looking good.

"Hello?" I called out loud, this time paying attention to the way the sound traveled above me. The ceiling was high. Six meters? More? It was impossible to tell when it was pitch black. I opened my palm and held it face up at chest level. Calling on one of my more mundane—albeit practical—abilities, I closed my eyes and summoned a glowing orb of light. My hand began to heat, and a faint vibration ran along my fingers. Any moment now, I'd hear the *pop*, and the room would be bathed in a faint white glow.

My brother got to fly, and I was an immortal flashlight. Odin's sense of equity was questionable.

"That's odd," I murmured as I opened my eyes. The room was still black as night. Where was my orb? I furrowed my brow and focused on my fingertips. The tingling sensation confirmed my magic was still within me, so why couldn't it summon the light? Maybe…

A chill ran up my arm and wrapped around my heart. *No.* It would take a *lot* of darkness to mute my magic. Did Runa take me to Helheim? Or did she find a way to summon enough darkness to cloak a building in Svartalfheim? It was a dark realm, sure, but nowhere near dark enough to cancel out my magic. *Oh gods, could it mute my abilities too?* I pushed my energy outside my cell, scanning the area for other signatures. My bubble recoiled as it bumped against a being a floor beneath me, emitting a pulse of malice. *Thank Odin.* I might have encountered a hostile element, but at least my magic was the only thing that was muted…my energy-based abilities remained intact. I supposed it made sense. Summoning my orb required I access light magic, which could be muted by a surplus of dark magic. But energy was a universal truth, not governed by the laws of magic or affected by anything beyond the user's will. Energy followed intention, and so long as I remembered that, my energetic abilities would be strong enough to manifest my desired outcome.

And right then, I intended to manifest that we all find our way safely back to Arcata. Fast.

After I pulled my energy back, I continued my assessment. My cell was so dark I'd have thought my eyes were sealed. I blinked against the cold air, willing my body to fight off the chill coming from my right. *Hold on.* I inched across the rough, uneven floor. It felt as if it was made of stone, and if the smattering of pebbles beneath my fingers was any indicator, the construction job had been a hasty one. My hands pressed on until I came to a wall. I moved up the rocky surface, and followed the curvature of the room in a careful exploration. *Interesting. The room is round.* I paused when the stone turned to wood, and knocked quietly on the surface of what I assumed to be the door to determine its density. My knuckles made a low thud, and I knew the barrier was too strong to break through without a heavy tool. My palms lightly traced the door's surface, and I made a note of the metal rectangle at face level. It must have opened from the other side— maybe it was some kind of a window so my captors could look in. For now, it was sealed shut, and I took advantage of the alone time to complete my evaluation.

The stone picked up where the door ended, and as I circled back to where I'd started, the draft grew stronger. I moved my hands upward until I felt the square-shaped break. *Thank Odin.* The room had a small window, sealed with thin metal bars. I didn't know how this would figure into my escape plan, but it sure as snow didn't hurt things.

Plus, it meant I had fresh air. Even if that air was freezing.

I ran my fingers across the metal bars. They were close enough together that I'd be able to fit my forearm through, but not much more. Climbing out wasn't going to be an option. Besides, I didn't know where the window led. Svartalfheim had one sun that only shone on the realm a few hours a day during the winter, and no moons. This meant the realm was blanketed in blackness most of the time. My friends would be able to use technology or their extra abilities to create light, but so long as I couldn't summon my orb, I was literally in the dark. *Fabulous.*

I shoved my forearm through the bars in case the block only worked *inside* this cell, and made one more attempt to produce light from my palm. When my orb refused to appear, I accepted my temporary fate. *Darkness it is. Move on to assessing an escape route.* I dropped to the ground and patted the stone surface until I found a pebble. Picking it up, I moved carefully back to the window, and felt the walls until I found the opening. I pressed my cheek to the metal bars so my ear settled between them, and dropped the pebble out of the window, listening carefully as it fell. My heart plunged as the silence stretched on. When I finally heard the faint plunk of the rock hitting water, I pressed my back to the wall and slid down.

Mom had read me plenty of Midgardian fairy tales in my childhood—the mortals' tales were much more lighthearted than our own, and Mom chose to infuse our lives with joy over fear, whenever possible. But for all the times I'd asked for the story about the princess locked in a tower...well...I suddenly wished I'd been more partial to the one about the Snow Queen. Or the one where the servant girl falls in love with the handsome prince, and lives happily ever after with a closet full of fabulous shoes.

But there was no sense in dwelling, when I needed to ascertain exactly whose not-so-ivory tower I was locked in. Then I could call my friends, enlist their help to break me out of here, and put this whole ordeal behind me.

I folded my hands in my lap and closed my eyes, preparing to push my energy outward until it came into contact with the malicious being I'd felt earlier.

But before I'd finished grounding myself, a sing-song voice came from the other side of the door. "Well, don't you look relaxed."

The creak of metal let me know the viewing square in the wooden door was opening. I stayed where I was, only moving enough to open my eyes. When I did, candlelight illuminated Runa's angular face through the window. The light cast an orange hue on her skin, and made her crimson hair look like it glowed.

Sure, she was pretty. But what had Forse ever seen in her?

"You might as well release me now. My friends will be coming for me." I spoke matter-of-factly.

"Oh, I'm counting on it." Runa's mouth turned up in a cruel grin.

"You *want* them to come here? If you wanted a fight, you could have just had it back at the mountain. Why drag everyone all the way out to…where are we, exactly?"

"Nice try, but I wasn't born yesterday. Tosk and Bagatha are having a little fun with your friends as we speak. If they survive what the dark elves have planned for them, I've got a few games of my own I'm going to play while they hunt for you." The candle flickered, and Runa's mud-colored eyes reflected the flame. Hate shot at me, the emotion so strong it nearly broke through my protective bubble.

"Why are you doing this?" I kept my voice even.

"Because you're hiding my dog."

"Fenrir?" My pitch shot up, betraying my surprise. "He's *my* dog, or he used to be. Now he's a prisoner of Asgard. And if you want him so much, why did you trade him for the stone?"

"We knew you'd never hand him over willingly, so we asked for the stone in his place. That crystal gave me the powers I needed to capture you, and now you're going to take me to Fenrir. The effects of this crystal will wear off, but the dog…" Runa chuckled. "His effects last forever. Don't they, *Elsa*?"

Rage bubbled inside me like a hot spring, and it took every bit of willpower I had to *not* react. I drew a cleansing breath, inhaling more forcefully than I would have liked, before exhaling. When I was positive I was in control of my faculties, I allowed myself to speak.

"We'll never give you Fenrir."

"Oh, I'm pretty sure you will." Runa's eyes narrowed. "Which will make Tyr responsible for the fall of everyone he loves. And your precious boyfriend will know he stood by and let it happen. If only he'd been a better judge of character when he was dating me." Runa threw her head back and laughed.

I leapt to my feet and reached for my dagger. My hand closed around nothing, and I patted my waist frantically. *Where is it?*

"What's the matter, *goddess*? Missing this?" Runa raised her hand. My dagger dangled between two fingers.

"When did…" *Ugh. She took it while I was unconscious.*

"Do I look like an idiot? I confiscated these when I brought you here." Runa held both hands up to the window. My phone and my dagger glinted in the sliver of light. I lunged for them, my hands reaching through the metal bars to close around my lifelines home, but Runa stepped back before I could make contact. "I'll let the Asgardians find you eventually, but I plan to have some fun with them first. A *lot* of fun."

Before I could respond, Runa jammed my arms back through the bars and slammed the window shut, encasing me in darkness once again. The rage turned to a swirl, bile churning in my gut as I took enough cleansing breaths to blow down the world tree, Yggdrasil. No way was that wench—I mean, that creature of Ymir—going to hurt another soul.

Especially not my friends.

I pressed my pointer finger to my wrist and murmured into the com. "Call Tyr."

And then I waited.

When a full minute went by and my arm was still just an arm, I gave up. There was no sense in drawing attention to the com in case Runa came back. It rang loud and clear on my end, a testament to Mia's *älva* dust-free design—the device worked even where dark magic rendered light magic useless. My inability to make contact with my brother must have been because of a problem on his end; maybe he was still in the heat of his battle. I'd have to rely on my abilities if I wanted a line out of here.

I grounded myself and set a protection around my aura. When it was secure, I pushed my energy outward, searching for the mind signature I knew almost as well as my own. All of Svartalfheim looked the same to me, and I tore across mile after mile of dark-sooted plain. An eternity passed as I scanned the ground for my friends. I could have been traveling in circles, for all I knew; the sky was the same black void as the ground. The only light cutting through the Svartalfheim night came from the homes of the occasional settlement, and the parliament building. *Hold on. The parliament building?* If the map Tyr made us memorize after last night's dinner was correct, that would mean I was three kilometers due north of our drop-in spot. If I could find the outcropping where Runa had captured me, I could follow my friends' energy trails until I tracked them down.

I pushed my energy south until I came to the mountains. Once there, I shot over the range, intent on picking up my brother's blazing red energy trail of fury.

I didn't have to look far.

On the cactus-strewn hill beneath me, Tyr, Forse, and Brynn remained locked in battle with the outlaws who'd conspired with Runa. Their auras were so dark I couldn't get a clear read on their strategy. The only thing I knew for sure was that they fought to kill. Rage practically seethed from their pores, the angry energy tainting the air with an unseemly smell.

All energy had a scent. It explained why easygoing souls like Henrik smelled like sunshine, protective souls like Tyr smelled like redwoods, and peaceful souls like Mia smelled like lavender. And right then, those dark elves filled the plain with the undeniable odor of an evil soul...sulfur.

I locked in on Tyr's brain and entered without asking permission, violating our self-imposed rule. The minute I dove into his head, I remembered how complicated Tyr's job was. His brain monitored multiple scenes simultaneously, each scene playing on its own screen like the inside of a mission control room. On the right, Forse wrestled Tosk's apparent second-in-command—the dark elf wore an insignia on his jacket that resembled Tosk's. He threw Forse on the ground with the confidence of a seasoned fighter. Forse rolled to the side, tucking his long legs beneath him and jumping back before the second could deliver a blow. When the dark elf crouched to attack, Forse leapt in the air, delivering a front kick to the elf's jaw that sent him reeling. The second stumbled backward, howling as Forse threw a series of punches that would have broken a mortal's jaw. His frenzied attack left me confident he had the upper hand, so I switched screens and assessed Brynn's situation.

Brynn's opponent was Bagatha—the white-haired female. She gripped a thick blade in her hand, expertly deflecting the parries of Brynn's rapier with her much shorter weapon. Where Brynn was the embodiment of power, a striking contrast of Asgardian warrior and ballerina-like fluidity, Bagatha battled like a viper. Her short, choppy strikes betrayed her rage, and each time she advanced on Brynn it was clear she struck to kill. If Brynn wasn't such a seasoned valkyrie, I would have been worried. But I knew she had this. She always did.

You go, Brynn! I cheered her on.

"Elsa?" Tyr grunted as he swung his broadsword. The weight of the weapon and the shock of finding me in his head must have thrown him off-balance, because his equilibrium shifted and he stumbled to the right.

Forse stopped pounding on his opponent long enough to steady Tyr. He pulled his gun, twisted his wrist, and fired at Brynn's attacker. The force of the capsule launched Bagatha off Brynn, who in turn took off running. As she distanced herself from the impending implosion, Brynn pushed off her toes and flung her body into the air. Tyr held Tosk's attention with a one-handed parry, giving Brynn the element of surprise. She landed easily on her toes, raising her arms above her head and driving her rapier deep into Tosk's back. Tosk's mouth fell open as he looked down, his bony fingers wrapped around the blade sticking through his chest. A tar-like substance oozed from the wound, and in the second it took him to reach behind his back and withdraw the weapon, Bagatha let out a wail. My focus shifted again as the implosive took hold. A pungent odor filled the air and Bagatha's hands shook as her bones, organs, then flesh were sucked inward. With a sickening pop she disappeared completely, her remains no more than an ashy film settling on black soot.

Forse's attacker looked up in horror. Forse's rage was palpable, and I knew him well enough to understand he needed a release. He holstered the gun and reached out so both hands circled the dark elf's neck. His eyes were dark as he wrenched the elf's head to one side, breaking the spine and declaring unapologetically, "That's for taking Elsa."

If the sight of a dangling dark elf head wasn't so disgusting, I would have kissed him. Though since I was nothing more than an energy signature in my brother's head, maybe a kiss wasn't exactly appropriate.

An anger surge in Tyr's brain brought my attention back to my host. As Tyr prepared to drive his sword through the still stunned Tosk, the elf pulled Brynn's rapier from his torso and flung it onto the ground. He twirled in a fast circle and disappeared, leaving behind nothing more than a thick pool of blood.

My brother, Forse, and Brynn swore in unison. Then they formed a triangle, backs pressed together, and turned a tight circle as they scanned the area for threats. Wanting to be useful, I pushed my energy out and felt for additional presences. Other than the occasional scavenging animal, my friends were alone.

You're clear, I signaled in Tyr's mind.

"Elsa?" Tyr grunted. "Where are you?"

Oh, sorry! I'm in here! In your head. I'm in your head. I would have asked, but you seemed kind of busy, I apologized.

"You think?" he muttered.

"Is Tyr going crazy again?" Brynn asked Forse.

"Shut up, Aksel. It's my sister," Tyr growled. Since I was viewing the world through his eyes, I couldn't see my brother's expression. But the way the sky turned a slow circle before the screen focused on Brynn, I surmised he'd given her an award-winning eye-roll.

"Elsa?" Forse flew into Tyr's frame of vision. He gripped Tyr's arms and shook. Annoyance flashed through Tyr's mind. "Where? Where is she?"

"She's in my head." Tyr removed Forse's hands from

his biceps. I could tell from the way his mind strained, it wasn't easy work.

Forse! Are you okay? I shouted.

"Else," Tyr complained. "They can't hear you. And that gives me a headache."

Sorry.

"Rule number one. When we're *inside* each other's heads, we use our *inside* voices. Remember?" Tyr chastised me out loud.

I said I was sorry, I huffed.

"She's in your head?" Brynn jumped in front of Tyr and waved with characteristic enthusiasm. "*Hei* Elsa! Where are you? Are you okay? Sit tight; we're coming for you." She adjusted her ponytail so her curls sat less chaotically atop her cherubic face. "Tyr, where is she? Which direction are we going?"

"I—" Tyr began.

"Well?" Forse's lips were drawn. "Where is she? Come on. What are we waiting for? Brynn, pick up your sword. Let's move."

Brynn dove for the ground and came up holding her rapier. "Ugh. Really?" She pulled a rag from her backpack and wiped the black blood from the blade. "Dark elves have the *grossest* blood. This will be caked on the handle for-freaking-ever."

"Where is she?" Forse placed his hands on both sides of Tyr's face and leaned close to stare into his eyes. "Elsa, I'm so sorry they got you. I never should have agreed to facilitate this exchange. If I'd just been able to reach you faster, I could have ported you out of here and…" Forse looked heartbreakingly helpless. "I'm sorry," he whispered.

"Enough already!" Tyr pushed Forse back. "You do realize you're baring your soul to the war god, don't you?"

"Elsa's in your head," Forse countered.

"Yes. But *you're* in my face." Tyr took a step back, distancing himself from our friends.

Move the other way Tyr! I like being that close to him, I complained.

"Enough! All of you!" Tyr bellowed. "Forse, Brynn, keep watch. Tosk might come back with new friends, since we killed his old ones. Elsa, tell me where you are so we can come get you."

I don't know. I sighed. *I'm locked in some tower but you know how it is here at night. It's pitch-black outside, and the tower's got enough dark magic I can't summon my orb. You guys are lucky Brynn has her brightener on, or you wouldn't be able to see anything.* Tyr glanced to his left, where the glowing sphere hovered over Brynn's backpack.

Right. Well, how did you find me? Do you remember passing any landmarks on your way? Anything that can help us? Tyr pressed.

I found you the same way I always do—I pushed my energy out until I picked up on your signature. I tried calling on my com, but you didn't answer. You were probably already fighting Tosk and his minions, and didn't hear it hum.

I'm sorry, Elsa.

It's fine, I reassured him. *I found you anyway.*

So where are you?

I'm not sure. I know I'm somewhere on the other side of the big mountain behind you. I passed the parliament building on the way in, and I know I traveled for a long time looking for you. Maybe you're seventy-five kilometers from the place Runa's holding me? Maybe more? I guessed.

Tyr swore. *You could be anywhere.*

"Where is she?" Forse interrupted. My heart tugged at the crack in his voice.

"Elsa, give me a minute with these guys," Tyr spoke aloud. "Forse, get the locator set up and set up two scans—one for Elsa specifically, and one for all towers within a fifty-to-two-hundred-fifty-mile circumference of the parliament building. Elsa, do you know how high up your tower is?"

Between twelve and fifteen meters. And it's surrounded by water. But Tyr, I think the tower's cloaked in dark magic—there's enough in my cell to mute my light magic, though thankfully my energetic abilities are intact. I guess you know that, though, since I'm in your head. But I think it will be too much for the locator to see through. So even if—

"Slow down. The dark magic's strong enough to mute yours? You're not in Helheim, are you?" Tyr sounded alarmed.

"Oh gods, is she in Helheim?" Brynn cried.

"I don't know. Let her answer! Elsa?" Tyr pressed.

I'm not in Helheim. You're still in Svartalfheim, and I didn't jump realms to find you, so I'm here, too. I just have no idea where.

"She's not in Helheim," Tyr voiced out loud. I heard Brynn and Forse sigh in relief.

Oh, Elsa. Regret clouded Tyr's vision as he directed his words inside his head. *I'm so sorry I put you in this position.*

You didn't. Runa did. You were right to want to bring her in. We just hit a little hiccup, but we'll get through it. I'll try to escape and get back to you guys, but in the meantime, I'll make myself useful and gather as much intel as I can—find out who she's working with, what she's planning to do with Fenrir...she really wants that dog. Be careful—I have the distinct impression that if you show up wherever I am, you'll be walking right into a trap.

Elsa, surely you know that I am un-trappable. Tyr's arrogance made me smile.

Of course. You focus on steering clear of Tosk, and whoever else he's working with. When I've gathered as much information as I can from Runa, I'll find a way to get out of here and track you down. If you guys happen to find me in the meantime, we can catch the next Bifrost out of here.

Tyr's view narrowed as he furrowed his brow. *Sorry, Sis, but finding you trumps everything else.* He spoke his next words out loud. "Forse, amend your scan to include all towers in Svartalfheim over twelve meters in height, surrounded by water. Don't worry about looking for Elsa's trace; she says the tower's cloaked in enough dark magic to render the locator useless."

"What the Hel?" Forse swore.

"I know. But that device can still track the towers themselves. We'll isolate all potential hostage locations.

And since there are only three of us, Forse, you're going to port us to each one until either that locator or our god hunt tracks down my sister."

"With pleasure." Forse put his hands on either side of my brother's head and pulled him close. Now his emerald eyes were just inches from my vantage point. They burned with an intensity that was equal parts adoration and agony. "We're going to get you out of there, Elsa," he vowed. "And then I'm never letting you out of my sight again. That's a promise."

My energy fluttered, and I willed Tyr forward so we could kiss the bridge of Forse's nose. But my brother's audible groan, coupled with his vigorous removal of Forse's hands from his temples, thwarted my plan.

Tyr, I complained.

"Both of you need to remember that you are talking through *me,*" Tyr growled. "And this is getting weird. Elsa, knock it off. Forse, get to work."

"Fine." Forse stepped back. He pulled the locator out of his pocket and set up shop beneath the rocky outcropping at the base of the mountain. He drew his shoulders back, set his jaw, and began pressing buttons like a god possessed.

You know he'd do anything for you. My brother's voice sounded inside his head.

I'd do anything for him, I said wistfully. *Tell him I miss him.*

You can tell him yourself when we pick you up. Förbaskat, Elsa, I can't believe they pulled one over on us.

Again. How are they getting through? I knew Tyr closed his eyes because the screens went dark.

Freya was—well, we'd never seen an attack like that before. And we've never seen anything like the crystal Runa ingested. It gave her powers, Tyr. Powers. We don't even know the extent of them. Did you know it could generate magic like that? I asked.

*If I did, I'd never have taken it out of the treasure vault, much less put it in dark elf hands. We don't need to give them any tools that might help them bring about the fall of Asgard. The Norns have been following the Ragnarok prophecy, but they don't see the end of days coming for decades, maybe centuries. Though they've been wrong before…*Tyr's screen brightened as he opened his eyes to stare at the sky.

Don't go there, I cautioned.

It's my job to go there, he growled. *But Ragnarok aside, these monsters are getting around us, Elsa. We've got to tighten up or…or…*

He didn't have to say it. I could see the flashback from inside his mind.

Stop, I ordered. *We aren't our parents. I'm going to be just fine. You guys will get me, and we'll head back to Arcata, and everything will be exactly the way it was.*

That's not good enough, Tyr rumbled. The way it was got a lot of gods killed. We're going to get you out of here and so help me, Forse and I are going to make Runa and Tosk pay.

You do that, big brother. Just make sure you don't give her Fenrir. She wants him too badly. I flinched as my energy went on lockdown. My ears picked up on something clanging outside the door. *Sorry, I've got to get back to my body. You know it's hard on it when I send my energy out for this long, and I think someone's coming. I'll gather intel on this end. If I break myself out of here before the locator finds me, I'll let you know where to come pick me up.*

Take care of yourself, Tyr thought softly.

You do the same. And take care of Forse, okay? I kind of need him around.

Will do, Tyr vowed.

Secure in his promise, I withdrew my energy from his head, pulling it at breakneck speed across the black space until I was once again back in my body.

It was the last place I wanted to be.

CHAPTER 7

"GET UP. YOU'RE GOING to show me where they're keeping Fenrir." Runa stormed into the cell, her stiletto boots clacking on the stones. A glow bathed the room as Runa lit a wall sconce I hadn't noticed in my inventory. *Interesting.* I filed its presence away and pushed myself to my feet. I pressed my back to the wall and kept my arms flexed in the defensive stance Forse had drilled into me before we left.

Runa laughed, the barking sound echoing off the walls. "You think you're going to fight me, *ko?*"

Well that was just rude. I was many things, but I was definitely not a cow.

"I think you're going to be angry when I tell you I don't know where Fenrir is. So I'm prepared to defend myself, yes." I held my breath as Runa stood directly in front of me. Even without the stilettos she would have towered over my five and a half feet. She was easily as tall as my brother, and her shoulders were practically as broad as his. I swallowed my anxiety and pushed out calming energy. Bullies preyed on fear, and I wasn't about to give this one any reason to strike.

"What are you going to do, meditate your way out of this?" Runa crossed her arms. "Don't forget, I lived in Asgard once too. I know you went through high school in the protected gods program. Those weaklings didn't get nearly enough fight training to take me on. Your little *gift* meant you never had to learn to fight for yourself—the rest of the gods trained hard to be able to protect sweet little Elsa." She snorted. "I remember all about your freaky mind powers. Now they're going to take me straight to Fenrir, so show me what you know and I won't kill you."

What I knew was that the cell door was open, and with my magic on lockdown, I might not have another window to get out of there. The situation wasn't ideal —a beast of a woman stood between me and freedom, and I was hardly athletic enough to overpower her. But I did have a modicum of Brynn's Asgardian super-speed, and one Hel of a lot of motivation to remove myself from my current situation. If I faked left and dove right like Forse had shown me back in the forest, I might be able to throw Runa off long enough to get to the door. And from there…well, there was a reason even gods in the protected program went through so many improvisational drills in school.

Here goes nothing.

I didn't allow myself to think about the risk, the odds, or the likelihood that I was about to incur severe injury. I simply shifted my weight to my toes and bolted.

I launched myself through the door and barreled down the narrow hallway. The grey stones were hard beneath the thin soles of my shoes, and I stumbled across the uneven surface before slamming into the thick slabs of a dark wood door. A high-pitched laugh pealed behind me.

"Just where do you think you're going?" Runa called.

"Home," I muttered, pulling on the heavy iron handle of the door. It took all of my strength to wedge it open enough to squeeze through, and I didn't bother pulling it shut behind me before I sprung into motion again. My arms pumped and my flats clacked as I raced down the circular stone staircase. I bit back a yelp as my elbow made contact with an uneven shard sticking out from the wall. Runa's laughter echoed through the rocky chamber, letting me know she was close behind.

"Do you honestly think this little escape act is going to work?" Runa barely sounded winded as she called from somewhere behind me.

"You achieve what you believe," I panted. And it was my absolute belief that if I didn't make it out of here *right now*, I might not get another chance.

The staircase filled with a bright blue light as a beam shot over my head. It struck the wall directly in front of me, sharp rocks raining down on my head and arms. I pushed forward, ignoring the pain as a dozen tiny tears erupted across my skin. I knew my Asgardian super-healing would fix the wounds in minutes. My magic might have been muted by whatever cloak Runa placed on this structure, but my energetic gifts remained mercifully unaffected. *For now.* I ducked as another beam shot past me, this one narrowly missing my arm. It struck the wall, creating a boulder-sized hole. Another beam struck the ceiling, and I covered my head as the stones from above clattered to the ground, blocking the staircase. I skidded to a stop just before I plowed headfirst into the rubble. A keening cackle came from behind me.

"Now what are you going to do?" Runa's voice sounded unnervingly close.

What *was* I going to do? Forse had told me to identify two plausible escape routes in any situation. But the staircase was blocked, and the monster trying to kill me was closing in. The only way out was…

I didn't bother to look down. No matter how high I still was, the freshly blasted wall was my only escape. I bent my knees and launched myself off the staircase, through the hole and away from Runa.

The second I was outside, panic wrapped me in its manacles, and I flailed wildly. *Oh, gods. I must be twelve meters high. And I'm…over a moat? If I hit the water from this height…but I won't. I jumped as far as I could from the wall, and there's no way Runa could summon enough dark magic to extend the blocker this far beyond the edge of the building; the cloak is going to wear off any minute.* I held out my hands and pushed energy at the rapidly approaching ground, secure in the knowledge that my magic would kick in and slow my descent.

Any second now.

It was about to happen.

Oh my gods. Why isn't it kicking in? How did she cloak the outside of the tower? I closed my eyes and braced myself for the collision, praying whatever injuries I incurred wouldn't prevent me from swimming to the shore and clawing my way back to my friends…wherever they were. But before I felt the sharp strike of the impact, my body was yanked upward. My head bowed under the force and heavy energy squeezed my heart. Darkness overwhelmed me, as I was ripped away from the moat and back through the hole.

"No!" I screamed, clawing at the air in a pointless attempt to overpower Runa and her blue beams of terror.

"Yes," she hissed, as the beam pulled me back up the staircase and down the narrow hallway before flinging me into the cell I'd just escaped. I landed on my hip and skidded across the uneven surface. The stones scraped through my clothes and left me feeling raw and bruised. But I pushed myself to my feet, refusing to give up.

Runa wasn't taking me without a fight.

"You're going to tell me where they keep Fenrir." Runa slammed the cell door behind her and stalked toward me. "And you're going to tell me *now*."

My gaze shifted between the closed door and the barred window. I needed to buy time while I figured out another escape route. I wrapped my arms around my stomach so my fingers grazed the worst of the bruises. They hurt, but I'd had worse. "I'd love to help you, Runa, but I can't. Nobody told me where they took Fenrir after we captured him. Maybe his guards knew it'd make me a target."

"Liar." Runa thrust out her arm, and thick fingers wrapped around my neck. The pressure against my windpipe was immediate, and my hands fell to my sides as I opened my mouth in a futile effort to suck in air. Was Runa always this strong, or...*oh gods. Exactly what powers did she get from that crystal? The ability to port with at least one captive. Blue beams. Super-strength...what else was she capable of? Oh gods, oh gods.* Forget gathering intel. Forget outrunning her. I'd be lucky if I could hold off Runa long enough to send my friends one final *jeg elsker deg.*

"What's the matter, snowflake? Didn't your brother teach you how to protect yourself?" Runa taunted as she squeezed.

I threw my arms up and gripped Runa's hands. While I pulled, I wrenched from side to side in a futile effort to relieve the pressure. The room grew hazy as my blood took a one-way trip south. I pulled harder, fighting the grip that robbed my lungs of air. A searing pain filled my chest as my body burned through the last of its oxygen, and despite my pathetic struggle, it was clear I was outmaneuvered. I let my torso go limp, dropping my hands and using the last of my strength to push loving energy at Runa. If I could disarm her, even for just a minute, it could give me another chance to run.

Or at least to breathe.

When the warm bubble of energy filled my heart, I pushed it forward. Runa must have been too focused on hurting me to maintain her defenses—the second my bubble hit her, she released her grip and stumbled backward. *Bullseye.*

I dropped to the ground, my chest heaving as I sucked in air. When the burning began to ebb from my lungs, I pushed myself up to run. The calculating gleam in Runa's eyes stopped me cold.

"That's what I'm talking about." The corners of her mouth lifted in a cold smile. "Use that little talent of yours to find the dog. Now."

Regroup, Elsa. Use her. My intuition sparked, and I rubbed lightly at my neck as I worked through my next steps. My first escape attempt had failed—her new power meant I couldn't outrun her.

But there was a chance *my* power could outmaneuver her.

I took a step closer to Runa. "Fine. We'll do this your way. But remember, what I can do is based on energy and feelings—it's science, not magic. If whoever's holding Fenrir doesn't want me to find him, I'm not going to be able to do it."

"Stop right there." Runa held up her hand as I approached. "After that stunt, I don't want you anywhere near me."

I shrugged. "Suit yourself. But this probably isn't

going to work if you don't let me tap into your energy. I need to use it as a cloak to block mine, so Fenrir's guards won't think to keep me out. But if finding him isn't that important to you…"

Runa narrowed her eyes. "I'm not welcome in Asgard. If they don't want you finding him, they're not about to let me do it."

"Who said they're keeping him in Asgard? He could be anywhere," I pointed out.

Runa exhaled forcibly. "Okay. But if this is a trick, so help me, I'll end you right here."

I pushed down my fear and forced an easy smile. "If you end me, you've got no chance of finding him."

Runa stepped closer, and I braced myself for the strike. But she didn't hit me. Instead, she just growled. "Hurry up."

I closed my eyes, relief coursing through me. *It worked.* "Give me a minute," I said. As I pictured the thick trunk of one of the redwoods behind our Midgard house wrapping around me and rooting itself to the earth, the unease I felt at Runa's nearness ebbed. She wasn't attacking me in this moment, and by forcing myself into the present, I released my fear at what she might do next.

Besides, it was what *I* was going to do next that scared me most.

"First, I'm going to push my energy into yours so I can hide myself. Then, we'll start our search. Is that all right with you?" It was a lie. There was no way I was tricking Fenrir's guard for Runa's benefit.

"Whatever," Runa grunted. But the tension coming off her body was palpable. She *needed* this to work. Retrieving Fenrir caused her a lot of anxiety.

"Okay."

I set heavier protections than normal around myself. Mingling my energy with that of another being carried a risk of a merge—an irreversible entanglement of forces. And the *last* thing I wanted was to have any part of my energy trapped inside Runa's body. Or worse, to get her energy trapped inside of mine. *Ick.* I doubled down on my protections, then added an additional layer, just because. It was better to be safe than infiltrated by a dark soul.

Secure in the knowledge I'd made my aura impenetrable, I retreated to the quietest spot in my mind and pushed out my energy. I knew the minute I made contact with Runa's aura—the outer edge of my bubble recoiled, its distaste practically visceral. My fingertips tingled as I brushed against the blackness of Runa's personal space. It stung. Runa's inner pain manifested in a series of needle-like pricks along her energy bubble. I tried to get closer, but my outer layer of protection refused. Even the secondary layer protested, morphing from a shimmering gold screen to a black Kevlar wall. *Fabulous.* How was I going to reach Runa if my own aura wouldn't let me through?

With a sigh I withdrew, pulling my energy back so it no longer touched Runa's. I'd have to use an external scan. And I'd have to be quick; I could sense Runa's unease as she waited. She expected me to produce

Fenrir's location, and if the tapping of her foot was any indication, she expected it fast.

"Just a few more minutes," I lied.

"Hurry," Runa barked.

Knowing my time was limited, I pushed my energy as close to Runa's as my aura would allow. It wasn't happy, but it let me get near enough to do a scan. *Good enough.* I focused on Runa's first energy center—the space at the base of her spine. There was something off there I couldn't quite put my finger on—a greyish blur, hidden behind a bright white light. I frowned. Of course Runa would be buzzing with an unusually high physical prowess. It probably had something to do with the crystal she'd swallowed. Odin only knew the extent of the powers it gave her.

I moved up to the second energy center, the spot behind Runa's belly button that controlled her emotions. It revealed a duality—darkness smothering light. *Interesting.* Although I generally believed in the innate goodness of most spirits, I'd taken Runa for one of the rare black souls. Maybe there was hope for her yet.

Runa's third energy center reflected low self-esteem, not surprising, given her proclivity to destroy. Her heart center showed a nearly total void where her capacity for compassion should have sat. But more importantly, it absolutely seethed of self-hatred. Where did that root? I moved up, quickly scanning Runa's fifth through seventh centers, but found nothing of significance. Then I worked my way back down, following the black thread of energy wrapped around Runa's heart. It laced through her third and second centers, ending in the grey blur at the base of Runa's spine. Of course! The family of origin center. Babies were born innately good—even jotun, troll, and dark elf babies. But their early experiences with the world could tarnish them beyond repair. And the individuals responsible for forming those early experiences in Runa had been...

Hold on. Who *were* Runa's parents? She'd come to Asgard in the middle of one school year, and lived with a "family friend" we never actually saw. When she'd started dating Forse, she'd told us her parents were dead. Beyond that, she never talked about her family. Or Vanaheim, where she'd allegedly come from. Or anything, really. She'd dominated combat club, thanks to her gargantuan height, and the seemingly impenetrable chip on her shoulder, but none of us knew much else about her.

Could this be why she was so cold? The blackness in her heart rooted from a bad experience with her family of origin. Runa must have felt adrift at sea, growing up without her parents.

Poor thing. My heart tugged, the wave of sympathy overwhelming me. I couldn't undo Runa's past, but if I could untie that black knot in her first center, maybe I could change the way she looked at the world going forward. And maybe I could divert her from this dark course she was so determined to hurtle down. A surge of light pulsed in my head. *That's it!* If I could untie that knot, I'd unblock Runa's first center, erasing the black cord choking her heart, and leaving her free to choose a more positive path.

A dim light flickered from Runa, something deep within her acknowledging the truth of my assessment.

What is that?

I scanned my captor from head to toe, but the light was gone. *Did I imagine it?* No matter—my intuition told me I was on the right track. Ignoring my aura's protests, I pushed into Runa's energy, directing a thick beam of white light at the knot. The light struck the darkness, filling the dense matter with the love and hope my parents had instilled in me. But instead of unraveling, the knot clenched tighter, closing in on itself and sending an angry blast at my light. I pushed harder, trying to drive a stake into what appeared to be the weakest part of the coil, but the bond wouldn't budge. And as I sent one more surge of love at the knot, my body was racked with an insurmountable pain that tore through me from head to toe. I screamed out loud as an unbearable weight bore down on my chest, the blast from Runa's knot ejecting me from her space and knocking me back.

"What the Hel was that?" Runa snarled. Cold hands gripped my shoulders as my captor leapt on top of me. The back of my head connected with the stone, and I heard the crack at the same as time I registered the pain. Blood rushed to the wound as the thick pounding built to an unbearable pressure. I knew that pain. I'd felt it once before…right before Fenrir sent me into the coma.

Just don't black out and you'll get through this.

"You little liar. Were you even looking for Fenrir?" Runa shrieked.

"I was trying to help you," I mumbled. What was wrong with me? First I couldn't get past the wall around Forse's heart, and now I couldn't unravel Runa's knot. My realm was depending on me to be their interim Unifier, and I was a total failure. *I'm sorry, Mom.*

Runa put a prompt end to my pity party.

"I need that dog." She slapped my face. The sting of her palm was a tickle compared to the raw agony pulsing in my head. "Stay the Hel out of my space or next time I send you back to your coma. You have twenty-four hours to get me Fenrir's location or your people start dying."

Runa snapped her fingers, and I dragged one eyelid open just enough to see a hologram projected above her open palm. *Fabulous.* I added *hologram making* to the list of abilities Runa had acquired today.

"Pay attention. You'll want to see this." Runa held her hand directly in front of my face, so there was no chance I'd miss her projection. In the image, Runa had me in a headlock while she fought both Brynn and Forse. She threw her arm out in front of her, and two beams of light shot from one palm. One wound itself around Brynn, the other Forse, circling them from torso to neck and constricting as they lifted, creating a magical execution device. My breath caught, and for the first time since my capture I couldn't divert my fear. It churned in my gut and rose, gripping my heart in icy tentacles. It didn't matter whether that hologram was a vision of the future or a trick to force my hand. The blackness inside Runa was so strong, I knew she wouldn't think twice about killing anyone who kept her from what she wanted. That vision was a nightmare.

But it would *never* come true.

I rolled to my side, placed my palms on the ground, and pushed myself up, ignoring the pool of blood. The room spun violently as I stood on one foot, then the other, scrambling for a plan. Hurting Runa was out of the question; she was just too strong. But maybe if I got close enough, I could eject some of her dark energy—enough to make her see the value in Asgardian life. Or even just enough to distract her so I could run.

Runa lowered her hand, and the hologram disappeared. I bent my knees and prepared to move. Before my feet could leave the ground, she turned on one heel and wrenched the door open, then quickly slammed it shut behind her.

I'd missed my chance.

"Twenty-four hours," Runa called through the wood. "Then Asgard loses one god a day until I get that dog. And just in case you dream up another of your little escape plans..." A light flashed outside the door. "Don't. You're sealed in tight."

Runa's boots clicked on the stones as she stormed

down the hallway. I sank to the floor and pressed my hand to my head. The blood came slower now, though the pounding hadn't eased at all. As I took a deep breath and willed my body to heal, I tried to ignore the panic that danced heavily along my spine. I'd failed to physically overpower her, and I'd failed to energetically outmaneuver her.

What was I going to do now?

"Elsa, thank gods. Where are you?" Relief coursed through me as Forse's face filled the surface of my arm. The familiar sweep of his golden highlights; the intensity radiating from grass green eyes; even the ever-deepening *V* between his eyebrows filled my soul with a much-needed surge of calm. Forse Styrke was a god-sized dose of comfort food on a hugely stressful day. Every last inch of me relaxed at the mere sight of his face.

"You're bleeding! Where are you?" Forse repeated. The urgency in his voice jarred me from my calm, and as I cradled the screen atop my forearm, I realized the justice god didn't exactly share my inner peace. The *V* atop the bridge of his nose wasn't the only sign of the toll this day was taking on him. His forehead was lined with the wrinkles of a god twice his age, and his lips were pale and cracked.

"Are you okay?" I asked him softly.

"Are *you* okay?" he countered. "Gods, *hjärtat*, there's

blood caked to the side of your head. Is Runa's cloak on your tower inhibiting your healing abilities too?"

"No, this injury's just a deeper injury than the ones I've been repairing lately, so it's going to take a while to fix itself."

"Can you perform a healing or does the dark magic in the structure block that gift?" Forse asked.

Good question. I brought my hands together and channeled restorative energy. A moment later I felt the small surge of power between my hands. It wasn't as strong as I was used to; my energy had been severely depleted by Runa's attack, and that would have a corresponding effect on my strength as High Healer. Even so, the tiny ball was better than nothing. I placed my hands on the side of my head, and sent the energy into my skull. The pounding decreased by half and my scalp tightened as my skin slowly resumed knitting itself back together.

"The tower still hasn't affected my energetic abilities, just my magical ones," I reassured Forse. "I'll be fine, Forse. I swear."

"Elsa, are you...you're curled up in a ball, aren't you? I'm going to kill Tyr for bringing you here. War!" Forse bellowed. "Get the Hel over here and see what you've done!"

"Shh," I urged. "There's not exactly a volume control on this com, and you're shouting through this end, too. She confiscated my phone and my dagger; I don't want Runa to figure out I can still communicate with you."

"Is she nearby? Let me talk to her. I'll make her—"

"What? You'll make her what? She's not exactly open to persuasion. Trust me, I'm trying to get out of here. It's just not that easy, so until I find a way to break myself out of this tower without getting any of us hurt, I'll do my duty to Asgard and try to figure out why Runa's doing all of this. She's on a warpath, and so long as I'm stuck here with her, I'll keep trying to tap her energy to find out who she's working with and why. It's not ideal, but it's not without its benefits. Once I leave, I'll lose access to her, and we'll lose our upper hand, so I'm taking advantage of the—hopefully limited—time I've got with her."

"You think having you locked up is the upper hand?" The vein popped across Forse's forehead, but at least he kept his voice down.

"Kind of. The last time she went nuts, we didn't see it coming and something really awful happened."

"Elsa..." Forse's red-rimmed eyes turned positively crimson.

"This time," I pressed on, "we have the chance to get inside her head and see what she's planning. So we can stop it *before* it happens."

"I thought Tyr was the only Fredriksen who could read minds."

"He is. But I can access her energy, which allows me to see what her motivation is for whatever heinous crime she's planning this time. And if I can isolate her motivation, maybe I can get her to talk to me."

"You think if you call her out on the root of her issues, she'll get all meadow-elfy with you and share her feelings, along with her diabolical plan?" Forse sounded doubtful. "I hate to break it to you, but she didn't get to where she is by being touchy-feely with anyone—even the High Healer."

"Maybe not." I closed my eyes. It was a good idea in theory, but Runa was a master of deceit. I doubted even her own spirit could see through her darkness. *Hold on...*The thought triggered something. "Forse, remember a few weeks ago when we were going through the boxes of my parents' things, and we found Mom's old journals?"

"You asked me to hold on to them until you were ready to take them. You said it hurt too much to see her handwriting and know she was never coming back." Forse's voice cracked. "My mom's still got them in our library. Why?'"

"Can you get a message to Freya? Have her scan the journals and e-mail them to you, and then forward the scanned pages to my com. When we found them, I just assumed they were personal—that she'd filled pages about her epic romance with my father, and that it wasn't my place to look at them." My own journal was peppered with sentimental nuggets—*Elsa hearts Forse 4-ever. XOXO.* I'd die if anyone ever read it, and figured I'd owed my mother her privacy. "But what if Mom wrote about her work life too? About being the Unifier? What if the answers we've been looking for have been right in front of us this whole time?"

Forse's eyes widened. "If that's true, then we're the thickest gods in Asgard. If the key to unifying is sitting in my parents' library, I'm going to be beyond mad at myself."

I nodded. "Me too. Forse, what if there's something in there that can help me figure out how to get through to Runa? I saw a flicker of light when I was evaluating her energy…it made me think there's still goodness in her. If I can figure out how to multiply it, maybe I can make all of this better."

"You think there's goodness in everyone." Forse shook his head.

"Because there is. Sometimes a soul gets confused, but most are inherently kind. Even if that kindness is *really* buried." The blood on my cheeks cracked as I smiled at Forse. That was a good sign—drying blood meant my wound was finally healing.

"Gods, I miss that smile." Forse held his fingers to the screen, and I followed suit. It was almost as if we were touching. *Almost…*"I'm so sorry about all of this, Elsa. We're doing everything we can to get you out of there. We've ported to three different towers but they haven't been the right ones. If only we could break through the dark magic barrier, we could Bifrost you out of there and—"

"It's not enough to get me out. You need to take Runa into custody. She poses too much of a threat to the light realms."

"I agree." Forse nodded. "But it's more important to me to keep you alive. Have you ever wondered why I call you *hjärtat*?"

Hjärtat was an endearment that was familiar but not

too romantic; the kind of thing you could get away with calling a good friend...or someone truly special. Forse had never confirmed which side I fell on.

"Why?" My heart rate tripled.

"Because you, Elsa Fredriksen, are my—"

"Are you talking to Elsa?" Tyr's voice came through the screen, cutting off Forse's declaration. My hopes were dashed as the face of the brother with the worst possible timing joined Forse in my communicator. "Thank Odin! We can't track you. Do you have any idea how many towers there are in Svartalfheim? A few dozen match the height specs you gave us. The first few were busts, so—"

"Um, could you give us another minute?" I asked Tyr hopefully.

"Can you give us a DNA sample?" Tyr countered.

"Excuse me?"

"A sample. You say your tower is cloaked in dark magic, but is there any passage to the outside of the building from where you are? A crack in the wall, or a window or something?" Tyr asked.

"I've got a window," I offered.

"*Perfekt*. If you can swab a piece of your shirt, or any loose article you can find in there, and throw it out the window beyond the perimeter of the cloak, the locator might be able to pick it up." Tyr wore a *V* between his brows that rivaled Forse's. At this rate, Idunn was going to have to double up production on the anti-aging apple serum.

"Breathe, Tyr. It's going to be okay."

"No it's not." Tyr clamped his jaw so hard I heard a pop.

"Tyr," Forse interrupted. "Look at her ear."

Tyr squinted into the screen. "Great Odin, she's bleeding. *Förbaskat*, we need to find her *now*. Or so help me—"

"Calm down!" I scanned my cell until my eyes fell on a pebble amidst the rubble of the floor. In one movement, I'd picked up the stone, pressed it against my bloodied wound, and flung it out the window. I gritted my teeth as I tried to ignore the searing pain. *Note to self—do not shove sharp rocks into open wounds. Ouch!* "Okay. I threw a bloodied pebble as far as I could, at a ninety-degree angle to the plane of this window. That probably doesn't help narrow down where to search for it, since you don't know where my tower—or its window—are located, but it's all the information I have. Is the locator picking anything up on the rock? Or did I not throw it hard enough to cross the perimeter?"

"It's too soon to tell." Forse looked frustrated as he stared off-screen. "Henrik wasn't lying; the locator takes for-bloody-ever. Maybe if...hold up. Tyr, look at this."

Tyr leaned over, staring at what I presumed to be the locator. "What is that thing?"

"Two beings just ported into one of the potential tower locations. And if the blood trace from Brynn's dagger is correct, Tosk is one of them. I bet this is where they're hiding Elsa."

I did a quick energy scan of my surroundings. "I don't sense two additional beings here. Are you sure?"

"I'm sure two creatures just showed up at one of our places of interest," Forse said. "It could be your tower—maybe they've found a way to cloak their energy signatures from you."

"Gods, I hope not." I shivered.

Tyr swore. "You can run, but you can't hide. Sit tight, Else, and be careful. We're on our way."

"I'll be here," I said lightly.

"Brynn!" Tyr shouted. "Pack it in. We're moving out."

As Tyr stormed off-screen, Forse turned to me with a small smile. "We're coming for you, *hjärtat*. And once you're safe, I'm never letting you go again."

"Is that a promise?"

"Absolutely." Forse eyed me with determination. "And I've never gone back on my word."

"I know you haven't," I said. "It's why I trust you."

Forse's gaze clouded, but before I could ask what was wrong he signed off. "See you in a few."

As the screen went black, I leaned against the stone wall and closed my eyes. There was nothing to do now but wait.

MINUTES TICKED BY, BUT nothing happened. My friends should have ported here by now; something must have gone wrong. Maybe the locator had misread the coordinates, or maybe my energy assessment had been right and Tosk had gone to another location. I grounded myself and pushed out my energy, but the only other mind I could sense in the building was Runa. I skirted around her, not wanting to alert her to my search, and pushed my energy to the border of the property. There wasn't another soul to be found. My friends had definitely gone to a different tower...and if Tosk was there, they'd probably entered an extremely hostile zone.

I'd have to go looking for them. If my intuition was right, they'd need all the help they could get.

I pulled back to check on Runa. Her aura was still a red ball of anger, but she didn't appear to be going anywhere. I pushed my energy out of the building and shot straight for the sky. The sun crept higher in the atmosphere, its filtered beams cutting through the perma-smog covering Svartalfheim just enough to lend visibility. In the light of day, I could see my tower was part of a large, abandoned castle, and that its moat was narrower than I'd previously thought. I made a note of the thick grove of trees circling the property, and the distance from the nearest mountain range. It was information I could pass on to Forse to help him track me if the locator failed to pick up my blood sample.

From my vantage point atop the clouds, I saw a sea of towers. Maybe it was a zoning ordinance—*all creepy gothic residences must come complete with one tower.* Thankfully the actual structures were few and far between, and my scan for energy signatures revealed most were unpopulated. Dark elves must winter in the southern region.

A pulse of light to the west caught my attention, and I zeroed in on the tower closest to the flash. The energy coming back at me sent a wave of calm though my chest, and I knew it had come from Forse. *Dang it.* They'd gone to the wrong tower.

And judging by the intense darkness bearing down on them, my friends had walked straight into a trap.

Tyr! I pushed myself into his head without asking for

the second time in less than a day, but the situation totally warranted it.

Elsa? He sounded confused. *Where are you? The locator still hasn't locked in on your DNA trace.*

Forget about me, I rushed. *Get everybody out of there. It's a trap. They're coming from the northeast—*

But before I could finish warning him, an explosion rocked the compound.

"*Skit!*" My brother swore out loud. "Abort. Elsa says it's a trap. Coming from the north—"

A second explosion blasted the area, sending my brother to the ground. Pain ricocheted across his mind, the sensation so intense I felt it along with him. *Is your back okay?* I rubbed the bottom half of my spine.

It's been better, he admitted. *You felt that?*

Yeah. I rubbed harder, until the stinging ebbed.

I scanned the screens in Tyr's head until I came to the one that viewed Forse. He remained standing as a third blast shook the stones loose from the base of the tower. "Are you positive Elsa isn't here?" Forse asked my brother.

"She says she's not," Tyr muttered through his teeth. He pushed himself to his feet. A second flash of pain across his mind sent my hand to my ankle. I sucked in a sharp breath at the knife-like sensation slicing through my tendon.

Are you hurt? I pressed into his head.

I'll be fine. Just twisted something. Tyr moved forward, limping across the soot just south of the tower. When he reached Brynn, he bent down to help her up. The movement sent a stabbing ache shooting up my own calf.

"You all right?" Tyr asked, ignoring the pain.

Brynn bobbed her ponytail as she stood. "Barely. That thing nearly took my head of."

Tyr's viewpoint scanned a car-sized boulder resting a meter from Brynn. "That's not from the tower. Where did it come from?"

Get out of there! I urged Tyr. *There's a blackness bearing down on you from the northeast mountains. Those explosions might have been activated remotely, but whoever's triggering them will be there any minute.*

"Forse," Tyr barked, as he pulled Brynn alongside him. The valkyrie unsheathed her rapier, and held it at the ready.

"If Elsa's not here, then where is she?" Forse growled.

I'll recap the landmarks I passed on my way to you later. Just get everybody out of there.

"I don't know yet. Just port us out of here so we can figure it out." Tyr shifted his gaze to the horizon. His viewpoint narrowed as he pushed Brynn to the ground. An arrow pierced the air, soaring through the exact spot where she'd been standing. "It's an ambush."

Forse swore as another arrow flew by. "Gather in," he ordered, holding out his arms. Tyr and Brynn moved closer. "We'll port on three. One. Two. Th—"

Before he could finish his count, the sky exploded.

A sea of shrapnel rained down on my friends. My body felt the sting of each impact as my brother's vision clouded with pain. The screens in his head dimmed nearly to black as he and Forse hunched their bodies over Brynn's. Through Tyr's mind, I could see Brynn escaped injury. But the blood soaking through the back of Forse's shirt showed he wasn't so lucky.

No! I screamed. *Tyr, Forse is hurt.*

"You okay, Forse?" Tyr barked.

"It'll heal." Forse shrugged, the blood dripping onto the soot. "We port on 'now.' Now."

And with that my friends disappeared, leaving my energy to scramble back to my body. I could only pray they'd made it to safety as the heavy footsteps of a monster thundered down on my cell.

"Have you decided to play along? Or do I actually need to go kill someone to motivate you?" The door banged against the wall as Runa stormed into my cell. The soles of my shoes scraped against the stones as I scrambled to my feet. Runa bore down on me with all the fury of an enraged fire giant. Her nostrils flared as she crossed the room, boots pounding on rocks. "Well?"

"I'm trying to track Fenrir," I lied. Runa pulled her arm back, and I threw my hands over my face. "Don't. I said I'm trying."

"I don't believe you," Runa spat. "Whatever you did

to me before made me sick. There's this…thing. Right here." She jabbed at the base of her spine.

"Thing?" I asked cautiously.

"Yes. It feels…fluttery. I don't like it. What the Hel did you do to me?"

My eyes widened. Had I actually loosened the black knot? Stopped Runa's dark side from completely choking out an innately good soul? Was it possible I wasn't a total failure as a Unifier after all?

"Stop smiling and undo whatever you did," Runa demanded.

"I can't undo it."

Runa drew her hand again, and I braced for the impact.

"I mean I don't know how," I protested. My eyes closed as Runa's hand struck my ear. *Ouch.*

"Figure it out. Now." Runa glared at me.

"In order for me to do that, you to have to let me back in."

Runa clenched her fists. "You better not screw with me again. I'll off your boyfriend *and* the valkyrie in one strike."

"I know you will," I whispered. *Come on, Elsa. She's giving you the chance. Don't mess this up.* I chose my next words carefully. "I'll do my best to fix what's wrong inside you."

"You will stop this awful feeling you gave me," Runa corrected. "I'm not playing some game with you. Mess with me again, and it's goodnight gods. Do you get that?"

"I do. Just…"

"Just what?"

"Just promise you'll be open to me? If you kick me out it's not going to do either of us any good."

"Just fix this."

I closed my eyes and drew a breath. After doubling up on my protections, I pushed my energy at Runa.

She pushed back.

"I can't fix you if you don't let me in," I reminded her.

The growl that came at me sounded more resigned than angry. If that was progress, I'd take it.

With a slow breath, I directed a stream of energy at Runa's knot. It raced through the tangled trenches, searching for something, anything, that might tell me what had happened to Runa to wrap that black cord around her heart. If I could find the root of her anger, I could heal her emotional injury and eradicate her darkness. Then maybe she'd stop hurting the gods I loved. As I traced the windy path of the cord, information shot back at me. The clarity of the images was fuzzy, but Runa's emotions hit me as if they were my own. All the while, I kept an eye on my mental stopwatch.

Five seconds passed.

A preschool-aged Runa sits alone outside a schoolhouse, waiting for someone to pick her up. A teacher comes out, shakes her head, and offers a hand. "Your parents forgot again? Well, I'm sure they'll send someone for you. In the meantime, you can wait in the classroom with me."

Ten seconds.

A young Runa cowers in a closet, cradling a toddler in her arms. She looks a year or two older than the toddler, who gazes up at her with confusion. Runa starts to hum, her voice drowning out the sobs of a woman being beaten. "Hide and seek is almost over," she reassures the tot. "Then I'll take you to a special park. A park far, far away from here."

Twenty seconds.

A primary-aged Runa stares in horror while a woman lies on the bathroom floor, screaming. "How can you be so selfish? Only a monster would stop me from killing myself. Why would you wish this never-ending pain on your own mother?"

My gut clenched, and my perception of Runa tilted on its head. The images from Runa's past were heartbreaking. They didn't excuse what she'd become, but for the first time I understood why she had so much darkness inside. Her life had been so different from mine…she'd never had a childhood. And now she would live out the rest of her days in Asgardian prison. What an awful existence. This girl needed help—the kind only a High Healer could provide.

As I readied myself to blast light at Runa's black hole of pain, one final memory flashed at me. It was so intense I felt myself sucked into its vortex as if it were a vacuum.

An adolescent Runa walks outside, head low and face strewn with tears. A male figure follows at a distance, hatred dripping from his words. "I knew it. I always knew you were the one who took him from us when he was a baby. You bring him home by nightfall or you are dead to me. Do you hear me? If you don't come home with your brother tonight, don't bother coming home at all."

My stomach churned, and my hands flew to my mouth. In the vision, Runa looked exactly the same age as she'd been when she arrived in Asgard. She even wore the same blue sweater she'd been wearing when Forse had first introduced her to us. I remembered, because I had one just like it. I'd tried to bond with Runa over our obviously similar fashion sense, but she'd blown me off. She'd blown everyone off, except Forse. He'd been the only one she let in.

Why hadn't I tried harder? If she'd had more friends, seen more kindness, maybe whatever goodness had inspired Runa to protect that little boy could have won out. Instead, Runa had become the very thing she grew up fearing. A killer. A monster. A—

"You. Little. Liar!"

The shriek made my energy retract like a recoiled spring. I pulled away from the pain inside Runa, retreating into myself and staring wide-eyed at the enraged face directly in front of me. The young girl from Runa's memories was barely recognizable behind the angular red face hissing obscenities. Runa grabbed my hair, her long fingernails stabbing my scalp as she forced me into the wall. The crack of skull on stone was almost deafening. As I fought to shirk the darkness that threatened to overtake me, I stared at Runa.

"I'm sorry," I whispered. "For everything that happened to you. For not trying harder to be your friend. For all of it. I'm sorry." A hundred mallets thudded at the back of my head, and my lids grew heavy as I gave in to the pain. I drew a raspy breath, and whispered the words I never thought I'd say. "And I forgive you."

Runa drew a sharp breath, and behind my closed eyelids I could have sworn I saw a flash of light within her aura. Was she feeling surprise? Disgust? I'd probably never know. In the next instant, whatever emotion she'd felt had passed, and Runa's rage took over.

"You're not half as sorry as you're going to be," she hissed. "You had no right to betray my trust. But turnabout's fair play, right? You take a memory of mine—I'll take something of yours. I hope your boyfriend's ready to die."

Panic squeezed my heart as Runa's heels clicked on the ground. But I was trapped. By the time she'd slammed the cell door, the pain was so intense my body had started to shut down. My hands lay limp at my sides, too weak to channel healing energy. And as I drifted into blackness, I sent one final thought to the universe.

I'm sorry.

I wasn't sure who I was talking to; I only knew that I'd failed. I'd failed Runa all those years ago, when I'd written her off as a mean girl instead of trying to find out why she was so cold. I'd failed my friends when I couldn't undo the energy block that would end up killing us all. And I'd failed Forse—who'd done everything in his power to help me fulfill my destiny—when

I couldn't perform my first and only assignment as Unifier.

I'm so, so sorry.

But it was too late. Runa was out on a mission to kill.

Again.

CHAPTER 9

I FLOATED IN A sea of darkness, lost somewhere between the searing pain that sought to end me, and the utter exhaustion I always felt after a healing—even an attempted one. As I drifted, too tired to grasp consciousness and too battered to want to try, my brain gave me a beautiful reprieve. It switched into sleep-mode, freeing me from the nightmare of my reality and releasing me to the dreamland of my past. In that unburdened state, my subconscious returned to one of the happiest memories it could recall—the moment I'd realized, even without the Norns telling me, that Forse Styrke was fated for me.

"Elsa?" Forse looked up as I barged into his study. When he glanced from my bare feet to my drawn face, he placed his hands on the desk and rose. "You're white as snow."

I shook my head, running my fingers through my abnormally messy hair. "I'm fine."

Forse threw his pen on top of a stack of paperwork and

walked around the desk in long strides. He wrapped his arms around my shoulders and pulled me to him. I rested my cheek against the thick muscles of his chest, raising both hands to press my fingertips into his back. If I held on tight enough, maybe I could stay in this moment, with my one constant, forever. Everything else had changed, or disappeared...or died. My parents had barely been set to sea, and now I had this to contend with?

"I want them back." My shoulders shook as I started to cry. I wept delicate tears of defeat, not the deep wracking sobs of grief. After the week I'd had, I didn't have the energy.

"I'm so sorry this is happening, hjärtat. " Forse rested his chin on the top of my head. "Your parents were like a second family to me. I can't believe they're gone."

"Me neither." I sniffed.

Forse rubbed the space between my shoulder blades with his thumb. The touch sent a warmth along the length of my back, and despite my pain, in that moment I felt...almost happy. My world had turned completely on its head. My parents were gone. My brother was tearing through the realms on a revenge rage. But Forse was still here, just as he always was. He'd been there my first day of primary school, when the kids made fun of my powers. He'd been there when Skadi's clique of mean girls had made everyone's life unfathomably awful. And he'd been the first to show up at our home last week when Fenrir did the unthinkable. He'd intercepted me at the door as I came home from school, steering me back to his house and making sure my last vision of my parents was Mom waving me to school from the front porch, Dad's arm firmly around her waist. His *parents took care of the bodies while Forse held me on his couch and delivered the news that would change my life forever.*

Now it was changing again.

My knees buckled, and Forse scooped me into his arms. Despite the fear tearing through me, relief tapped lightly at my heart. Runa had done her best to try to keep him away from me, but Forse was always there when I needed him. And he always would be. Thank gods.

"You want to sit down?" Forse asked.

Being cradled in the strongest arms I'd ever actually touched was an infinitely better offer, but nodding seemed to be the appropriate response. Forse furrowed his brow and carried me to the couch that faced the window. He sat, placing me next to him so my legs hung over his lap. The contact evoked another wave of relief, leaving me light-headed. I rested my head on his shoulder and closed my eyes. My entire body melted into his, and I sat very still—barely breathing, just soaking in his presence. When the warm glow filled my heart, I let out a ragged sigh and buried my face in Forse's chest. His nearness filled me with a peace I'd never experienced. At the same time, it sent my nerves into a frenzy. It felt like for once, I was exactly where the Norns wanted me to be.

"Elsa?" Forse's voice deepened with worry.

It took a lot *of effort to wrench my nose away from Forse's T-shirt. He smelled like mint and cedar—awareness and strength. He smelled divine.*

"Elsa?" Panic shot from Forse's eyes.

"Sorry." I drew a piece of paper from my pocket and

placed it on Forse's lap. "I got this from the Norns. And no, even with my abilities, I did not see this coming."

Forse unfolded the paper and held it in one hand. With the other, he gently stroked my thigh, sending my pulse into a near frenzy. How was one god capable of creating such disparate reactions in a matter of seconds?

"What the...?" Forse exhaled forcefully as he read. "How is this even possible? You don't have the Unifier gene. Your parents had you tested."

"I remember! It was unbelievably awkward! Back then, the Norns said I was to fulfill my Key role as High Healer. It's what I've been preparing for my entire existence. My. Entire. Existence."

"You're yelling." Forse furrowed his brow. "You never yell."

"Wouldn't you yell? How the Helheim am I supposed to do my mom's job on top of mine? Unifier? I don't know the first thing about that! And gods, Forse. Without a good Unifier, Asgard's going down. The minute word of her death reaches Jotunheim, or Odin forbid, Svartalfheim, we might as well pack up and move to the safe houses in Midgard. It's over. Asgard's going to fall. There's no way I can protect the realm on my own."

"You wouldn't be on your own," Forse reminded me. "There's a whole team charged with safeguarding Asgard's security. Besides, the Unifier was never responsible for day-to-day protection of Asgard. That's the God of War's job."

"My dad's dead," I said drily.

"Then your brother's going to have to stop throwing a

hissy fit and god up. Odin will appoint your parents' successors today, and the odds are on Tyr for war god."

"Dad prepared him. We just didn't think it'd happen so soon..."

"I know." Forse squeezed my leg.

"But this?" I jabbed the paper. "Mom didn't prepare me to be Unifier. We thought the Norns would let her know when her successor came along. We figured it might be Tyr's future wife, or a convert from Vanaheim, or someone else. Nobody ever said anything about it being my job."

Forse tilted his head and looked at me. "You're scared."

"Of course I'm scared! Wouldn't you be?"

Forse looked out the window. "I don't know," he answered honestly. "I've always known my fate. The Norns declared me God of Justice the day I was born. That reality has shaped every decision I've ever made. If I woke up tomorrow and it changed...ja, I guess I would feel a little scared. But also liberated."

"What do you mean?"

Forse continued to stare at the trees outside his study. "When my friends were going off to combat club, I was in the library researching laws of Midgard. When they were cheering at the rugby match, I was on a work-study trip to observe war negotiations with Odin. I would have loved to choose my extracurriculars, my classes—Hel, even how I spent my Friday nights. But I knew what rested on me claiming my title at graduation, and I couldn't afford to take my eyes off my course."

"You are a pretty intense guy," I agreed. "But I saw you at

combat club for a while there. And you didn't need the extra lessons. You're scary with a broadsword."

"I had to learn fast so I could move on." Forse paused and stared out the window for a long moment. When he spoke, his voice was thoughtful. "This might end up being a really good thing for you. You're going to discover all kinds of things about yourself. You'll push yourself to perform tasks you never knew you were capable of. You're going to discover exactly how strong you really are. You're already a force to contend with, but once you develop this skill? Watch out, realms." Forse winked. "This could be the best thing that's ever happened to you."

"It doesn't feel like it," I argued. "It's overwhelming. I know how much rested on my mom's ability to bring people together. She spent years preparing for her role. I've got a day. And according to this"—I jabbed the perfidious paper —"the Unifier hat will rest firmly on my head. Until such time as..." I re-read the prophesy for the hundredth time in twenty minutes. "'Until a daughter not of Asgard unites with War.' Whatever that means."

Forse looked thoughtful. "I'd wager it means until your brother gets married. Huh, Tyr isn't going to end up with an Asgardian. Go figure. Wonder who it's going to be...not a light elf; they're too flaky. They're hot though..."

"Forse!" I swatted his leg.

"Sorry." Forse set the prophesy on the end table and turned so his body faced mine. He took my hands in his and held tight. "Listen to me. This is a change. And change can be frightening. But you're not in this alone. You've got me. You've got your brother. I know," he interjected as I opened my mouth. "He's out of his mind at the moment. Henrik and I will talk him down. He'll step up and make a fine war god, just like he'll continue to be the support you need while you transition into your new role. Being a dual Key isn't going to be easy, but I'll be right beside you at every step. We'll figure this out together. Okay?"

I leaned forward so my forehead rested against Forse's. "What about Runa?" I whispered. "She doesn't like it when you spend time with me."

Forse's jaw clenched. "Runa has left Asgard permanently."

"Oh gods. I didn't know. I'm so sorry." No, I wasn't. But Forse didn't need to know that.

"Don't be." Forse pulled back. His eyes narrowed, and goose bumps broke out along my arms as I stared into two angry, green orbs.

"What happened?" I whispered.

"It came to my attention that Runa performed an act of treason. I intend to hunt her to the edge of the realms to ensure she pays for her crime. The next time you see her, she'll be in our deepest prison cell...if she isn't executed."

Forse's voice was so cold. It was the first time I'd really seen the lethal edge to his deceptively calm character. I'd known the justice god hid a hardness beneath his cool exterior, but I'd never actually experienced it. Whatever Runa had done, it must have been really bad.

"Forse, you're scaring me. What did she do?"

He drew his shoulders back. "Runa's a war criminal now. If she approaches you, run straight to me. I'll protect you."

"Forse...what's going on?" I reached up to smooth the

wrinkle between his brows. Icicles danced along my fingertips.

"I'll tell you when the dust settles."

"Promise?" I asked.

Forse's face softened. "Have I ever gone back on my word?"

"No." A smile played at my lips, and despite myself, the light fizz of happiness bubbled back into my heart. Forse was predictable. He was comfortable. He was steady. He was my rock.

I had no idea how I was going to get through the next week; the next month; the next century. But I knew exactly who I was going to get through it with.

"Hey." Forse cupped my jaw in his palm. The pad of his thumb wiped the moisture from my cheek. "Why are you crying?"

"Because you've always been here for me." I sniffed.

"And I always will be." Forse pressed his lips to my fore-head, testing my overworked nerve endings. It felt like a thousand tiny fairies danced a jubilant ballet across my skin.

"I know you will be," I whispered gratefully.

"What do I always tell you?" Forse looked at me mean-ingfully.

Moisture pricked at my eyes. "A kind heart can brighten the darkest realm," I recited.

Forse nodded. "Your mom taught me that one. I know it feels impossible right now, but I need you to be that heart for me. For Asgard."

The weight of his words hit me, and I blinked away a fresh wave of tears. "Okay," I whispered.

Forse pulled back and slung his arm across the back of the couch. "Come here, hjärtat," *he murmured. "Let's just sit for a while,* ja?"

I nodded, nestling into Forse's side and letting his rhythmic breathing lull me into a quiet peace. My parents were gone, and my brother was out of his mind. But as I curled against the God of Justice, I felt safe. Protected. Happy.

I was exactly where the Norns meant for me to be—with my perfekt *match.*

CHAPTER 10

MY HEART CLUNG TO my dream as if it were a life preserver in a churning sea. I knew the minute I withdrew from the sweet surrender of my subconscious that something terrible would happen. I wasn't yet awake enough to remember what it was, but a sense of foreboding hovered just at the edge of awareness, urging me to stay inside my memory. *Five more minutes. I can just stay in Forse's arms and...*

Forse!

With a jolt, I ripped myself from sleep's comforting embrace. Forse would be nothing more than a memory if I didn't get to him *right now*. Runa might need me alive to finish off whatever sick plan she had in her twisted head, but since she didn't strike me as the sentimental type, I doubted she'd have any qualms following through on her threat to kill the god I loved.

And that simply couldn't happen.

Sending my energy to my friends hadn't been enough to keep them safe. So long as my body was trapped in this tower, they'd keep on risking their lives, trying to rescue me. I needed to get more than just my spirit out of Runa's prison. I needed to physically escape.

I activated my com and released a sigh of gratitude when Forse's face filled my forearm. *Thank gods, he's still alive.*

"Elsa? You look terrible. Great Odin, what's she done to you now? Why aren't you healing?" The vein in his forehead throbbed.

"I am healing." I was, albeit slowly. I'd undergone some regeneration while I was blacked out, but my body wasn't accustomed to fighting off injuries of this severity. And I simply didn't have the time—or the energy—to perform a full-on healing. "Listen, I can't talk long. I just need to warn you that Runa's on her way to find you. Forse, she wants to kill you."

"Elsa—"

"I'm going to break out of here and find you, so we can all go home. I don't know how long she'll leave my tower unattended, and I need to work fast. Promise me you'll be careful," I pleaded.

"Elsa, I—"

"I'll be there as soon as I can." With that, I pressed my finger to my wrist and de-activated the com. My arm began buzzing immediately, but I ignored the call. I didn't have time to reassure Forse. I'd told him about Runa, and I had to trust that he'd be able to protect himself—and warn Brynn and Tyr of the incoming attack—while I got myself out of here.

How am I going to do that?

Since walking out of the room wasn't an option, I'd have to send my energy on one final recon excursion. I'd just have to work fast—with my body already compromised, I wouldn't be able to leave it unattended for long. It needed the strength of my spirit to regenerate.

This would be a quick trip, then.

I closed my eyes and grounded myself through the rubble of the tower floor, all the way to the center of Svartalfheim on an energetic lightning flash. With a steady breath, I widened my stabilizer, strengthened my aura, and let my spirit soar. *Stay safe, body. I'll be back soon.*

A quick scan of my cell revealed no changes; the door remained securely closed, and the bars on the windows were still too narrow for a body to climb through. My spirit, however, slipped easily through the cracks, and moved along the tower's exterior, flying downward toward the moat. A gaping hole in the tower wall confirmed Runa hadn't yet patched the remnants of my previous escape attempt. *Perfekt.* The hole was close enough to the moat that if I could scale three meters of tower exterior, I could safely jump from there. I just had to get to the hole.

But how do I get through the cell's door? It's locked tight.

I flew through the hole and moved up the spiral staircase, resolving to scour my cell for a makeshift tool, maybe a rock shard that I could use to bludgeon my way out of my prison. I was so intent on identifying a means of escape, I failed to notice the blazing red energy flashing toward me. Runa sprinted along the hall toward the door of my cell, flinging it open at the exact moment I registered her presence.

No. My body couldn't take a hit without my spirit—it would shut down. And if my body shut down, the energy cord that linked it to my spirit would be severed. I'd be locked out until my physical self could regenerate…if not forever.

"Get up, *ko*," Runa shrieked. She charged into my cell as I flew after her. By the time I made it through the doorway, she held my body against the wall. Her fingers were wrapped tight around my neck as she slammed my head against the hard stones. I should have felt each strike throughout my spirit, but it remained pain-free. The lack of sensation could only mean one thing—I was too late.

I dove for my body as Runa forced it against the wall again, aligning my energy centers for quick re-entry. But my spirit bounced back, as if it had struck the tower wall. I shook myself and tried again, then again, to no avail. My body had sustained too many injuries to be my spirit's physical host.

We were separated.

"I said wake *up!*" Runa howled. "Your friends weren't where I thought they'd be, so I was going to give you one more chance to find Fenrir. But if you're going to play dead"—she threw my body onto the ground, where it crumbled into a lifeless heap—"then all bets are off. It's lights out for Forse."

With that, she transported out of the cell in a flash of crimson fury, leaving my bloodied body on the floor. There was nothing I could do to help it—without a cord to connect us, my spirit was as foreign to it as Svartalfheim was to Asgard. Leaving my body alone at that moment meant I risked permanent disassociation, but I couldn't let Runa ambush my friends…even if I had to spend the rest of my existence as nothing more than an energy signature. I sent a silent prayer that my body would heal enough to allow me to re-enter soon, *or ever*, and I dove through the window, intent on finding my friends. That monster wasn't going to hurt one more god that I loved. Not today, not ever.

My spirit soared over Svartalfheim, covering kilometers of barren desert interrupted with the occasional cactus-like vegetation. But though I encountered a handful of castles, and even scoured the settlements surrounding the parliament building—there wasn't an Asgardian trace to be found. Wherever my friends had gone, their energy was imperceptible. And I couldn't afford any more time away from my body—if I had any chance at rejoining, it would have to happen soon. After two hours of separation, the risk of permanent disassociation spiked significantly.

I was butting up against that all-important one-hundred-and-twenty-minute mark.

With a burst of speed, I returned to Runa's castle, soared through the window and assessed my body. It was still on the floor, but now it was curled in a tight ball. That was a good sign—it had moved since I left. I aligned my energy centers and pushed against myself. I made it halfway in before my body ejected me. Pulling back out, I studied the corporeal heap. The blood caked against the back of my skull indicated that wound was my most severe injury. It made sense, given this was my second head wound of the day. *Note to self—bring a helmet on my next unifying mission.* A ripple of excitement ran through me as I studied the shallow cuts and light bruises. My energy remained low, but I'd fixed worse wounds as High Healer. Even without a physical form, I was confident I'd be able to heal this one, too.

I hoped.

I held my fingers a half-foot apart, channeling restorative energy. When I felt a malleable ball between my palms, I turned my hands downward, pressing the energy into my body's skull. The bleeding ebbed, and I felt a light tug at my first energy center. *We're connected!* I pressed another wave of energy into the wound, and the pulling sensation intensified. *Good enough. I'm going in.*

I pushed the remaining restorative energy into my body and lined up my centers, this time slipping easily back into my physical form. Pain exploded across my mind, resonating from every nerve ending that was still operational. But pain was better than darkness, and I welcomed the agonizing waves, knowing the alternative was far worse.

After an excruciating eternity, the darkness gave

way to grey, and I managed to claw my way to a sitting position. At least two hours had passed since Runa had set on her murderous march, and there was no telling how much damage she'd inflicted. My spirit may have failed to help my friends, but now that I was back in my body my tech could still get the job done. I pressed my fingertips to my forearm and issued my command with a scratchy voice. "Call Forse."

When he answered, the stressed face filling the screen did little to reassure me. "*Hei*, Elsa." His image bounced up and down against the backdrop of black soot and red lava. Was he running by the molten river we'd seen when the Bifrost dropped us in Svartalfheim?

"Where are you?" I rasped.

"Are you okay? Did she hurt you again? So help me, Odin, I'm going to kill her." Fury laced Forse's voice.

"I'm fine," I lied. "Forse, you have to evacuate Svartalfheim. Runa's reached a whole new level of crazy. She is seriously going to kill you. You need to get Tyr and Brynn out of the realm *now*."

"Nobody's leaving this realm without you. We're on our way to another tower. The locator hasn't tracked your blood sample, but it picked up a trace on Runa."

"I thought it needed DNA to track someone?"

"It does. Henrik uploaded a hair from an old hat Evidence kept." The screen showed Forse's hip as he pumped his arms.

"Forse, you need to be running away from Runa, not toward her. Are you not hearing me? She's going to kill you." My heart pounded at the words, sending another wave of pain across my skull.

Pain's better than dead, pain's better than dead...dang it, this hurts.

"She won't get the chance. I'm going to kill her first." Forse's face came back on the screen. His jaw was set.

Oh gods. He wasn't kidding. "That was never part of the plan."

"*Ja*, well. Neither was you getting captured on me, was it, *hjärtat*? Plans change."

"Turn around. She's leading you into a trap."

"I've got this under control." The lava stream behind him blurred as Forse ran faster. "Sit tight. I'll reprogram the locator and force the *förbaskat* thing to get a read on you the minute we find Runa."

"I might be able to help narrow the search. I never got to tell Tyr that I picked up a few more landmarks the last time I was in his head. When I left my body, I saw that my tower is roughly three kilometers from a pretty substantial mountain range, and that a thick grove of trees surrounds the property. Does that help?"

"Not really," Forse grunted. "Most of the towers that are tall enough to fit the specs you gave us are guarded by both mountains and woods."

"I traveled west to reach you," I offered. "So my tower should be east of the one you were ambushed in. Get yourselves out of Svartalfheim, call the Elite Team, and send them to come find me *after* Runa calls off her god hunt. Just evacuate, now!"

"We've got this, Elsa." Forse's voice was steady.

"Elsa?" Brynn's upbeat voice rang through the device. Forse tilted his arm so I could see our friend running alongside him. "*Hallå, flicka!*"

"Hey girl, to you, too. You guys have got to get out of this realm. Runa's homicidal." My plea fell on deaf ears.

"You want me to miss a fight this epic? I don't think so." Brynn's ponytail bounced as she ran. "Gotta go. We're at the location, and holy Helheim, where'd they get a dragon?"

"A what?" I squeaked.

"I'm signing off, Elsa." Forse sounded tense. Of course he did.

"Don't turn the screen off!" I begged. "How will I know you're okay?"

"You can watch through my head," Tyr chimed in. "Maybe having your calming presence in my brain will keep me from killing every demon I—*skit*, there are two dragons. And I've got visual on Runa. She's fifty meters due north. Weapon up. Forse, are your guns fully loaded?"

"*Ja*," Forse confirmed.

"Good." I heard the swish of Tyr's sword as he drew it from his belt. "Shoot first, ask questions later. Elsa, see you on the inside. *Do not talk* when you're in my head, okay? I need to concentrate."

"Thank you," I whispered to my brother. "I'll be right there. I'll do what I can to diffuse the hostiles so long as they let me near their energy. And Forse? Please be careful. I need you guys to come out of this alive."

Forse's image jostled as he drew his sidearm. "I have no intention of dying today, *hjärtat*. We're coming for you. Right after we take care of a little pest problem." Forse winked at the screen before it went black.

Oh, Hel.

I doubled down on protections, enforcing my aura with the thickest walls I could visualize. Leaving my body when it was compromised *again* carried a degree of risk, but if my spirit could help my friends in any way, staying behind wasn't an option. With a deep breath, I closed my eyes and pushed my energy at my brother. It took less than a minute to find him, but by the time I'd dropped into his head, he, Forse, and Brynn were under fire. Literally. Two dragons circled the sky above the stone structure where Runa, Tosk, and a dark elf I didn't recognize waited. The grounded monsters stood in a straight line in front of the building, smiling like a crazed welcome wagon, while their winged counterparts breathed streams of fire into the lava river separating my friends from Svartalfheim's un-finest. A wall of fire erupted from the lava, creating a twenty-foot barrier between my friends and my captors.

Double Hel.

My brother's mind whirred. I could sense him running through attack plans, evaluating each for risk, duration, and effectiveness. A light flashed as he settled on the best one, and he took action without second-guessing himself.

"Forse, you're going to port us across the stream. Once we're on the other side, Brynn, you take the unknown hostile. I'll take out Tosk. Forse, I'll leave Runa to you. Seems you two have some unfinished business. Try not to hurt the dragons. They're most likely being controlled by one of these demons, and in the event they're acting of their own accord, keeping them alive will be our goodwill gesture to their king, Nidhogg. He'll owe us a favor, and I have no doubt we'll need one."

"Like we don't need one now?" Brynn muttered.

"Two dragons, two dark elves, and an ex-pat?" Tyr sounded confident. "We've got this. Now move out."

Brynn nodded. She and Tyr moved close to Forse. Forse wrapped his arms around his friends, gun still in hand, and held tight. The next instant, the three of them were on the other side of the fire wall. They hit the ground running, dodging dragon fire as they tore across the blackened ground. My back warmed as a blaze landed just behind Tyr, the dragon breath narrowly missing his shoulder blades. He gripped the hilt of his broadsword, and a perverse sense of pleasure flowed through his head. I knew he wanted to end Runa himself, but because of her prior relationship with Forse, the justice god was in a better position to assess her weaknesses. And to Tyr, removing Runa's dark elf counterpart would be nearly as fulfilling. Tosk had been an accomplice in my kidnapping, after all. And nobody hurt Tyr's baby sister.

Aw! I love you too, big brother.

No talking! Tyr growled inside his head. *I'm trying not to die here.*

Sorry.

Ugh. Screw running. Tyr bent low and launched himself off his toes. A stream of dragon fire seared the spot seconds after he vacated it.

"Must be nice to be able to *fly*," Brynn chirped. Tyr glanced down, affording me a view of Brynn bounding up the gentle slope. Fire rained down as she danced toward the stone structure. The dragons were relentless, shooting flames in a near continual stream of rage. Their wings flapped angrily and they whipped their tails back and forth, the flames fanning beneath the forceful gusts of air.

"Just end the elf, Brynn," Tyr commanded. My viewpoint shifted as Tyr alternated screens in his head, glancing between the dragons he flew level with and the team he oversaw on the ground. My brother's ability to compartmentalize blew me away.

No wonder Odin gave him Dad's title.

"I'm on it." Brynn covered the ground in a leap worthy of a classically trained ballerina. She came down directly in front of the unidentified dark elf, who wore a mask of shock—he probably hadn't expected such a tiny female to cover such a substantial distance in one jump. He pulled his arm back to throw a punch just as Brynn brought her combat boot up in a powerful roundhouse that landed squarely across his face. The elf stumbled back, cradling his cheek in his hands. If the sound of foot on bone was any indication, he'd be nursing a broken jaw.

Crack.

And a broken nose. Brynn planted a series of jabs in the center of her target's face, earning a heavy grunt and a spray of blood from the dark elf.

"Is that all you've got?" The elf ducked, then threw himself at Brynn. He wrapped his arms around her waist and tackled her. They rolled across the soot, colliding with Tosk's tall, black boot. The unknown elf pulled his head back and pinned Brynn to the ground. She struggled beneath his gnarled hands, arching her back and kicking violently, but the elf was in control. He leaned to the right, giving Tosk a clear shot. As the monster raised his knee to kick Brynn in the head, I switched screens and the ground flew at my face. My brother dove, closing the gap between his bodyguard and himself in the time it took me to blink.

"I don't think so," Tyr growled. He connected with Tosk's boot before Brynn's face did, wrapping his fingers around the dark elf's ankle and yanking him off his feet. He flung Tosk to the ground. Tosk tucked into a ball, narrowly avoiding a shot of fire probably intended for Tyr. Tyr flew so he was level with the dragons and held his hands out.

"Ceasefire?" Tyr offered. The dragon reared its scaly head, sending a new stream of flames at my brother. "Guess not," Tyr muttered as he dove back to the earth.

Tyr's view shifted as he caught sight of Forse, locked in a battle with Runa. My chest constricted as I noticed his gun lying on the ground, most likely knocked out of his hands by Runa's freakishly strong kick. Her leg whipped forward like a wind-up toy on repeat, while Forse side-stepped to avoid becoming a casualty of her stilettoed boot. When Runa shifted her weight to kick with her other foot, Forse dove to the side, sliding across the soot on his stomach and picking up his sidearm. He gripped the handle and rested his fist on his wrist, firing a steady shot as he slid. Runa howled as the bullet grazed her shoulder. She held up her palm and sent a blue beam of light at Forse.

How the Helheim can they fight that?

"Tyr?" Forse bellowed. "What's the deal with the subject's blue hand laser?"

I pressed a thought into Tyr's head.

"Elsa says it looks like the same blue beam Runa used to capture her, only in that case the beam acted as a pulley, not a blaster. Runa must be able to manipulate it at will."

"Great," Forse muttered, as he dodged another beam.

"Elsa also thinks it's a temporary ability stemming from the crystal Runa ingested, and that whatever powers it gave her will wear off. Hopefully soon," Tyr relayed, as he drew his sword and swung at Tosk. Tosk met the strike with one of his own, the clang of metal on metal echoing off the stone building.

"*Ja*, well." Forse rolled behind a boulder as Runa fired again. "Any time this particular power wants to go away, I'd be okay with that."

Forse popped up, holding his arm straight and taking two quick shots with his pistol. A loud shriek pierced the morning air as Runa let out a wail. Her arm hung limp at her side, a fresh current of blood dripping from her shoulder.

"You need backup, Justice?" Tyr forced Tosk's sword to the side. He took the opportunity to drive the elf to the ground with a firm front-kick. Tosk landed hard on his back, skidding across the dust and dropping his sword in the process. My brother pounced, sword drawn as he launched himself at Tosk. Tosk hissed, rolling out of the way as Tyr pierced the empty ground with his blade.

"Arugh!" Tyr growled, withdrawing his sword and gripping the hilt with two hands. He swung in a perfect arc, his weapon landing where Tosk should have been. But the elf rolled again. Tyr swore so loudly, Odin probably heard him all the way in Asgard.

But Tyr's curse didn't drown out the sound that paralyzed my soul with a fear I'd felt on just one other occasion. Although Forse's cry barely registered on the screen in my brother's mind, I zeroed in on the image of the god I would have done anything for. Forse lay on the ground, clutching his chest and gasping. On the other side of the boulder, Runa shot one final beam. It missed Forse by inches, striking the rock near his head and causing an explosion that sent shards of stone flying across the field. She held tight to her bleeding arm as she turned around and ran.

My world sank to a singular viewpoint, as I gave in to the fear coursing through my energy.

Tyr! I mentally shook my brother. *Forse is down!*

CHAPTER 11

MY BROTHER CALLED OFF his elf hunt and switched viewpoints, zeroing in on his fallen friend. "Brynn," he barked. "I'm flying Forse out of here. Finish what you can and catch me as I go by."

"Yes, sir." Tyr's view alternated, showing Brynn driving her rapier through the heart of the unknown dark elf. She wore a perverse look of pleasure as she withdrew the blade, the heel of her boot pressed firmly against the elf's stomach. His eyes bulged as blood spewed from the hole in his chest. He drew one last gurgling breath, and as I watched, his spirit withdrew from his body, speeding through the sky and off to whatever level of Helheim the goddess of the underworld deemed appropriate. If its muddied color was any indication, the spirit was heading for Hel's inner sanctum.

Please let Forse be okay, please let Forse be okay, I chanted to myself.

I won't let him leave us. I'm almost to his side, Tyr pointed out. And he was—while I'd been wrestling with mind-numbing fear, he'd been flying. He dove behind the boulder, scooping Forse into his arms and dodging dragon fire as he carried our friend toward Brynn. She jumped as Tyr passed, grabbing onto his leg and holding tight while he flew them away from the wreckage, past the stream of fire, and through the forest.

Hurry, I pleaded.

I am. Tyr's focus didn't shift until he reached the shore of a small lake. He dove, depositing Brynn on the ground and cradling Forse as he touched down. I tried not to sob as I took in Forse's strong form, crumpled in the arms of War.

We need to heal him! I urged.

A tense rumble emanated from my brother's chest. "Brynn, confirm there are no intruders in a twenty-meter radius. I'll shield the perimeter once it's secure."

"On it." Brynn blurred around the circle, returning in the time it took Tyr to lay Forse on the ground. "Perimeter's secure."

"Excellent." Tyr held his hand to the sky. A silvery dome encased the area. Forse drew a shaky breath, and Tyr zeroed in on my love. He shut off every screen in his mind but two—the one that continually scanned the dome for threats, and the one that studied his friend. Forse's skin was unnaturally pale, and his lips were lightly tinted blue.

They're blue? Oh gods!

I know. Tyr's eyes narrowed. *This isn't good.*

Tyr placed his hand to Forse's chest and waited six seconds. His mind registered the slowing of Force's heartbeat.

"Skit," he swore. "What the Hel did Runa do to you?"

Forse kept his eyes closed and opened his mouth to speak.

He can move! Relief surged through me.

Forse opened his eyes slightly as he rasped out his words. "One of Runa's crazy hand beams hit my chest. I think it hit my heart."

Oh my gods. A blast to the heart under any circumstances was dangerous, but Odin only knew what kind of powers the Svartalfheim crystal had given Runa. If it was dark magic, and Runa had blasted Forse's heart… we were lucky he hadn't been killed on impact.

My heart thundered in my ears as I shouted at my brother. *Fix him!*

My magic extends to protecting, defending, and killing. War-ish things. You're the High Healer. Got any ideas?

One look at the entry wound and I knew the restorative energy ball I'd used to heal myself wouldn't be strong enough to overcome what Runa did to Forse. My rapid-fire pulse and nausea-inducing adrenaline surge did me no favors as I scanned my mental medical journal, honing in on several ways to heal an ailing heart. Each depended on knowing the exact specifications of the injury.

What do we know about the crystal that gave Runa her powers? I asked.

"Brynn, did Henrik get back to you with the crystal specs yet?" Tyr barked out loud.

"Hold on." Brynn checked her communicator. "Kind of. He's still doing research, but he e-mailed limited findings while we were fighting."

"Convenient." Forse coughed while I sent a prayer of gratitude. If he still had his sense of humor, then we still had time to heal him. But first I had to get a grip on my energy, and calm down enough to be of use.

"Isn't it though?" Brynn ran her finger along her arm. "He knows it's a miliant crystal, but he hasn't confirmed any of its properties yet." She looked up. "Is Elsa in your head?"

"*Ja,*" Tyr confirmed.

"Does that help you diagnose Forse, Elsa?" Brynn asked. "Sorry we don't know more."

It'll have to do. I'd done more with less hundreds of times. If there was one thing healing had taught me, it was improvisation and calm under the face of stress.

But it was hard to keep my panic at bay as I watched Forse's eyes squeeze shut with a fresh wave of pain. Justice was strong—stronger than my brother, in a lot of ways. Seeing him hurting like this was agonizing.

Hurry up, Else, Tyr urged.

On it. I took a deep breath and processed Brynn's words, running Henrik's classification through a mental diagnostic. Miliants were extremely rare. Like, once-in-a-blue-moon, two-horned-unicorn, cheerful-jotun rare. They were indigenous to Svartalfheim and so far as I knew, there was only one other documented case of ingestion in…in ever.

And that hadn't ended well for anybody.

"Arugh." Forse groaned and gripped his chest. "It's burning."

Oh gods. Burning wasn't good. *Tyr? Get the emergency healing kit out of Brynn's backpack.* I pressed my thoughts into his head.

"Brynn, hand me your backpack," Tyr snapped.

Brynn threw the bag at Tyr. He plucked it out of the air with one hand, and withdrew the kit.

Now what? he asked.

Pull out the necklace—it's a blue and green crystal that looks like it's glowing. Hold it against Forse's wound. A larimar crystal is a really powerful heart stone, and it will work especially well on Forse because of his connection to it. It won't solve the problem, but it should strengthen his heart enough to slow the progression of the injury for a few minutes.

Then what? Tyr's thought sounded panicked.

Then I think fast. Just get the crystal in place.

Tyr did as instructed while I mentally scanned pages of medical journals, online reports—everything I'd read during the last two hundred years about miliant crystals. It felt like an eternity. My heart pulled every time Forse winced under the pain, but I finally stumbled on something that might work.

I've got an idea. Your region of the realm should have hemian flowers and tomad roots, probably somewhere near that lake to your north. Tell Brynn to go by the water and look for a black-petaled flower that looks kind of like a rose, and a greenish moss that's growing at the base of one of those big trees.

Elsa, he's really pale. Look at him.

I drew a sharp breath as I took in Forse's graying pallor. His cracked lips drew uneven breaths at alarmingly slow intervals, and a faint sheen lined his forehead. What the Helheim was going on? He was Asgardian—his heart should have healed on its own. Coupled with the larimar stone, and its powerful connection not only to its patient, but also to the High Healer who was using it, Forse should have been nearly out of the woods. He most certainly shouldn't look like he was two steps from Hel's gate. Whatever breed of miliant crystal Runa had ingested, it must have contained *really* dark magic...the kind that could kill a god.

Tell Brynn to gather those two flowers, roots and all, and get back to you immediately, I ordered.

Done.

Brynn nodded as Tyr voiced his command, removing her now shredded fingernails from her mouth as she blurred to the trees. My attention shifted to Forse while she searched. This particular healing would require a direct application of physical elements, which meant I couldn't separate my energy from Tyr and heal Forse as a spirit—I'd have to rely on my corporeal brother to do this with me. I'd never helped someone through another god before, but healing was more science than magic, and while Tyr was hardly what anyone would call a stellar student, we had enough experience sharing a mind that I knew he could be an exceptional instruction-follower.

Gods, this had to work.

"Got 'em." Brynn blurred to Forse's side, holding uprooted samples of the plants I requested.

Good. I nodded. *Tyr, start with the hemian flower. Magic out its heart.*

Since when do plants have hearts? Tyr's head whirred as he looked the plant over from roots to petals.

Since always. Not like our hearts, but they have an energy center like every other living being. Look at the top of the stem; where the petals meet the stalk. Use your abilities to extract the ball that's giving off a subtle pulse. I made a note to explain energy systems to my brother *yet again* after we all got out of here.

Tyr's brain hummed as he narrowed his focus. Silvery sparks bounced around his head, a sign he was accessing his magic. When he touched the base of the flower, a sparkly energy raced through his mind, down his arm, and out his fingertips. It circled the hemian's heart until it created an iridescent bubble. Tyr held a finger up and pulled it back slowly, withdrawing the bubble-encased-heart.

Now what? Only my brother could make a thought sound like a grunt.

Now take off Forse's shirt and inject the hemian heart.

Tyr ripped Forse's black T-shirt over his head, and I was momentarily distracted by the image of Force's spectacular stomach.

Try to stay with us, Sis.

Shut up! Warmth flooded my energy, and a series of images from a *very* vivid dream I'd had once upon a time flashed through my mind.

Elsa, that's gross! You're my sister! Tyr shuddered. Sometimes, our little mind mash-ups ended in total mortification. We'd both seen things we wished we could unsee.

Then don't look, I hissed. Forse's teeth began to chatter and his pallor dimmed a shade. *Warm him up!*

"Brynn," Tyr barked. He pointed at Forse's exquisite, goose bump-covered chest.

Hurry, I pressed.

"Got it." Brynn knelt behind Forse and slid her knees underneath his head. She folded herself over him so her arms enveloped his, and rubbed her hands along the bare skin.

Now what? Tyr brought me back to the present.

Now magic the flower's center into his heart. Hold your free hand over his chest.

"Brynn. Lean right." Tyr barked. "You're blocking my access."

Okay. Free hand over the chest, check. I need you to scan his aura to see if that iron wall's still around his heart. Do you know how to do that?

Please. Tyr gave a mental shove. *I was scanning auras and reading minds when you were still in diapers.*

Just do it already.

The silver sparks pinged around Tyr's mind as he scanned Forse's heart. *No blocks. His heart's wide open.*

And it is absolutely overflowing with love. Guess who it's for? Tyr couldn't help but smile as warmth flooded my energy once again.

But my happy dance would have to wait.

It's good there's a clear path to his heart, but I don't understand how it's unblocked. There was a wall around it a few days ago—one so thick even a bomb couldn't have burst it open...That's it! My energy sparked.

What? Tyr paused, his hand over Forse's heart.

The beam didn't hit his heart; it hit the wall. The barrier he built to protect his heart is the reason he's alive! I couldn't believe it. Forse's typically cautious approach to our relationship—and to everything in his life—suddenly seemed like our saving grace. If the exploding rock back at the battle site was indicative of what Runa's blue beam of death could do, Forse's heart should have stopped beating the minute he was hit. The fact that he was still breathing, albeit barely, meant the beam hadn't touched his heart at all. His heart had been pierced by his own defenses. Granted his wall had probably been charged with the energy from Runa's beam, but he would have received a transitive dose of dark energy, not a direct one.

And that was something Tyr and I could definitely fix.

Okay. Put the blue crystal aside and send the flower directly into his chest. Try to apply it to the spot where his heart was struck. It should look like a small bump, either an angry red one or a black one, depending on how much magic already got in.

I see it, Tyr confirmed. The silver sparks in his head lit up as he held the hemian heart over Forse's torso. As glitter rained inside Tyr's mind, the flower passed inside Forse's skin and through his sternum, then deposited itself neatly in the pebble-sized hole in his heart. The organ emitted a gold glow as it accepted the plant, absorbing its regenerative properties. Besides being an exceptional binding agent, hemian was known to promote honor and fidelity, virtues both innate in Forse's genetic makeup and drilled into him as justice god. I knew its structure would repel any dark magic interfering with Forse's healing ability.

Rule number one of being High Healer: Darkness loathes light.

It worked, I confirmed. The light show in Tyr's head dimmed, and I felt him relax into relief.

So he's good then?

Not yet. The hemian heart is repairing Forse's, but you need to withdraw the lingering dark energy. Isolate the tomad root and use your fingertips to grind it into a powder. Then magic that on top of the hemian, I instructed.

Forse shuddered as Tyr rubbed the root between his finger and thumb.

"Is he doing okay?" Brynn asked.

"Keep warming him," Tyr ordered. "Elsa says we have to extract the dark energy now."

"Elsa," Forse murmured. His head rolled to the side, a small smile playing at his lips. His energy pulsed weakly beneath pale gray skin. We needed to get that darkness out *right now.* He was delirious.

Hurry! I urged.

I am. Tyr sounded frustrated. The light show began anew as my brother magicked the tomad powder through Forse's flesh. Forse's skin brightened the minute the dust broke through his chest bone, and by the time it settled around his heart, Forse's breathing had almost returned to normal.

Leave the powder for thirty seconds then pull it out. The tomad should work like a magnet to draw all the dark energy out of Forse's system. He'll be exhausted and sore, but Odin willing, he'll survive.

Tyr followed my instructions, and within a minute Brynn cradled a healing, albeit battered, justice god in her arms.

"He's still cold," Brynn's fingertips grazed the goose bumps that peppered Forse's arms.

"Here." Tyr threw Forse's shirt at Brynn. She tugged it over his head, sliding his arms through the holes and covering the loveliest view in all the realms with disappointing ease.

I can still hear you, Tyr complained.

Shut up, Tyr! Fasten the larimar necklace around his neck. Its heart-healing properties will work on both energetic and physical levels, and should speed the recovery process. I waited while Tyr followed my instructions.

"It's on." This time Tyr spoke out loud.

Brynn looked up. "That was scary. Is Elsa doing okay in there?"

Tyr met her gaze. "She's upset you took away her view."

Brynn giggled, and even Forse gave a small smile. His eyelids flickered, then opened, and he looked up at Tyr with a reverence that filled me with joy. *He's okay!*

"You saved me," Forse whispered quietly. He stared at Tyr, his eyes glowing with warmth.

"It was nothing." Tyr shrugged, but I could feel his relief. Tyr had been nearly as anxious as I was. "I owed you one from that time in Jotunheim when you jumped in front of that frost giant and—"

"Not you." Forse rolled his eyes. "Her. Is Elsa still in your head?"

Yes! I screamed.

"She is," Tyr answered. "But if you don't stop staring at me like a lovesick puppy, I'm going to ban her from my brain for life. This little infatuation fest is getting weird."

Tell him I miss him, I pressed.

Tell him yourself, Tyr groaned. *He's awake. You can call him on the communicator now.*

Oh! That would be infinitely preferable to using my brother as a walkie-talkie.

You said it, Tyr agreed.

"Tell Elsa I miss her," Forse murmured. I couldn't help my grin.

I miss you too! I shouted in Tyr's head.

"She misses you too," Tyr muttered begrudgingly. "She's going to call you any minute."

Forse smiled. His eyelids closed, no doubt heavy with both physical and mental exhaustion. I stared at his peaceful form, knowing underneath his shirt, his chest wound was already regenerating with fresh skin. The process would involve a good amount of pain, and he'd be wiped out for a few hours, maybe even a full day. But he would survive. And with his wall gone, he might finally be able to *live*—which was what I'd always dreamed for him.

We need to let him sleep this off, I told my brother. *That was a big-time healing, and his body's going to need time to catch up. Ask him to call me when he wakes up.*

Will do. The minute he's well enough to travel, we're coming after you again, Tyr vowed. *But I don't think it's smart to split up this soon after an attack.*

I agree. Just take care of Forse. And be careful, I warned. *Runa is on a warpath. She wants Fenrir, and she's willing to kill Forse to get me to give up his location.*

You don't know the dog's location, Tyr said.

She thinks she can make me use my gift to track him.

She doesn't know you very well, does she? I could hear Tyr's smile in his words.

Nope.

Tyr sighed. *We'll get out of here together. Be safe out there. Wherever you are.*

I love you too, big brother.

With one final look at Forse, I withdrew my energy from Tyr's head and made my way back to my body. It was cold in my tower, but I didn't care about the chill. As soon as Forse woke up, I'd get to talk to the god I loved. And on a deep, knowing level, I could sense that he loved me back.

I just had to wait for him to realize it.

"*HEI*." **I EXHALED AS** I spoke, releasing the tension of the past few hours into one breath. My fingers loosened their grip on my forearm, my knuckles cracking as they stretched for the first time in thirty minutes. Apparently, willing my arm to ring hadn't been particularly efficient.

"*Hei*," Forse repeated. "I'm sorry that I slept for so long."

"Don't be. Your body needed the rest." Physical beings took *much* longer to recover than their energetic counterparts. We'd removed a significant amount of dark energy from Forse's heart. It would have taken a mortal days to recover from a healing of that level, if they'd been able to recover at all. Thankfully for my nerves, Asgardian bodies were much more efficient.

"What I needed was to talk to you." Forse looked so serious, it caught me off guard.

"Are you okay?" I asked cautiously.

"Thanks to you, I am."

"It was nothing,"

"It was everything," Forse corrected. "But why am I wearing your necklace? How did you get it to Tyr?"

"I tucked it into the emergency kit before we left, just in case," I admitted. "I was afraid I'd lose it if I wore it around my neck on the Bifrost trip, but it was too special to leave behind. I'll expect you to return it to me the minute I see you."

"Deal." Forse smiled. "You know I'd be dead if it wasn't for you."

I waved my hand. "It was a group effort. Tyr technically performed the healing; I just talked him through the steps. Besides, that necklace did half the work for us. Larimar heals the heart on both physical and energetic levels, and because that particular crystal was a gift from you to me, its tie to both of us increased its potency. So in a way, you saved yourself."

"When are you going to realize how incredibly special you are?" Forse rubbed his jaw. "Your gift is unlike anything I've ever seen."

"Thanks, but that's not true. We have lots of healers," I reminded him. "Any one of them could have extracted the dark magic."

"*Ja.* They've worked on me before, and it was nothing like what I felt when you did…whatever it is you do. Hel, it was even different from the other times you've worked on me. Did you change your approach?"

No, you did. You dropped your wall and you can actually feel *now, you robot.* I wanted to shout the truth at him, but Forse's feelings were something he'd have to sort through on his own. It would have been nice if he'd sorted them *before* I got trapped in a lunatic's tower, but one worked with the hand one was dealt.

"I think you're going to find you're seeing things with a lot more clarity from now on," I answered honestly. "Runa's beam knocked some, erm, extraneous matter loose, and Tyr and I just cleared out the remnants."

"Huh. Well, whatever you did, thank you. My mind feels more refreshed than it has in years. If I had my caseload in front of me, I'd be able to work clear through my spring sentencings in two, three hours tops."

"Good. Then I did my job."

Forse held up his forearm so I could see him as he lay on his back. If the bags beneath his eyes were any indication, the poor guy was still exhausted.

"You need to go back to sleep," I advised.

"Not while you're still out there. Thank Odin your bruises look better." Forse squinted. "Does your head still hurt?"

"It's fine." I reached up to touch the skin behind my ear. It was a little sensitive, and dried blood matted my hair, but my energy ball had knitted the wound back together nicely.

"You holding up okay otherwise?" Forse tucked his free arm behind his head.

"I guess."

"What does that mean? Talk to me, *hjärtat.*"

My teeth worried my bottom lip. Forse needed to focus on healing, and capturing Runa before she made good on her promise to kill him. Everything else was superfluous.

"Elsa," Forse warned. "If you don't tell me, I'll never bring you Coke in a bottle again. You'll be forced to drink that inferior canned variety, into perpetuity."

"No need to get mean." I couldn't help but smile. "I'm worried about how far Runa's going to take this fight. We're a strong team, but she captured me, she almost killed you…things aren't going well *at all*. It was my job to keep the peace on this mission, and I failed. My inability to master unifying could very well be the weakness that gets us all killed."

"What are you talking about? We were all responsible for bringing Runa in. And I promised I'd keep you safe on this mission. If anyone's a failure here, it's me.

"You couldn't have known she'd ingest some superhero pill," I argued. "And you may have had one off moment in Svartalfheim, but I've had tons." I quickly recounted my attempt to turn Runa into a kinder, gentler sociopath. "We both see how that ended," I finished, pointing at my head. "This is my first actual mission, and I've been abducted, beat up, and sent my charge off in a rage to kill you. Nobody could accuse me of doing a decent job this round. What if it's like this every time? What if I never figure this out? Asgard needs a real Unifier, not some lousy interim. If I can't master this skill, then I can't teach Mia how to do it. And if neither of us get it together, the realm's going to be susceptible to attack all the time. Then the light realms will fall. And it's going to be all my fault."

"Don't be so hard on yourself. You're new at this. And you haven't had anybody to train you. We need to figure out how your mom did it." Forse looked at the sky for a moment. "Mmm." He typed something into his arm and waited. A moment later, he swiped his finger across the screen. "That's what I was hoping for."

"What?" I leaned forward.

"Freya finished scanning your mom's old journals. I've got them in my inbox. Let me send them to you." Forse typed again. When he finished, my arm hummed lightly. *I've got mail.*

"I see them." I swiped the flashing image on my skin, and my mom's journal appeared, splitting the screen with Forse's face. "We are so blind, Forse. We should have looked at these weeks ago, when we first found them. There's definitely something we can use in here."

"Agreed. If you read them from your end, and I read from mine, I'm sure we'll find a tool that helps us figure this out." Forse's finger moved across the screen as he scrolled through the document.

"I need you to focus on healing," I told Forse softly. "I've got this, please rest until you feel better."

"I will," Forse promised. "In a minute."

"Forse—"

"You have my word." Forse met my gaze and I sighed.

"Five minutes. Then you rest," I confirmed.

"It's a deal." Forse winked at me, then turned his attention to the text.

I leaned back against the cold stone wall as I stared at my mom's familiar handwriting. The chill dancing along my spine barely bothered me. At this point, I was pretty much numb.

One minute passed before Forse spoke again. "Here's something interesting."

"What?" I looked over from my reading, meeting Forse's gaze in the screen.

"Your mom mentions spirits." Forse rubbed his jaw. "When you worked on Runa—before you sent her off in a homicidal rage—"

"Hey," I protested.

"I'm kidding. But when you worked on Runa, did you push your energy at her like you do during a healing?"

"*Ja.*" Where was he going with this?

"What if unifying isn't about energy?" Forse asked.

"Don't be silly; everything's about energy."

"Hear me out." Forse closed his eyes, like he was deep in thought. "What if unifying is about connecting with someone on another level. A spiritual level."

Intuition pinged from the recesses of my brain. Forse was on to something. "Go on."

"Sometimes you call your energy your spirit. And you've said before that you can tell whether someone has a light or dark spirit." Forse opened his eyes. "But have you ever communicated with another spirit?"

"Like, talked directly to someone's spirit?" I paused. "No. I never have."

"Do you think it's possible?" Forse asked.

"I don't know," I answered honestly. "I've never tried."

"Want to try with me?"

My breath caught. Did I? That could get *really* personal. "I don't know. What if I...do something wrong?"

Forse shrugged. "Then you do something wrong. It's just me. I won't tell anyone."

That was true. Forse never divulged my confidences.

"You are pretty trustworthy," I agreed. "My parents never found out about the time you snuck me home three hours after curfew."

"You were a sophomore. They would have shipped me straight to Helheim if they knew I took you to a junior party. Especially one with that much mead."

I rolled my eyes. "Letting me have one drink wouldn't have killed you."

"Maybe not. But your brother would have. Don't forget, he was there too."

"Isn't he always?" I grumbled.

"Mmm. And speaking of your brother, I also never told him about the time you asked me to teach you how to kiss." Forse raised one eyebrow and heat flooded my face.

"Oh my gods! You can't bring that up, *ever*. I was, like, twelve."

"You were six hundred and eighteen," Forse corrected. "Plenty old enough to know what you were doing."

"That's twelve in mortal years," I hissed. "And there's a statute of limitations on bringing up embarrassing memories. That one passed."

"Let me check my law books." Forse pretended to scan through the communicator. "Huh, would you look at that? It says I have your whole entire existence to bring up any and all kissing memories. Sorry, *hjärtat*."

"You're terrible," I muttered.

"Am I? Or am I an exceptional secret keeper, one you owe big time for never telling the headmaster those sick notes you gave him to get out of combat class were fake—since you actually spent fifth period reading in the woods behind school."

"I'm sort of wishing I'd read less and combat-ed more right now." I gestured around my cell.

"It wouldn't have made a difference. You had a solid grasp of the self-defense maneuvers I taught you before we Bifrosted in here. And you did everything right when Runa grabbed you. That crystal she consumed had properties nobody expected. None of us could have fought her off."

"Thanks." Forse's words loosened the feeling of failure that had dogged me since my capture. "Will you teach me more when we get home? Maybe some offensive stuff, too? It'd be super fabulous if this could never happen again."

"You want me to pin you to the wall and watch you

squirm? Why Elsa Fredriksen, what would your brother say?" Forse drew his brows up in mock surprise.

"My brother can just deal. Besides, he owes you one. I do too. For bringing Tyr home when he went on that rampage after our parents died. I thought we'd lost him —that he'd finally given in to the darkness he's always been so afraid of." My stomach felt hollow as the memory passed through me.

"It was no big deal. He was easy enough to turn around."

"What did you say to him?" I raised an eyebrow.

Forse shifted, repositioning his arm beneath his head. "I told him he was an idiot for leaving you alone when you needed him the most. And that if he didn't get his sorry butt back to Asgard and look after you, I'd have him put on my list and brought into custody until he got control of himself."

"You threatened to put the God of War in jail?" I laughed. "That's not a nice thing to do to your friend."

"You were hurting, Elsa. Your brother needed to god up and be there for you." Clear green eyes met mine through the screen. They were impassively cool, as they always were, but beneath the façade Forse maintained for the worlds rested a warmth only a few got to see.

Right now, that warmth was lighting a spark some-where just south of my navel. If I hadn't been stuck in his psycho ex-girlfriend's tower, I'd have asked him for another kissing lesson right then and there.

"Thanks for always looking out for me," I whispered.

Forse shrugged. "I'd do anything to ensure your happiness. You know that."

"I know," I murmured. "And I want to do the same for you."

"You already do." Forse repositioned himself so he lay on his side. His coloring still hadn't returned to normal, and I knew our five minutes were nearing their end, but since I didn't know when I'd get the chance to talk with him like this again, I pressed forward with the question I'd been waiting decades to ask.

"Forse?" I ventured.

"Mmm?"

I pulled my bottom lip between my teeth for a beat. When I released it, my words tumbled out. "Why did you date Runa? She was so awful to everyone—why did you choose to be with her back then?"

Forse closed his eyes. When he opened them again, they were clouded with remorse. "I know it's hard to believe, but she was different with me. Maybe it's because of who I was fated to become, or the code I was bound to uphold as Justice, even when we were still in high school. But the Runa I knew in private was very different from the Runa she showed to the rest of the worlds. She was softer, more vulnerable. There was this sweetness to her that's unfathomable now. It was obvious someone had hurt her very badly, and that she lashed out from fear. Back then, I didn't believe she was the girl she presented to the rest of Asgard; I thought her coldness was just a mask to cover the vulnerability. Someone did a number on her Else, though I never was able to get her to open up enough to tell me who—or what—had hurt her. And I honestly believed I could help her—or at the very least, be a non-damaging presence in her life." Forse shook his head. "Talk about a gross misjudgment of character."

For the millionth time, my heart tugged at Forse's actions. He was just so very *kind*. And I so very much adored him for it.

"I don't think you misjudged her back then, Forse. Runa changed, but when you were together, I believe she still had a chance at choosing a good life. Maybe she still does." I sighed. "You're a good guy, Forse Styrke. I didn't understand your previous assessment of Runa, but I know you saw more good in her than the rest of us did when you were together. And I respect you for wanting to be there for someone who needed a healthy dose of light."

"Yeah, well, look where it got us." Forse nodded at his arm. "Let's take an hour and comb through your mom's journals—see if your mom explains *how* the whole unifying thing works; if it has anything to do with spirit communication or not. Do you want to stay on the coms and read together?"

"Yes. But your five minutes are up and you promised me you'd rest. Another few hours of sleep will do you a *lot* more good than reading old diaries with me."

"I promised I'd rest, but there's no way I'm waiting a few hours to come and find you." Forse didn't blink.

"Okay, let your body regenerate for an hour and call me again when you wake up."

"I feel fine," Forse protested.

"Your energy says otherwise. And I'm sorry, but I'm not letting you go back in the field without being fully charged."

"I'm not a battery," Forse groaned. "But I know you see things I can't, so fine. You have thirty minutes. If Henrik's guesstimate on the locator's performance time was right, that's the earliest it might be able to pick up a trace on you. The minute it does, we can move out."

I smiled. "Then I'll expect you here in thirty-five."

"It's a date." Forse's eyes crinkled. "And Elsa?"

"Hmm?"

"I miss my *hjärtat.*"

With that he signed off, leaving me with a warm feeling in my chest. Runa's blast might well have been the best thing that could have happened to Forse...and to me.

It had opened up Forse's heart.

CHAPTER 13

WHILE I WAITED FOR Forse to come for me, I positioned my back against the cell door and turned on my communicator. Runa wouldn't be able to see me through the window at this angle, and if the door opened I could just turn off my screen. My arm hummed, and I opened the document to the first journal I came across. It was dated before I was born.

June 3. Today I accompanied Ragnar to Jotunheim. Things have gotten so dark there. Their king lost all sense of compassion when his would-be daughter-in-law disappeared. Although I empathize with his heartbreak for his son, I cannot comprehend his path. Instead of reaching out to the girl, who clearly wants nothing to do with the giants' reign of cruelty, he put a hit on her. Ragnar believes the girl returned home to Vanaheim, but I doubt she would expose her loved ones to the tyrant's wrath. Most likely she sought protection among the dwarves. Their alliance with the dragons all but ensures peace in their realm, and their dislike of the frost giants would make them sympathetic to the girl's plight. I will continue my own search for Lifa, but I will do so with extreme caution. The king's rage is terrible.

While we were in Jotunheim, Ragnar negotiated a treaty with the ruler's youngest son. The prince was reluctant to enter into an agreement with Asgard, but I located a weakness in his emotional center—a pebble-sized hole near his heart, awaiting the return of his runaway bride. When I spoke to his spirit, I saw it was only partially dark—not yet fully tarnished. And so we were able to come to a meeting of the souls. For now.

I read the last few lines twice as Mom's words sunk in. Forse had been right. Unifying *was* about connecting with another being on a spiritual level. I mentally kicked myself *again* for not reading Mom's journals earlier. Of course my mother's journals would be about more than falling in love with my dad. If I'd stopped to think it through, I would have realized her grown-up journals would have more depth than my teenage ones. But I'd been so wrapped up in my grief and fear, I'd failed to see the lifeline she left behind. All those tears over not having anyone to teach me...and the textbooks had been in a box labeled "Stuff From Mom's Closet" all along. *Sigh.* It was such a universal truth. So often the answers were right in front of us— we just had to get outside our own heads to see them.

I scanned through the communicator, reading entries that confirmed Forse's theory again and again. I lost myself in my mother's words, her familiar scrawl embracing me in comfort as I imagined her reading her journals aloud. When I finished that file, I clicked it closed and opened another, reading until I came to a page that stopped my heart cold. *No. Way.* I read it again, my pulse accelerating as I realized how connected my mother had been to my fate. If only she'd done what she set out to do, maybe none of this would be happening...

December 12. Lifa's daughter arrived at my home today. I haven't seen her since her mother's death—Runa has rebuffed my offers to do a healing since Lifa's passing, and continues to deny my requests to perform a cleansing. Sadly, this refusal precludes me from giving her a permanent Asgardian placement, and she remains in the custody of her temporary guardian. Seeing her today came as a shock—the girl has her mother's eyes. It was the first thing I noticed when she came over with Forse Styrke to help me bake for St. Lucia's. From what I gather, they are together. I should be happy that Lifa's daughter found such an upstanding young man—Forse certainly will not repeat Runa's father's crimes —but I cannot help but feel unsettled. Forse has always been so close with my children, I feel as if he is a part of our family. His soul is filled with light, despite the heavy path he must walk as God of Justice. He deserves a partner who emanates an equal brightness...and truth be told, I have always seen him ending up with my Elsa.

Me too, Mom!

Runa can sense something between them. She watches my Elsa with unsettling calculation. She looks angry, or maybe jealous.

When I reached out to her spirit today, her energy was

cold. She has a good dose of her father's darkness, but tempers it with what little she inherited of her mother's light. Her spirit is torn—it has not completely given itself to her father, but I sense his energy pulling on her. No doubt he will pull out every stop to bring her into his fight. I will do what I can to keep her on the path her mother wanted for her, but Runa keeps her spirit locked so tight inside her heart, I am not sure if I will be able to reach it.

And I am afraid of what will happen to her...and to us... if I fail.

My arm dropped into my lap as I finished reading. Of course my mother knew Runa. Forse, Tyr, and Henrik were pretty much joined at the hip all through *forever*, and once Forse started dating Runa she invited herself along everywhere he went. Thanks to my parents' open-door policy, the boys—and Runa—were at our house a lot. But I hadn't known Mom knew Runa's mom. Until today, I hadn't even known Runa had a mom. If Mom's journal was correct, Runa had been lying to us from day one. It sounded like Lifa had passed away before Mom wrote that journal entry. But if Runa's father was still trying to pull her into his darkness, whatever that meant, then he was still alive when Runa showed up...and might even still be alive now.

Anger filled my chest. She'd lied to Forse. He'd trusted her enough to hand her his heart, and she'd stomped all over it. She'd betrayed my mom who, apparently, had done everything in her power to help her. And then she'd destroyed our family, and knowingly aided and abetted Fenrir in the murder of the God of War and Unifier of Asgard. I wanted to hate her. Turn her blue-beam-of-death hand on her own heart and do to her what she'd tried to do to Forse.

But I couldn't help but remember the images I'd seen when I'd tried to unravel her knot. The day she protected her brother; the way she soldiered on as her mother pleaded for her own death; the night she bore her father's rage after she sent her brother away.

Hold on. Had Mom known Runa's brother too? And her father? I knew Mom had helped thousands of souls during her reign as Unifier, but her story about Lifa seemed more personal—like she had a deeper connection to this group of spirits than some of the others.

BANG.

A loud noise jarred me from my thoughts, and I quickly scanned the tower and the rest of the building for energy signatures. Instead of feeling my friends' presences, I felt a bird. Its energy was confused, and I deduced it had flown into one of the tower walls. *Ouch.*

The clock on the communicator indicated it would be at least another ten minutes before the locator might be able to track me. I swiped the screen, jumping documents to read an earlier journal entry, this one dated before Tyr or I were old enough to start school. As I read, my heart tugged.

I wish you were still with me, Mom.

I wiped my tear and resumed my reading.

May 19. Ragnar and I took the kids camping this week-end. He is just so sweet with them. I don't know how he checks his war god hat at the door and becomes simply Daddy, but he does it with a grace all gods should envy. This weekend was no different. He and Tyr shared an enthusiastic stick fight with willow branches. Tyr will make a fine swordsman one day. Elsa preferred to cheer from the sidelines, and when the battle ended, Tyr helped me grill the caribou while Ragnar read Elsa one of her favorite fairy tales. After supper, he led us all on a nature walk, lifting the children on his shoulders in turns so they could peek at the bird nests in the aspen trees.

As crazy as our work lives are, I truly cherish these moments we have as a family. The children are our greatest blessing. Tyr adores his sister unabashedly, and his fondness for his father radiates from every inch of his aura. No matter what the Norns throw at him, I know we have given him a foundation of love that will see him through his darkest day. And my Elsa...our baby girl has a heart so beautiful, I doubt there will ever be another like it. I hope she retains that unparalleled blessing for all her existence, and that she always remembers a single act of kindness can brighten even the darkest realm.

I turned off my communicator and rested my head against the door. Gods, I missed my parents. They were honorable; kind; full of love. They were everything the realms needed, and they'd given me the most beautiful childhood. I was so thankful for that. And though I felt their absence every single day, I was grateful for the love they instilled in me. They'd taught me to find the best in everyone, to make the most of even the worst situation. And although I might not be able to hug them anymore, I knew they were with me; in every act of kindness, I saw a reminder of the mother who'd taught me hope, and the father who'd taught me compassion, and the good that could come of change.

Change. I might not have the family I was born with anymore, but my parents were proof that family was more than just what Odin gave you at birth—it was what you built for yourself. And just as they'd taken in my brother, Tyr and I had built a circle of friends we were lucky to call our new family. We'd been blessed with so much love, even in the face of unbearable loss. And with the addition of Mia, Asgard wouldn't be without its rightful Unifier much longer. We'd face a lot of challenges, but with Mom's journals as our guide, we'd be able to figure it out together. And then Mia, Tyr, Forse, Henrik, Brynn, and I would do everything in our power to maintain peace throughout the realms.

A sharp pain racked my skull as the door slammed against my back. *Holy Asgard, that hurt.*

"Get out of the way, *ko*," Runa hissed. "You're going to find that dog, and you're going to do it *now*."

I scooted to the side, rubbing my spine as Runa stormed into my cell. Her aura was heavy as the Svartalfheim soot, all trace of the goodness I'd seen before extinguished by the dark. When I tapped into her energy, I sensed a blackness I hadn't seen before.

Odin's beard. The hit on Forse was only the beginning. She's actually going to kill every last god until she gets Fenrir.

With a deep breath, I drew my shoulders back. The

time for training had passed. I had no choice but to appeal to Runa's spirit. And if I failed, I'd have to try even harder to find my own way out of here. There was no way I was leading my friends straight to this lunatic.

But would I be strong enough to overpower a monster?

Runa took a step closer, and my energy recoiled at her heavy dose of darkness. "Your boyfriend's dead. The valkyrie's next. Do you feel like doing what I asked now or do I need to keep killing?" The cell spun a dizzying circle as Runa's words sent an ice pick through my chest. It took several panicked gasps before I realized Runa didn't know that her blast hadn't killed Forse—Tyr and I had saved him.

"Well?" Runa slammed the door behind her and stood over me. "Answer me! Are you in shock or are you just stupid?"

"Your shoulder's bleeding?" My voice went up on the last word. According to my mother's journals Runa's mom was from Vanaheim, which would make Runa the recipient of a partial healing gene. If her shoulder wasn't knitting itself back together, that meant she was seriously injured. I pressed the heels of my hands to my eyes, seemingly to stop my tears, but actually to give myself time to process this information. There had to be a way to use it. "Did Forse do that before...before?"

"Before I killed him? Yes. He went down fighting. Too bad he turned out to be so weak." Runa sneered. "*Now* are you ready to cough up Fenrir's location?"

The light in my brain flashed. *Got it!*

"Don't you want me to fix your arm first?" I fake-sniffled, playing along with Forse's presumed death. "You can't go anywhere near Asgard if you're bleeding like that. The guards will smell you before you even touch down, and they'll take you into custody before you get anywhere near Fenrir."

"So he *is* in Asgard!" Runa declared triumphantly.

"I don't know," I answered honestly. "But most of our high-security prisoners are. And you should know, the facility I'm thinking of has more than just Elite Team guarding it. It has some...animals. That much blood is going to agitate them, even on an energetic level. They won't smell blood since we won't be corporeal, but they will smell injury and weakness. If I hide myself in your energy the way that it is, they're going to sniff me out long before I can track your dog."

Runa pressed her lips together. "How do I know this isn't another one of your tricks?"

"You don't." I wiped my nose on my sleeve, keeping up the act. "You just killed the only god I've ever loved. I have every reason to retaliate."

"You're not fighting me." Runa furrowed her brow.

"In case you hadn't noticed, I'm not exactly a fighter." I shrugged. "Besides, I don't want you to hurt Brynn, or my brother, or anyone else for that matter. But before I look for Fenrir again, do you want me to heal your arm or not?"

The line was cast. Now came the wait.

Runa glared at her arm, and then at me. She knew

the facility I alluded to; we'd toured it in high school, as part of our Law and Justice course. Asgard had upped the security since, but even back then it had plenty of sentinels of the carnivorous variety.

"Fine," Runa spat. "Heal it. But if I get the slightest feeling you're up to something, I will track down your idiot blond friend and put a blast through her head so fast, she'll never know what killed her."

"Fair enough." I held up both hands. "Why don't you sit down? This can be kind of draining."

"I'll stand." Runa crossed her arms. She winced as the motion jostled her injury, but otherwise didn't move.

"Okay then. This will take a few minutes. You'll feel my energy moving inside you. Just let it pass through your body, and don't try to eject it. I won't be able to fix your shoulder if you do."

"You heard what I said about killing blondie, didn't you? I won't hesitate to—"

"I got it." I interrupted through gritted teeth. "Now, try to relax. It goes faster if you're not…clenching."

The last thing I saw before I closed my eyes was Runa's angry glare. *Typical.* It must have been exhausting to live in a state of perpetual fear. Because as much as Runa played angry, anger itself was only a mask. It wasn't a real emotion—rather it covered up a deeper, more vulnerable one. And from the little I'd seen of Runa's black knot, she'd lived her life in a state of constant fear—fear for her safety, fear for her little brother, fear of losing her mother, and fear of being alone after her father banished her. If she wasn't so unbelievably awful, I'd have felt sorry for her.

But she was awful. At least, a part of her was. Now I needed to see if there was any trace of that good soul that had risked her own life to save her brother's. I hoped the boy was safe and happy, wherever he was. Runa's sacrifice was worth at least that much.

With a grounding breath, I retreated to the quiet part of my mind. I uncoupled my consciousness, and allowed my spirit to control my thoughts. It was surprisingly easy to do.

Hei, I greeted Runa's spirit cautiously. When I didn't get a response, I waited a moment before trying again. *Hei?*

Still nothing. I retreated into my mind, and took a quick scan of Runa's energy. There was a heavy blockade surrounding her mind; no doubt she'd braced herself for the worst. She'd thrown up a mental wall, probably thinking I was a mind reader like Tyr.

I snorted. If only my gift was as simple as my brother's.

"Are you laughing at me?" Runa growled.

"I am *sniffling,*" I said indignantly. "You just killed Forse. How am I supposed to feel?"

My lie seemed to mollify Runa. "Just hurry up."

Fine. I directed a stream of positive energy at the wall around Runa's head, and in moments I'd dissipated the block. With my hands raised, I whisked it away, flicking it into the ground, where it would be reabsorbed and recycled like the fertilizer it was. *Good riddance.*

This time when I retreated to the quiet spot in my mind, I felt the desperate pull of an anxious soul. *Bingo.*

Hei, I tried again. *I'm Elsa. I'm here to help you.*

I know who you are.

My jaw fell open when the spirit presented itself. I honestly hadn't expected this to work. The spirit looked kinder than I expected. It had Runa's sharp features—her angular jaw, strong nose and full lips. But it had a softness that Runa lacked. Its cheeks were a rosy pink; its hips were gently rounded. And although it flickered with a dark energy it obviously tried to repress, its heart emitted a strong light. There was hope for Runa yet.

Are you going to kill me? I asked the spirit.

I don't want to, it answered back.

Is that because you need me alive to find Fenrir?

No. I don't want you to find Fenrir. The spirit sounded vehement. I wasn't sure if I should be relieved or alarmed.

Why then?

It's because I don't want to kill anyone. The darkness flickered, and the spirit held itself very still. Blackness covered its form from head to toe, draining it of all color. Then a dim light flashed from its heart, and the spirit permitted itself a breath, drawing the light upward. When it reached the spirit's face, relief washed over its features, and the blackness ebbed.

What was that? I effectuated an air of calm. A freak-out, even a spirit-level one, wasn't going to win me any friends.

That was the real me, the spirit said sadly.

No, it's not. You're talking to me. If Runa had a black soul, it—you—would have killed me by now.

I killed my mother. That's black enough.

I scanned the spirit's energy. *No, you didn't,* I confirmed.

I might as well have. I'm the reason she's dead. I left her alone with him.

You lost me.

"Are you fixing me or are you screwing with me again?" Runa's voice broke through our interlude.

"I told you this would take some time," I reminded her. But in the interest of sending up a red herring, I sent a pulse of healing energy at Runa's arm. It would numb the pain enough to make her think I was playing along, when in reality I was searching for information that would help me break her dark streak.

All's fair in love and war.

"Hurry up. I don't have all day." Runa sounded agitated.

With another grounding breath, I retreated into my mind.

What happened with your mom? I asked the spirit.

The spirit's shoulders drooped. *When my father told me to leave, my mom begged him not to kick me out. She said I was the only good thing she had left in her life, and she'd die without me. My father didn't care. He made sure every guard in Jotunheim knew to kill me on sight if I tried to come home. He gave me twelve hours to gather my things and get out.*

I'm so sorry. I was. Despite being God of War, my own father had been nothing but kind. Even on his darkest day, he'd made himself fully available for any games Tyr and I had wanted him to play.

My mother was heartbroken, but she knew better than to defy my father. She had a friend in Asgard who offered to protect me.

My mom, I surmised.

Yes. The spirit smiled. *Your mom was one in a million. She said the needs of a child outweighed the needs of a realm, and offered me refuge in Asgard. She'd offered it once before, but I'd been too afraid to leave my mother alone with him to accept. This time, things were different. Even so, your mom sensed my father's darkness in me, and she worried about what I might do if I snapped.*

Sadness colored my aura.

I'm so sorry. My mother would have been horrified at what I became. The spirit looked as downcast as I felt. *She wanted us to move away together, to live a better life, but she knew she had to plan our escape carefully. She reached out to your mom, and asked her to bring me to Asgard for safe keeping. Mrs. Fredriksen wanted to remove my dark energy before I entered the realm. But my mother was adamant that I needed immediate placement, for my own protection. Mrs. Fredriksen agreed to set me up in a house with a transitional guardian until she could do a cleansing— she couldn't in good conscience place a partially darkened spirit with another family. And my mother didn't want to leave my father until she knew I was secure in Asgard. So Mrs. Fredriksen stationed a female warrior in the house with me. She was supposed to stay until Mother showed up—then Mrs. Fredriksen could cleanse my energy.*

Let me guess, I interjected. *My mom never got around to that cleansing.*

Exactly. My mother was supposed to join me after a few days, but she never came. My father found out she was planning to leave him, and he had her killed. She'd still be alive if I hadn't left.

Maybe, I agreed. *But* you'd be *dead if you'd stayed. Your father all but promised as much.*

The spirit wrung her hands. *I know,* she whispered. *But look at what I've become. The realms would have been better off if I'd let him kill me instead.*

Don't talk like that, I urged. *Your father's choices were his to make.*

And my choices were mine. The spirit met my gaze. *The darkness took over when I lost my mother.*

How so? I questioned.

The part of my physical form that took after my father got stronger. It grew to the point that it all but choked out any goodness I'd cultivated in Runa. At first it was just the genetics; my father's physical traits manifested in acts of aggression—fist fights, screaming matches, normal teenage goddess things. But then the psychological eclipse occurred.

Psychological eclipse?

The spirit sighed. *Your mom reached out to me, but I pushed her away. A cleansing would have meant severing my ties with my father, and awful as he was, he was the only family I had left. When I looked at you and your friends, all I could see was what I'd never have. Loss wasn't foreign to your families, but you stuck together and made the best of what was left. When I realized how different my life could have been if my parents had made different choices...well, that's when I lost all sense of humanity.*

Boy, had she. *Was that when you left Asgard?*

Almost. First I went to my father. He hated the Fredriksens, so he said if turned their pet on them, he'd let me come home. I did what I thought I had to do to earn my father's approval. But it didn't work. There was always one more task my father needed me to complete before he would welcome me home. And as much as I hated hurting people, my host body has been consumed by her need for his approval.

Your host body? The choice of words surprised me.

I don't identify myself with Runa. I haven't been allowed to guide her choices in years. The spirit paused. *You know she's about to snap again, don't you? My father declared that if I don't deliver Fenrir to him by midnight, I'll be dead to him. He'll close my home realm to me forever, and I'll be stuck on Svartalfheim, praying nobody turns me over to Asgard.*

My blood chilled. Odin only knew what Runa would do if she went on another true warpath. Though her dad cutting her off would probably be the best thing for her. *Hold on. What about your dad's other son? Could he take you in? What ever happened to your brother?*

Runa's spirit blinked. *You really don't know?*

No.

The spirit gave a sanguine smile. *He's just fine.* She pressed her lips together, indicating the matter was closed.

Fair enough.

"Why don't I feel better yet?" Runa hissed. "You said it would take a few minutes, but it's been a *lot* longer than that."

Uh, I'd better go. I raised a hand in farewell. *Until next time?*

The spirit smiled sadly. *I'll be in here.*

I'll work on your host for you, I promised. *I'll try to make your living arrangements if not better, then at least less awful.*

Stay safe, the spirit warned.

You too.

"Elsa!" Runa shrieked.

"Sorry!" I sent another beam at Runa's shoulder. The energy cleared out the region's darkness, which enabled her demi-god genetics to kick back in. Her muscles rejected the bullet, dislodging it from the bone, and allowing the skin to knit itself back together. As the flow of blood ebbed, Runa leaned against the wall in relief.

"About time." She swore. Her eyes flew open and she stared at me, her gaze shooting the fire of a thousand Muspelheims. Runa hated me; there was zero doubt about that. The question was, how far was that hatred going to take her?

And how many gods were going to die because of it?

CHAPTER 14

"**P**ICK UP, PICK UP, pick up." *If I will it, he will come...*Positive thinking began working its magic. The communicator buzzed against my arm as I waited for Forse to answer. Runa had slammed the door on me just moments before, her newly healed shoulder severely weighed down by its enormous chip. She'd run out of patience with my fake attempts to track Fenrir, and she'd decided killing Brynn would convince me to do her bidding.

"Pick up!" I pleaded.

After a slow eternity, my wish was granted.

"*Perfekt* timing." Forse stared at the screen. "We adjusted the search parameters with the additional info you gave us, and the locator's narrowed your where-abouts to two potential sites—searching only the towers east of the ambush site cut our prospective locations down a lot. As soon as it confirms a single location, I'll port us to the forest at the base of your tower. Get ready for company."

His easy words did nothing to soothe my panic. "Forget finding me, just get out of here. Bifrost back to Midgard, or port to the far side of the realm. Runa thinks you're dead, so you're in the clear, but now she's on her way to kill Brynn."

Forse clenched his jaw. "Tyr," he muttered through his teeth. "Some cover, please."

My brother grunted in the background, and a shimmery bubble appeared behind Forse. My lower lip quivered. I'd never been so relieved to see one of Tyr's protective shields. Brynn would be safe, at least for now.

Forse swiped his finger across the screen. "Oh, *skit.* Henrik just sent his full analysis of the crystal Runa ingested."

"What does it say?" Brynn's face popped into the background. "Oh, *hei*, Elsa."

"*Hei.*" I waved halfheartedly.

"Double *skit*," Brynn swore. "This is so not good."

Tyr leaned over Forse's shoulder, nodding at me as he read. "*Hei,* Sis."

"Tyr, Runa is crazy. Your little bubble isn't going to do anything. You have to get Forse and Brynn out of there," I begged.

My brother scrolled through the screen. "*Skit* doesn't begin to cover it. The good news is that the crystal's effects last one to three days from the time of activation. So it could be wearing off any time now.

Then we'll only have a regular-issue crazy goddess on our hands, not a hyped-up crazy one."

"Unless she pocketed a shard when the crystal exploded and ingests another piece," Forse countered. "Then the clock would start all over."

Tyr and Brynn swore in unison.

I leaned against the stone wall of my cell. "What powers did it give her, exactly? Did Henrik break them down?" I asked.

"She's got the hand blast, as we saw. Henrik thinks it's a dark magic-laced gas that's being funneled into a condensed stream. The gas acts as a conductor for the dark magic." Forse swiped the screen.

"Fabulous," I muttered.

"Then there's the porting. The crystal should give Runa the power to open and close portals within the realm. Apparently the crystal's power is tied to Svar-talfheim," Forse explained.

"Interesting." Tyr sounded thoughtful. "So if we got her out of here, even if she's still hyped up on crystal juice, its powers would be impotent?"

"Probably. But this dose should wear off in a few hours. Let's try to bring her in before she goes for round two, *ja*?" Forse rubbed his jaw.

"Obviously," Tyr grumbled.

"Or you could wait out her rampage in Asgard, and come back when she's off her uppers?" I offered.

"We're not leaving you here alone, Elsa." Tyr glowered.

Gods are so stubborn.

"Fine." I tapped my chin with one finger. "Do you think she could have any other powers?" I asked.

"The crystal is enhancing what's in her. She was already strong; now she should be stronger. She was already fast; now she's like a cheetah on caffeine. You get the idea." Forse rubbed the deep *V* between his brows.

I knew exactly why. "Her darkness is growing too, isn't it?"

Forse nodded. "If Henrik's specs are correct, this crystal is enhancing everything in her genetic makeup, from physical to emotional traits. Runa had a rough life, and I always believed those circumstances made her do the things she did. But now...I can't help but wonder if evil was bred into her all along. Maybe her soul is coded for malice."

"It's not," I interjected. "I talked to it. Her soul is really nice."

"You did *what*?" Brynn squeaked. "Oh my gods, how?"

"Forget how, did you say her spirit is *nice*?" Forse's eyebrows shot up.

"It's a long story." I glanced over my shoulder, but my cell door was still closed. Thank Odin. "The most important thing to know is that you don't have much time. Runa has some major daddy issues, and unless we turn over Fenrir, she's going to lose the only god she seems to care about—her bat-poop crazy father."

"You been talking to Mia lately?" Tyr chuckled.

"You know what I mean." I rolled my eyes. "Runa is

determined to kill Brynn. I think her plan is to keep offing Asgardians until we turn over the wolf."

"If she's serious about hurting our people, then we'll turn over the wolf." Brynn shrugged. "We've trapped him before; we can get him back again."

"It's not that simple," I argued. "She's planning to use him to destroy Asgard. Apparently, the dark elf prophets say Fenrir will play a key role in Ragnarok. And Runa claims that if Tyr hands him over, he'll die knowing he was responsible for the end of the realms as we know them."

My friends stared at the screen without blinking.

"The dark elves have prophesies about Ragnarok, too?" Brynn tugged at her ponytail.

"Apparently," I confirmed. "I know we don't like to talk about the end of Asgard, but if there's a chance this could be true, we need to prevent it."

The vein in Forse's forehead bulged. He was seriously mad. "Under no circumstances are we to turn Fenrir over to *anyone*. Our Norns say Fenrir will play a key role in Ragnarok as well. But they have nothing but heroic things to say about Tyr's role."

A loud crash interrupted our strategizing.

"What was that?" Brynn pointed. My friends looked up, but my view was restricted to three furrowed brows.

I tapped the screen on my forearm. "I can't see. What is it?"

"I think a bird fell out of the sky." Brynn flinched.

Crash. "There's another one. Is someone shooting them?"

Tyr closed his eyes. "I'm not picking up any mind signatures," he surmised.

"Well, something's making them fall. They aren't dropping on their own." Forse ran his hand over the golden highlights of his waves, and I wished I could reach through the communicator and do the same. His carefully constructed layers were slowly unraveling as his inner warrior clubbed his outer scholar over the head, preparing for battle in the name of survival.

A disheveled justice god was unfairly sexy.

At the sound of a third crash, Forse swore. "They're not birds. They're drones in bird's clothing."

"Let me see," I urged.

Forse angled his arm to show me the perimeter of the silvery bubble, where a fourth black blur fell at the protection. It struck the shield with a force that sent it bouncing back, hitting a nearby tree with enough impact to shake its needles loose. As it spiraled to the ground I caught a view of its feathered head, bent wings, and broken beak. The drone convulsed, emitting a series of red sparks before shooting a flare twenty meters straight up.

Oh, gods.

Tyr growled. "It's a scout drone. Whoever's sending them will be here any—"

He never got to finish his sentence. Before my friends could draw their weapons, a sea of black birds rained down on the protective shield. And a voice I wished I would never hear again broke through the peaceful quiet of the forest.

"Come out, come out, wherever you are!"

Runa was ready to play.

Dear Odin, help us all.

"So, my little friends found you. How lovely." Runa's voice crackled, sounding far away.

Panic clawed at my heart. "Get out of there!"

"Drone birds are equipped with speakers," Force said. "She's not necessarily on site." As he glanced up, a trio of drones struck the shield directly above his head. How much longer could it last?

"Whether she's there or not, you need to leave. Get back to Asgard and send the Elite Team in to take her down. Don't get yourselves killed!" I pleaded.

One corner of Forse's mouth turned up as the locator emitted a series of beeps. "No Asgardians are getting killed today. We *finally* found you." Forse picked up Brynn's backpack and tossed it to her. "Brynn, you and Tyr hold Runa's attention while I port to Elsa and get her out of the tower. I'll have Heimdall drop the Bifrost to bring her home, then I'll come back with—"

The loud boom jarred Forse. His lips parted as he took in the silvery bubble, now streaked with so many breaks it looked as if it'd met the business end of a Helbeast. The cracks popped as they traveled the length of the shield, until the whole dome was covered in jagged lines.

"*Forbåskat*," Tyr swore.

"Incoming." Runa's voice rang triumphant as another bird dropped out of the sky, dive-bombing the apex of the shield. It sent a single crack from the peak to the perimeter of the already splintered dome.

"It's going to give soon," Brynn warned. "That last one hit the stabilizer."

Tyr glared at the sky. "Forse, go get my sister, now!"

Forse wrapped his hand around the hilt of his sword. With the other, he saluted Tyr before drawing a small circle in the air with his pointer finger. My last image before Forse ported out was of the silver glitter raining down on my friends, a sparkling contrast to the sweeping sea of drones. The fake birds filled the sky like a thick fog, blocking the sunlight and casting a haze over the forest. The communicator went dark for an endless beat.

Oh gods, come back. Come back!

As my heart thumped to a standstill, the beautiful image of Forse's face filled my screen. Behind him stood a sea of thick, soot-covered trees.

"Oh thank Odin. You're okay." My teeth released their hold on my fingernails.

"For now. There's no telling where Runa's drones will turn up next."

"Where are you?"

Forse turned a circle. "I'm in the woods due north of your tower, probably a good two kilometers away. If Runa's super-senses are wearing off, I don't think she'll be able to detect me at this distance."

"That was good thinking." I glanced out my window.

"That's why they pay me the big kroner. We need to get you out of there, but I've got to assess the castle to figure out the best exit strategy." Forse squinted. "Is she still in the building? Or has she left to put a hit on Tyr and Brynn?"

I scanned the castle for energy signatures. "She's here," I confirmed. "And she's really angry. Her spirit's still good though—I'm going to talk to it and try to get her to call off her attack."

"Nobody's that powerful, Elsa." Forse's voice was low. "You think I didn't try to save her a hundred times over the years? She doesn't want our help. She doesn't want to be saved."

I stared into the sorrowful green eyes in the screen, finally realizing what this recon must have cost Forse. Coming face to face with the ex-girlfriend who betrayed him in the worst possible way; seeing how far the goddess he once loved had descended into darkness; watching helplessly as I was taken away. This trip had been a living Hel.

And now I was asking him for more time.

"I'm sorry, Forse," I apologized. "I have to try. My mother would have wanted to know we did everything we could to save Lifa's daughter."

Forse raised his eyebrows.

"I'll explain everything later. Just move toward the castle. I'll try to talk to her, and hopefully get her to call off the drones—maybe even let me go. If I'm not in the forest closest to the tower in ten minutes, you'll know I didn't succeed. In that case, come up after me."

Forse sucked in a sharp breath. "And if you don't succeed? Then what do you want me to do with Runa?"

I closed my eyes. "Then you do what you have to do to protect Asgard."

"This is too risky. Let me come and get you, and we can—"

My eyes flew open. "I am the Unifier of Asgard. For better or worse, I'm all our realm has. This soul needs my help. You have to trust me."

Forse's features softened. "I do trust you, *hjärtat*. It's that monster I don't trust."

I took a deep breath. "Ten minutes. That's it. Oh, and Forse?"

"Mmm?"

"I love you. You should probably know that." With that, I pressed my finger to my wrist, the communicator's screen darkening on the image of the God of Justice, with his mouth open and eyes wide.

My hands shook as I tucked my hair behind my ears. As terrifying as that was, I knew something even scarier lay ahead.

I gritted my teeth and sucked in a breath. *Here goes nothing.*

ERM, *HEI*. I REACHED out to Runa's spirit. *Are you still here?*

Silence.

You don't have to talk to me, but you need to call off this god hunt. They're going to bring in assassins to kill you.

Still nothing, but my spirit felt the pulsating anger from Runa. My breath came in ragged gasps as I absorbed the rage burning within her. My heart sunk with the realization that I'd failed—Runa's spirit was almost completely black. There was only a tiny flicker of light left within her—barely even a spark. The darkness had all but snuffed out the spirit that had once been a protective big sister and loving daughter.

Gods, what did it take for someone to go from being that pure, to this…this evil? What kind of blow had she been dealt since the last time I spoke to her spirit? Was there any point in trying to reason with her anymore? Or should I turn tail and save myself?

My gut tugged. Runa might have made some horrific choices, but so long as there was a spark of goodness within her, this poor soul deserved my best effort.

I pulled my shoulders back and pushed my spirit forward.

Runa, I know there's still good in you. I'm so sorry you never had the family you deserved. I'm sorry you never knew the unconditional love every child should have. I'm sorry my mom, and Forse, and now even me, all failed to help you overcome your pain. I don't know how to reach you, but I need you to know that if you continue down this path, you won't be able to turn back. Right now there's still a spark of light in you, but if you go and kill Brynn, and—

I don't want to kill anyone. Runa's spirit broke through. Oh, thank Odin!

You're there! My joy was so overwhelming, I wanted to reach out and hug Runa's spirit. But I wasn't about to do anything that might send the vestiges of Runa's goodness back into hiding.

You have to stop my host. She snapped. Runa's spirit spoke hurriedly, like she was afraid she might be snuffed out.

What happened?

Her father upped his deadline. She didn't deliver the wolf, so he banished her. It's exactly like—

It's exactly like what happened when he punished her for protecting her brother, I surmised. Suddenly Runa's energy shift made sense. *He triggered an emotional memory of abandonment; the one that sent her on this path to begin with. And now he's forcing her to complete the journey. Gods, what kind of a demon is this guy?*

The spirit shuddered. *You have to stop her. If she kills Brynn, and unleashes Fenrir...your brother will blame himself. He'll spiral down the same path Runa is on. Only when he falls, the aftermath will be devastating. Because he's not just Asgard's God of War; he's—*

"Enough!" Runa's shriek rang across the castle. The sound reverberated throughout the floors, bouncing off the stones and sending waves of pain through my heart. Heavy footsteps pounded outside my cell door, and when Runa wrenched it open, her face was nearly unrecognizable. Her eyes burned like two blackened coals, and her lips were pressed together so tightly, they made a thin line. She shot a beam at the wall sconce with her hand, and the lava rocks within began to smolder. Their light cast eerie shadows around my cell.

Block her, the spirit said.

Excuse me? I cringed as Runa stepped inside my cell.

Block her. If you have your mother's powers, you can make her see—or feel—whatever you want her to. Push a thought into her head and take her off this destructive course.

My mother did that? How? I asked. Runa raised her hand, and I covered my face.

Just do it!

A blue light sparked in Runa's hand, and I knew the beam was coming. Without knowing how, I pressed the image of a flower-filled meadow into her mind. Confusion colored Runa's features, but her hand remained raised.

"What the Hel? Did you transport us to a meadow?" She pointed her palm at me.

It worked? I questioned. *How?*

Forget how, just do it again. But flowery fields aren't going to work with Runa. Goodness won't hold her off. You have to access something darker, the spirit urged.

Oh, I can't use dark magic.

I'm not asking you to. I'm asking you to debilitate her. Fill her head with darkness, *not light. It's the only thing that will save your friends.*

A Unifier would never do—

Your mother did it. I saw her. Runa's spirit spoke quietly.

My mother filled someone with a dark vision? There was no way that was true.

Your mother filled many someones with dark visions, the spirit corrected. *She had to. Her job was to bring beings together, right?*

I nodded.

Well, sometimes she had to work with beings like me—a spirit whose host rejected the virtues she tried to instill. In those cases, so long as she had the consent of the spirit, your mom pressed dark visions into the host to distract it when it was on the verge of committing a truly heinous act. In stopping that act of evil, she increased the strength of the spirit's goodness. It was the only way she could preserve that being's light. And it was the only way to save them from themselves.

I processed this quickly, as Runa's hazy eyes came

into focus. Her spirit was right—the flowery field wasn't holding her off for long.

Even if my mom did that, I'm not sure I'd be able to. I've never willingly hurt anyone before—

You won't be hurting Runa. You'll just be taking her to a dark place.

Yes, but—

My protest was cut off by a blue beam shooting past my head. It struck the floor of the cell, searing a six-inch hole in the stone.

Oh, gods. She was going to kill me.

You have my consent; use a dark vision to stop Runa. Do it for me.

I didn't have time to ask what exactly constituted a *dark vision*. I grabbed hold of the first picture that came to me and lobbed it at Runa before her blue beam of death could take me down.

Darkness. I pushed the cloak of night into Runa's mind, blanketing her vision in a thick field of black. It was admittedly a softball interpretation of *dark vision,* but I hoped it would be enough.

"What did you do?" Runa screamed. "I can't see!" Her hands swung around wildly, the blue beam firing in a chaotic stream. It ricocheted off the stones of the tower, and I threw myself onto the ground to avoid being hit. The moment I broke my focus, I lost whatever connection I'd forged to Runa's brain. *No!* When I looked up, clarity colored Runa's eyes. Now she held her hands steady, pointing them directly at me.

Use something darker, Runa's spirit pleaded. *I don't want to hurt you. And I really don't want to kill your friends.*

I'd tried sending lightness. I'd tried sending darkness. With a lurch, I realized the only thing that could truly debilitate Runa was…physical pain.

Hurry, Runa's spirit begged. And I understood that in this moment, hurting Runa was the only thing that could save her spirit—could save us all. I opened my mind to hers, and consciously forged a link directly to her brain. This time, I wouldn't let it go.

I didn't have a choice.

I took a breath and strengthened the connection between our minds. Darkness charged at me, barreling down the thick tube that joined us. But I pushed it back, sending my own energy at Runa with a force that made her step back. *Here goes nothing.* I closed my eyes and set my course.

Pain. I pictured a cluster of molten lava rocks percolating like an angry popcorn ball, and pressed my vision at Runa. It funneled down the center of her body, releasing a stone into each of Runa's energy centers. *Now.* On my command the rocks exploded, setting off a fiery inferno of agony within each of Runa's centers. The tiny balls seared her from the inside out, and she cried out. My stomach curled at my action, but I knew the consequences of *not* hurting Runa would cause far greater injuries.

Pain, I pressed again, praying I had enough power to

halt Runa's destructive path. A second cluster of lava rocks made its way down her spine, depositing explosives in each of her centers. *Now.* Runa clawed at her stomach, shrieking as the new blast set fire to the nerves throughout her body. As her face contorted, the blue spark at her palm extinguished.

"What are you doing?" Runa wailed.

Harder, Runa's spirit urged.

This is horrible, I sent back.

Hurry, Before it's too late.

Runa released her hold on her torso and held up her hand. The spark flickered.

Again, her spirit urged.

I fortified our connection. *Pain.* I dialed up the intensity, mentally coating the outside of each lava rock with a jagged layer of shrapnel laced with a paralyzing venom. I pressed the fortified cluster through the cord that bound us, depositing the enhanced weapons in each of Runa's energy centers before detonating the devices. My heart tugged as I watched Runa drop to her knees, the blue flame extinguishing as she fell.

"Stop that!" She brought her hands to her head.

"I'm sorry," I whispered, as I sent another burst directly to her sixth energy center. She squeezed her eyes shut and fell to her side, writhing on the ground.

Her loss of control provided the window I'd been waiting for.

Pain. I pressed one final wave of explosives through

Runa's body as I released the cord that connected us and turned for the door. In my haste to escape, I failed to realize that breaking our bond would terminate my control. Razor-like fingernails gripped my arm before I'd taken two steps, pulling me onto the ground just before a spiky heel thrust against my chest.

"Whatever the Hel that was, it ends now." Runa panted as she spoke, wiping sweat from her forehead. "After I take out the valkyrie, I'm going to wipe out Odin's entire council. Then it's goodbye, Asgard."

"No!" I screamed as Runa stormed for the door. I scrambled to my feet and raced for the exit, trying to forge another connection between our minds. *Pain. Pain. Pain!* I sent the intention, but I was too late. In one swift movement Runa was gone, slamming the door behind her.

Stop her! I pleaded with the spirit. Its signature grew fainter as Runa raced down the stairs and out of the building.

I'll hold her off as long as I can. But that's all I can promise.

I nodded. *Just tell her how sorry I am. It's not her fault she's my first assignment. I wish I was better at this.*

Elsa...

It's true. I'm a terrible Unifier. But you know who's really, really good at their job? Forse. And if Runa just calls off this god hunt, leaves Brynn and Tyr alone, and lets me go, it will show Forse her soul is capable of choosing what's right, and he'll mitigate her sentence. Runa might be on a path she thinks she can't turn back from, but she still has a choice here. There's always a choice. And if she makes the right one, then Forse will ...hei? Are you still there?

But she wasn't. The spirit was gone, either snuffed out completely, or ported to another part of the realm by the goddess who'd seen too much loss in her life to recognize her chance at redemption. My shoulders dropped. I'd failed Runa. She'd made her choice.

She'd chosen fear over love.

I leaned back against the wall and resisted the urge to give in to the weight of my failure. Instead I scanned the room, looking for something that could help me break out of this cell. I couldn't have Forse charging into the castle; the way Runa operated these days, he'd be killed before he made it to my cell.

My eyes lit up as I saw the smoldering ember of the lava rock at the base of a sconce. Either Runa didn't know the power it held, or she was too preoccupied to bother to extinguish it. Either way, her oversight was my salvation. That rock was my ticket out of here.

Since the cell lacked any creature comforts, including potholders, I tore off the bottom of my shirt and wrapped the fabric around my hand. With great care, I picked up the rock and crossed to the window. The heat from the stone passed through the thin fabric in no time, searing my palm with its white-hot inferno. But I gritted my teeth and ignored the pain, sawing through the metal bars of the window like a crazed inmate. If Forse and I didn't stop Runa *right now*, Tyr's life would be forever changed—he'd be dead, or descending on a path to darkness that would break him.

And I couldn't let either of those things happen to my brother.

Blisters formed as I sawed through the remaining bars, dropping the rock the second I'd created a space big enough to squeeze through. Then I climbed out of the window, closed my eyes, and sent my energy to my brother.

Hold on, Tyr. We're all going to get out of here.

Elsa? Tyr's confusion resonated inside my head.

Runa's headed your way. Whatever you do, don't engage her. Grab Brynn and fly out of there right now.

I think it's a little late for that. Tyr's thought radiated tension, but I didn't have time to scan his vision screens to see what he was up against.

Just stay safe and get out as soon as you can. I'll grab Forse, and we'll port in to pick you up.

Else, I don't think—

Our connection broke as I lost my footing. I pulled my energy back from my brother and scrambled to gain hold of the rocky outer structure of the castle, digging my nails into the stones as I slid down the wall. When I'd regained control, I didn't dare focus my energy on anything but a safe descent. For the millionth time, I wished I'd gotten my brother's flying ability. *One minute. One minute and I'll be with Forse in the forest, and he can port us to Tyr and Brynn, and get everybody out of here.*

My stomach plummeted as I chanced a look down. One minute might as well have been an eternity.

Here goes nothing.

When Forse suggested we take up rock climbing last year, I'd thought he was insane. But as I descended the rocky wall of my Svartalfheim prison, I was grateful I knew the best angle to dig my rapidly chafing fingertips into the spaces between cold stones. And when I accidentally dislodged a pebble from the castle's exterior, and it took a slow eternity to plunk into the moat, I realized I'd miscalculated the tower's height. After thirty seconds of climbing, I was still fifteen-plus meters off the ground. *Oh, well.* There was no turning back now.

My toes sought purchase on a slight outcropping, and I descended with more caution than a hypochondriac in a sick bay. Odin hadn't given me my brother's flying gene, or even Henrik's semi-gene that let him jump—or fall—ridiculous distances without getting hurt. For me, one wrong move on a tower cloaked with this much dark magic would mean a stay in Asgard's healing ward...if the lower healers could even handle an injury of that magnitude.

Focus, Elsa. I pushed fear out of my consciousness and channeled happy thoughts, or at least less morbid ones, as I continued downward. *Fingers, fingers, toes, toes.* The tips of my fingers were raw by the time I made it halfway down, and I hoped any nearby drone birds weren't equipped to sniff out blood. If they were, the skin around my nails would drive them into a frenzy.

I'd made it three quarters of the way down when I heard the rustling. Something shifted in the window just above me, and I pressed myself to the tower and held my breath. After an endless pause, I chanced a look up. A deep purple bird sat on the window ledge. It turned its head as I studied it, and its eyes dilated with unnatural speed. They formed a geometric pattern and widened, almost like the aperture of a...

Oh gods. The drones found me.

There wasn't time to think about how much the landing would hurt. I bent my knees and pushed off the side of the tower. It only took a second to drop onto the thin patch of land between the tower and the moat, but in that time I heard the whoosh of the drone's wings as the bird leapt from the windowsill. It let out a cry as my legs absorbed my impact, and I knew Runa would learn of my escape soon. There was no time to catch my breath, or even remove the rock firmly lodged in the heel of my shoe. I had to run. Fast.

Despite possessing more emotional gifts than physical ones, I managed to build enough momentum to launch myself off the sooty bank at the base of the tower, and clear the width of the moat. It should have been a moment of glory for a girl who was, admittedly, more indoors inclined, but the succession of bullets chasing my heels kept my celebration in check. My toes pushed off the grainy earth as I funneled everything I had into driving forward. I pumped my arms back and forth, and focused on their movement instead of the burning sensation rising in my legs. I sorely regretted not working out every morning like Brynn suggested. She'd been right about my post-coma fitness level.

Stupid Fenrir.

The shrapnel exploding in my path jolted me from my "should haves," and I ran harder, making a beeline for the edge of the forest. If I could get under tree cover, I might be able to lose the bird, or at least evade it long enough to find Forse. He was somewhere in the trees; our paths were bound to cross if I just kept running.

A boulder exploded to my right and I darted left, running a serpentine pattern until I reached the forest. Then I put my head down and sprinted. If I hit a tree, so be it—the drone was closing in, and I couldn't afford to waste energy on something as trivial as navigation. My focus was so singular that I almost didn't hear the familiar voice calling through the trees.

"Elsa! I said get down!"

Forse's warning finally registered, and I threw myself onto the ground. The drone's wing grazed my back as it dove for the exact spot I would have stood, if not for Forse's heads-up. Another shot rang through the trees, and as I rolled I saw Forse standing at attention with his pistol pointed at the bird. It plummeted to the ground, destructing in an explosion that rained faux feathers, wires, and a shower of black-sooted soil in a ten-foot radius. I curled into a ball and covered my head so my back bore the brunt of the impact. The razor-tipped feathers pierced my skin, and a stream of pain erupted at each point of entry. My body contorted of its own accord. I writhed on the ground, careful not to roll onto my back, and even more careful not to scream. Most drones signaled their controller when they self-destructed, and I didn't want to give Runa any reason to come to this particular spot.

As if I could have kept her away.

"Elsa!" Forse's voice sounded far away. Footsteps pounded behind me, but I couldn't roll over to watch his approach. The razors sent their poison through my bloodstream, and pushing them in farther would only expedite the process. "Elsa, don't move. When I get there we'll port you to the healers and—"

"Stay back!" I yelled. A wave of darkness passed over me, alerting me to the third presence. The residual anger filling the forest confirmed my fear. "She's here."

"Who? Runa?" Forse sounded like he'd moved closer. He was almost at my side.

"I said stay back!" I pled. I wrapped my arms around my knees as a fresh wave of pain rocked my back, shooting up my neck and settling into the top of my spine. A drawn sob escaped my lips as the poison shot down my vertebrae, filling my nerves with fire before rendering me stiff.

I couldn't move.

"*Förbaskat,*" Forse swore at the same time as a sharp energy filled my body. I was jolted upward, and drawn, as if along a pulley, into the arms of the psychotic creature I'd come *this close* to escaping.

"How many times do I have to kill you?" Runa screamed at Forse. Her claw-like fingernails scraped my arms as she cuffed my hands to restrain me. It wasn't necessary; the poison had essentially left me frozen stiff from neck to toe. Only my facial muscles escaped paralysis, allowing me to watch as Forse drew his sword and charged at Runa. My avenging angel was stopped short by a blast from Runa's left hand. The beam of energy sent him flying against the thick trunk of a nearby tree, and he crumpled to the ground, narrowly avoiding impaling himself on his own sword.

"Forse!" I shrieked.

He stumbled to his feet and raised his sword just in time to deflect four more beams from Runa's hand. One ricocheted so close to her head she had to duck to avoid decapitation. As she stood, her glare intensified. Forse began to close the distance between them.

"I wouldn't do that again," she warned. "Your girlfriend can't defend herself. And it would be a shame for her to lose a limb...or worse."

Forse froze. "What do you want, Runa?"

"I told you," Runa hissed. "I want Fenrir. You gave him to me before, the day he killed the Fredriksens. I want you to do it again."

"Forse didn't give you Fenrir. You broke into his cage and turned him on my parents." As I spoke, Forse's face turned the off-white of the late-spring snow.

"You never told her?" Runa's lips pulled back in a terrifying smirk.

"Elsa, I—" Forse's eyes looked haunted. What was going on?

"Forse, give me the wolf, like you did when we were together," Runa demanded.

"He never gave you Fenrir," I repeated. "And there's no way we're turning him over now. He's too dangerous."

"I know." A cruel smile stretched across Runa's face. "Forse is the one who allowed him to kill your parents."

She was trying to bait me. I kept my mouth shut and focused on Forse's *perfekt* face.

"Don't listen to her," Forse pleaded.

"Why not? Afraid your little snowflake can't handle the truth?" Runa stepped between Forse and me, and placed her hands on either side of my face. Without the ability to fight back, I had nowhere to look but into her mud-colored eyes. "Didn't you ever wonder how your pet managed to procure the key to his cage and unlock his own door?"

"I know you stole Forse's key and set Fenrir on my parents." Despite the tumult swirling in my gut, I kept my voice void of emotion. "I know you're the reason they're dead. Is that what you want to hear?"

Runa laughed. "Oh, Elsa. You really have no idea. I'm only *half* the reason your idiot parents are no longer with us. Have you really spent all these years believing Forse would be stupid enough to let someone steal that key? Especially when that someone was *dating* the god responsible for locking Fenrir up and keeping that key safe?"

I moved my eyes back and forth, trying to see around Runa to Forse. "What's she talking about?"

"Elsa, I—" Forse interjected.

"Save your breath." Runa waved her hand. "We killed her parents together, didn't we, *Justice*? Oh, Elsa. Don't look surprised. Forse happily gave me the key."

"I didn't give you the key; you stole it." Forse circled closer. His hand flexed over the hilt of his broadsword.

"Mmm. But Fenrir was on your watch list, wasn't he? That's why the Fredriksens started keeping him caged up. And who left the key to a volatile subject's cell on his kitchen counter, when he knew his girl-friend was coming over?" Runa clucked her tongue. "A responsible god would have made sure that key was locked in his high-security vault, not just lying around where *anyone* could pick it up. What happened to Elsa's parents is as much your fault as mine."

Runa stepped aside, giving me a full view of the god I thought I knew better than anyone. Forse's shoulders drooped, and he averted his gaze. His lips turned in a tight frown, and even his eyes dimmed. Everything about him positively seethed defeat. Runa's words had struck a chord, and from the way Forse's aura turned a pale chartreuse, I knew he believed everything she said. He felt sick. He genuinely thought he was as respon-sible as Runa and Fenrir for my parents' deaths. And it very clearly haunted him.

But there was no way what happened was Forse's

fault. Runa wasn't a sociopath back when she'd dated Forse—or at least, she hadn't appeared to be. She'd fooled us all, right up until the day she'd set Fenrir on his killing spree. Forse might have left the key out, but he hadn't told Runa to use it. And he hadn't told her to unleash Fenrir, or order the dog to kill my parents. Forse might have been fooled by the goddess Runa pretended to be back then, but he would never knowingly help her hurt anyone. Especially not my parents; he loved our family too much.

Forse's energy pulsed at me, and my spirit stirred with recognition. He didn't speak a word, but I felt the truth of his intention with a knowing more intense than any I'd ever experienced. As much as Forse loved our family, he loved me more. He loved me wholly. The truth resonated in my currently-immobilized spine.

Without stopping to consider the repercussions, I closed my eyes and reached out to Forse's spirit.

Is this why you're so afraid? Of us, I mean? I asked.

I listened for what felt like ages as Forse's soul peeled back layer after layer of his carefully guarded emotions. And as I watched him shed his protections, everything that had frustrated me while I waited for Forse made *perfekt* sense. Recognition bloomed and my world turned a shade lighter. Forse had loved me all along. But he'd held his emotions back because of *guilt*. He held himself accountable for what happened to my family, and his innate sense of justice wouldn't let him embark on our relationship until he'd made this right. *That* was why he was so insistent in tracking Runa all these years. *That* was why he wanted to catch the first Bifrost out of Midgard the minute he found out where she was. And *that* was why he was so adamant that I stay behind. After everything we'd already sacrificed, he couldn't handle losing me too.

My eyelids flew open and my grin stretched so wide, my cheeks ached. "Why didn't you tell me?" I blurted.

"I couldn't," Forse whispered.

"I…" I glanced at Runa. Her eyes practically spewed venom as she watched our exchange. No doubt she'd thought her news would break my spirit enough to make me cave, but it had done just the opposite.

It had let me see the truth.

"Let me go, Runa." I kept my voice level. "Let me go and Forse will cut you a deal."

"Excuse me?" Runa spat.

"You heard me. Release me and he'll ensure Odin doesn't execute you."

Runa bent down and held her hand to my head. I shirked away from the radiant energy. "Oh, you're not going anywhere."

"Is that so?" Tyr dropped into the clearing, carrying Brynn on his back. She jumped off, and they moved in opposite directions, circling my captor. Runa watched their approach with careful eyes. Tyr took a step toward Runa and she shot a beam from her hand, forcing him to sidestep the blast. *Seriously, when will that crystal wear off?* With Runa's attention focused on Tyr, Brynn charged from her other side, but Runa moved quickly, sending a beam at the valkyrie. The cycle repeated itself twice, ending when Forse let out a roar.

"Let her go, Runa. You're outnumbered and frankly, none of us will think twice about killing you." Forse raised his sword and stormed toward my captor, his boots making determined strides in the soot.

"I told you to stay back!" Runa moved her hand from side to side, sending shots at Forse, Tyr, and Brynn. Their light magic-charged swords enabled them to deflect her beams, and my friends circled us, pounding a path only six meters away. If I could have moved my legs, I'd have kicked Runa and run to them, but the poison still had me immobilized, and a very bitter goddess was about to blow somebody's head off with her magic hand.

This was so not a good week.

"You have until the count of three, Runa. After that, your death is on you." Tyr crouched in a fighting stance, his knees bent and sword held at eye level. Forse took up the same position, while Brynn angled her rapier. "One. Two." Tyr leaned back, preparing to jump.

"Three." A deep voice boomed from the sky. I craned my neck to see an enormous figure drop in through a black portal. He landed with a thud, the weight of his eight-foot-plus, pale-skinned frame sending a deep vibration throughout the forest. A flock of birds took flight, screeching as they fled, and a chill descended over the treetops. Forse leaned into his crouch, Brynn let out a gasp, and my normally stoic brother turned the color of a fresh Asgardian snowfall.

Runa kept her hand at my head as she turned to the monster with a self-satisfied smirk. When she spoke, her voice rang of victory.

"Welcome back, Hymir."

CHAPTER 16

HYMIR ROSE SLOWLY, HIS knees no doubt tender from bearing the impact of his fall. I'd never seen him in person, but I quickly realized Tyr had downplayed his biological father's scary factor. The giant had wild white hair that stood in unruly waves, as if he'd just stuck his finger in an electrical socket. Large bulbous knots rose from pale-grey skin, and his knuckles were bloodied, as if he'd come fresh from killing something.

In all likelihood, he probably had.

Tyr held up a hand, signaling Forse and Brynn to stand down. He held his sword at his waist and walked steadily toward me. Though he was the outward appearance of calm, his voice shook with barely contained anger. "Hymir, stay out of this. Runa, give me my sister, and walk away."

Runa let out a laugh so jubilant I thought for a

moment her spirit had finally broken through the infinite layers of darkness imprisoning it.

That was me. Always the optimist.

"Accept your fate, *war god*," Runa taunted, debunking my hopeful theory. "The longer you fight this, the worse *Daddy* will make you hurt."

Hymir's barking laugh cut Runa's words short. The giant stormed toward us, his massive legs covering the distance before Tyr could reach out to pull me to safety. Hymir's thick hands closed around my neck, blocking the flow of air as he lifted me from the ground. I couldn't move my arms to fight him off; I couldn't even kick. The poison still rendered me paralyzed, and all I could do was gasp for air as my brother's face gradually shifted from white to pink to red.

Hymir didn't know who he was messing with.

"Team," Tyr commanded. "Let's kill him."

My mouth gaped as I sucked what little oxygen I could through my painfully constricted windpipe. No doubt the bulge in my eyes alerted Forse to my fear. He shifted his sword to one hand and drew his pistol. He gave me a small nod as he fisted both weapons. Relief washed over my air-starved insides as I noted the confidence in his eyes. Forse had a plan.

"Gladly," Forse said. He lifted his gun to eye level. Before he could line up his shot, Hymir's voice thundered through the forest.

"That's enough!" The deep reverberations made the trees quiver, and needles dropped onto the soot, leaving a purplish layer of foliage. Hymir kept one hand around my neck as he stepped to Runa. My vision blurred in and out of focus as Runa beamed up at him. Her smile disappeared when Hymir wrapped his other hand around her neck, holding her alongside me as if we were dispensable.

"What are you doing?" Runa squeaked, her features turning red as she struggled to breathe. My own face tingled with the thick haze of oxygen deprivation.

"Shut up." Hymir shook Runa violently, and her eyes rolled closed. She'd resigned herself to her fate, as terrible as it was. Her energy pulsed with sadness.

Are you okay? I reached out to Runa's spirit, to no avail.

"You know what I'm here for, Tyr," Hymir declared. "I hoped you'd return to me on your own. But since you're so determined to waste your abilities for Asgard, I've had to resort to Plan B."

"What is he doing?" Brynn hissed at Forse.

"No idea." Forse raised his sword again. He still held the pistol in one hand and his blade in the other, but from the look in his eyes, whatever plan he'd come up with had changed.

"Drop your weapons," Hymir commanded. "All of you." He pulled his arms apart so his body formed a cross, me dangling from one hand and Runa from the other. "If you don't comply, Son, *both* of your sisters will die."

My mouth fell open and Forse's eyebrows shot practically to his hairline. *What did he just say?*

"What did you just say?" Tyr echoed my thought.

"Oh, Tyr." Hymir clucked his tongue in a very unconvincing demonstration of sympathy. "Didn't Odin tell you about your sister?"

"Elsa's my sister," Tyr growled.

"Elsa is your *adopted* sister," Hymir corrected. "But biologically speaking…"

No. Freaking. Way.

"No," Brynn gaped.

Tyr narrowed his eyes. He glanced at me and pressed a thought into my head. *His aura's too clouded. I can't tell if he's lying. I don't remember having siblings, but our parents adopted me when I was young, and I wouldn't put it past Odin to have wiped my pre-Asgard memories under the name of "realm security"…*

I closed my eyes and scanned Hymir's energy. Sure enough, it was mottled with dark clouds and black holes. If I lingered too long, he'd suck me in, and I might never break free. Pulling back, I strengthened my protection and reached out to Hymir's spirit. *Is Runa really your daughter?*

Yesssss. Hymir's spirit spoke in a hiss, and I immediately shut down our communication. His soul was black. *Truly* black. And *not* to be messed with.

Tyr. I struggled to retain consciousness as I pressed my thought into his head. *He's not lying. But you need to get out of here. Take Forse and Brynn and port or fly or Bifrost or whatever, as far as away you can. Hymir's homicidal.*

I'm not leaving you. Tyr sounded insulted. *And I'm*

sure you realize a herd of Helbeasts couldn't make Forse port us out of here without you.

I smiled, even as I rasped for breath. *Then hurry up and kick some giant butt.*

The corner of Tyr's mouth curled up in a smirk. *Gladly.* He held up two fingers to signal Brynn and Forse. "Now!"

And then all Hel broke loose.

Forse holstered his pistol and charged at Hymir with all the fury of a raging bull. He leapt into the air, sword drawn, on a trajectory to strike the giant's chest with his blade. But Hymir swung the arm restraining me, using my body to swat Forse out of the air. Since the paralysis hadn't worn off, my stiff body vibrated like a baseball bat, waves of agony piercing my already screaming nerves. *Gods, that hurts!*

Forse hit the ground with a sickening thud, skidding across the soot toward a thick boulder. Brynn leapt in his path, pushing him to the side so his head missed the rock by inches. At the same time, Tyr leapt at Hymir, his arms flexed and his sword held high. Hymir's grip loosened enough that I was able to draw a ragged breath. As my focus sharpened, I made out the pulsing vein in my brother's neck, the clenched muscles of his jaw, and the way his normally steady hands shook with anger as he flew through the air and sliced his sword through the leathery skin of his biological father's right arm.

Air flooded my lungs and I fell to the ground in a

heap, Hymir's now severed limb releasing its death grip on my neck.

"Arugh!" Hymir let out a guttural cry. He released Runa and brought his remaining hand to his shoulder, which spewed blood everywhere. A thick stream of the sticky liquid struck my back and I rolled to the side. It took me a moment before I realized what my rolling meant. The venom had worked its way through my bloodstream—I could move!

I didn't get to celebrate for long. With a fierce battle cry, Tyr charged at Hymir, and Forse and Brynn pushed themselves up from the ground. As they moved, Runa found her footing. She held out her hand and shot a beam at my kneecap, sending an intense wave of pain coursing through me.

Forse let out a roar, and I looked up in time to see him charge Runa, using his sword to deflect her shots. She kept her hand high and alternated beams at him and Brynn, bending down to wrap her free hand through the chains that still bound my hands. As she yanked me to my feet I screamed, my injured knee buckling in protest. I dropped to the ground and flung my head back, ignoring the pain as my skull made contact with her shin.

"You little—"

Runa dropped the chain and wrapped her hands around my hair. She pulled me to a seated position then slammed my head into the ground. I ignored the sticky gush of blood through what felt like a broken nose, and threw my head back again, this time earning the crack of what sounded like a broken kneecap.

An eye for an eye...Sis.

Runa screeched and fell to the ground, giving Forse the window he needed to come to my rescue. He closed the distance between us in the amount of time it took for Runa to cradle her shattered bone. Forse lifted me into his arms and sprinted to the thick trunk of a nearby tree. My hands were still bound in front of me, but I used my fingertips to trace the firm planes of his chest as he ran, closing my eyes and inhaling the familiar scent that enveloped me like a warm blanket. I knew in that moment that everything would be okay.

"Gods, Elsa, you're a mess. Screw orders, I'm porting you out of here," Forse declared. "Tyr and Brynn can handle Hym—"

But before he could finish his sentence, a tiny black hole appeared behind him. The circle grew at an alarming speed, opening to a door-sized portal in the time it took me to gasp. "Forse! Look out!" I cried, as the hooded figure of a dark elf stepped through the blackness and back into our lives.

"Well, well, well." Tosk's voice brought our exit plan to an abrupt halt. "You couldn't just hand over the dog like we asked, could you? Maybe a gift will motivate you."

As he opened his hand and threw a bird drone at the god I'd have given my life for, I arched my back and flung my body to the side. The motion pushed Forse off-balance, pulling him out of the path of the poisoned feathers. As we landed, I rolled on top of him, covering his body with my own and bearing the fallout of Tosk's *gift*. Forse looked up in horror as my face scrunched in pain.

"Elsa, what did you do?" Moisture filled his eyes. As pain wracked my body, an uprooted tree soared through the sky behind Forse's shoulder. It landed with a thud, and Tyr emitted an enraged roar. Hymir cackled in response before launching another tree. Tyr ducked out of my frame of vision and I held my breath, praying he'd avoided the projectile. I exhaled when I heard the vicious swiping of my brother's sword—the welcome sound meant he was still alive. As he flung himself at his birth father, I turned my attention to my legs.

"I can't move. Again," I said unnecessarily, as the drone poison overtook me for the second time that day. If history was any indication it would only take a few minutes for the drug to wear off, but in the meantime I was in a world of hurt. "Go take care of business for us, okay?"

Forse brushed my forehead with his lips before he lifted me off him. "With pleasure."

As Forse leapt to his feet and reached for his implosion gun, Brynn jumped on Tosk from behind. "Nobody fake-bird poisons my friends!" she screamed, wrapping her legs around Tosk's waist and pounding his temples with her fists.

"Brynn, get off him! I can't take the shot with you there!" Forse yelled.

But Brynn continued to pummel the dark elf as if she hadn't heard Forse. If the bulging vein in her otherwise delicate forehead was any indication, she was in another zone.

"Brynn! Clear out. That's an order," Forse repeated himself. My heart thumped at his command. Sometimes I forgot he was a high-ranking titled god, and a member of Odin's cabinet.

Bossy Forse was ridiculously hot.

Brynn continued her attack as if she hadn't heard Forse.

"Brynn Aksel," Forse growled. But Brynn continued to beat Tosk. Her punches clearly annoyed him, but the weaponless assault wasn't likely to do much damage. If she'd had command of her reason, she'd have followed Forse's order and let the senior officer remove the threat, but thick pulses of anger leapt off her skin, showing me Brynn wasn't acting with her mind. She was acting with her heart.

That lapse of judgment was going to get us all killed.

"Let me try to reach her." I closed my eyes and reached out to Brynn's spirit.

Brynn, I pressed words at her. *Brynn!*

After a long pause, her spirit shook itself from the anger frenzy. With a tremendous sigh of relief, I registered its panicked reply. *What?*

You've got to calm down. Forse needs you to clear Tosk so he can use the space gun.

Nanomolecular particle accelerator, Brynn's spirit corrected.

Right. We really need you to step down. Like, right now.

Brynn's spirit pulled back with a nod, and she drew a long breath. Either she was assessing the situation or she was trying to rein in the fury that still colored her aura. Either way, her pause had the desired effect—the anger radiating from her body dimmed several notches, and while I watched, Brynn leapt off Tosk's back and rolled away from his body. "Now!" she yelled, and Forse took aim. He fired the space gun at Tosk, but Runa hurtled a beam directly in front of the elf, intercepting the bullet and diverting the implosion. A nearby tree took the hit, leaving nothing but dust in its wake.

"Förbaskat," Forse swore, and I echoed the sentiment. Out of the corner of my eye, I registered a boulder shooting into the sky. It hit the earth with a crack, just before Tyr's growl filled the forest. The swish of his sword was punctuated by an agonized cry from Hymir. Tyr must have survived the boulder attack, and dealt Hymir a painful blow.

"You're not getting rid of me that easily." Tosk's voice redirected my attention. He and Runa moved together as Brynn scrambled to her feet. Forse holstered the space gun. If Runa could intercept the implosions, she could redirect the bullets at us. The space gun was too dangerous to deploy.

It was all down to the blades.

Forse raised his broadsword, and Brynn pulled out her rapier. They positioned themselves in front of me, which gave me a small amount of comfort. Though I couldn't exactly run away, I knew Brynn and Forse wouldn't let anything hurt me. Not so long as they were still standing.

Oh, gods. I closed my eyes and called on my spirit to project calm, rational energy to theirs. We'd need every possible advantage to get through this.

When I opened my eyes, Brynn's shoulders were pulled down, and her breathing was even. Forse's posture showed a similar level of presence—they were completely in the moment, their minds clear, and our safety their primary concern. From what I could tell, neither anger nor revenge clouded either of their judgments. Their physical and emotional beings existed in *perfekt* balance.

There was just one more thing to take care of.

Ignoring the lurch in my gut, I opened my mind and linked my brain to Runa's. Dark energy pressed against me but I shoved it back, sending a different kind of vision at her. Runa had proven she operated from a place of fear—fear of losing her father's approval, fear of being alone and unloved forever. I'd failed to debilitate her by inflicting physical pain, but if I filled her with the vision of her worst nightmare come to light, maybe the emotional pain would be enough to force her into a different choice. Maybe I could make her choose love over fear.

If I failed, we were certainly no worse off than we already were. *Here goes nothing.*

Loss. I sent an image of utter desolation. In my vision, Runa sat in a filthy kitchen, aged and wrinkled and completely alone. There were no family photos lining her walls, no cards from friends taped to her refrigerator, no messages waiting on her phone. She'd lived her life without ever truly connecting to anyone, and nobody, not even her father, came to visit her anymore.

She had no one.

Runa's knees buckled as the vision surged through her. When it reached her heart, she clutched her chest and stumbled backward.

Message received.

I released the vision and pressed a different one into Runa's mind. Now a wrinkled Runa sat in the same kitchen, but this time the room was filled with the scent of a freshly cooked roast, the laughter of grandchildren, and the warmth of friendship. A large group was gathered together in the small room, their easy familiarity evoking a warm glow. I pressed love through Runa's centers, and she stumbled farther, shock coloring her features as she glimpsed a reality she'd never let herself imagine.

This can be your future, I said. *You just have to choose it. Choose love, Runa. Save yourself.*

Runa let out a low growl and drew herself to her full height. She snarled at me as she reclaimed her place beside Tosk. But something akin to confusion muddied her eyes. Some small part of her must have registered my plea.

My work was done. Now it was up to my friends.

A silent communication passed between them, and before I could blink they'd launched themselves at our assailants. Brynn leapt at Runa, her rapier swiping the air as she batted away Runa's blue beams of death. My breath caught as I watched the beams change trajectory, twice narrowly missing Forse and once coming dangerously close to my legs. But the light that smoldered in front of me was dimmer, its blue a few shades less brilliant. *Thank Odin!* The crystal was starting to wear off. If we could restrain Runa now, we might have a chance of winning this thing.

Think positive, Elsa. I regrouped. We *would* restrain Runa, and we *would* win this thing. We absolutely would.

We didn't have an option.

I pushed energy at Forse, trying to keep him grounded as he battled Tosk. Not for the first time, I appreciated that Forse's talents extended beyond the desk job I was used to seeing him perform. There was more to doling out justice than reading reports and issuing sentences. Forse was a lethal fighter. A deep sense of peace settled through my chest as I watched him attack.

We were *so* winning this thing.

While Brynn moved away from me, fending off

Runa's laser blows, the normally even-keeled Forse used both hands to swing the full weight of his broadsword at Tosk. The dark elf drew his own sword, a slimmer blade that sliced through the air with a musical tone. The weapons clashed. Forse had the height advantage, and he drove his sword down, challenging Tosk's resistance with the pent-up rage of a god who'd spent the past two days hunting down his sociopathic ex-girlfriend. Tosk's elbows buckled, and he dropped to the ground, rolling out of the way before Forse could pin him under his considerable weight. Forse swore loudly, then leapt to his feet. Tosk jumped up at the same time, and they paced a slow circle, two angry predators looking for blood.

"What's in this for you?" Forse held his sword at the ready as his feet traced the circumference of their self-drawn arena.

"I serve my master," Tosk sneered. "The better question is, what's in it for him?"

"Hymir's your master?" Forse didn't take his eyes off the elf.

"Who else?" Tosk spat. He continued his slow circle.

Forse narrowed his eyes. "Does he really think he's going to convince Tyr to become like him?"

"He doesn't have to convince Tyr of anything." Tosk let out a twisted laugh that sounded like grating nails. "Tyr *is* like him. He already brought about the fall of Asgard by keeping Fenrir alive. The wolf will begin what your *friend* is still too weak to finish. Our prophets have seen it."

"There's only one set of prophets, and the Norns haven't mentioned anything about that to me. So you're going to leave our boy—and all of his friends—alone." Forse's low tone and menacing stance made it clear his words were more command than request.

"And if I don't?" Tosk leaned back on one leg and held his blade at eye level.

"Then we've got a problem." Forse gripped the hilt of his sword and prepared for the attack. When Tosk pushed off his feet and flew through the air in a graceful arc, Forse swung. He struck the dark elf in the ribs, eliciting a sickening crack as his blade broke through bone. Tosk let out a screech, but rather than debilitate him, the pain seemed to fuel his anger. He shifted his weapon to the hand *not* nursing a broken ribcage, and struck at Forse, the blade singing with each swipe in time to my pounding heart. Forse ducked as the weapon came at his head, but he raised his shoulder to his face, and I caught the drop of blood sliding down his right cheek. He'd been hit just below the eye. And the wound didn't seem to be healing.

Tosk broke into a wide grin at the sight of Forse's blood. His head whipped back and forth and he drew a deep breath. The smell of the sticky red liquid appeared to push him into a trance, and he whirled his sword in front of him in a figure eight pattern. My throat caught as Forse stumbled, backing away from the weapon that whirled so fast it had become a silver blur. But as Forse caught his footing he glanced at me. Determination filled his features, and with a wink he lowered his broadsword so it was parallel with the ground. Then he swiped Tosk's calves in a lightning-quick move. It was enough to throw the elf off-balance, and with Forse clearly gaining the upper hand, I felt safe enough to check on my brother.

I immediately wished I hadn't.

CHAPTER 17

MY BROTHER AND HIS biological father couldn't have been more different, in virtue or in fighting style. While Hymir raged like a caged bull, uprooting trees, boulders, and everything else that came across his tyrannical path, Tyr fought almost reservedly. He'd done this long enough to understand the importance of assessing an assailant, and with each unearthed sapling mutilated by Hymir, my brother gained another grain of knowledge. While Tyr sidestepped the effects of Hymir's tirade, I knew he'd be forming a mental checklist. Right arm severed below the shoulder, so he'd be less quick to defend against a jab to the right ribcage. Trees uprooted at chest level, so Hymir wasn't inclined to bend over; possible back or knee weakness. Five out of six boulders kicked with the right foot; it would be easier to throw him off-balance with a blow to the left. Head tilted slightly to the right; an attack from the left would be less notice-able. And the aim…Hymir must have been nearsighted. He only grabbed the foliage directly in front of him, and each time Tyr stepped beyond a certain point, Hymir narrowed his eyes in concentration.

When my brother did the same, I knew he was preparing to strike. And when he lowered his head and charged at Hymir's left knee, I knew I'd read his check-list spot on. He drove his sword through the flesh just below Hymir's kneecap, then wrenched his hands to the left, slicing through flesh and tendon and eliciting a surge of blood. The thick liquid quickly covered Hymir's lower leg, and his knee gave way under his weight. He shifted to his right, but not before Tyr delivered a second blow to his thigh. Hymir howled. His left leg was all but useless, and he was down an arm. How much more would he really be able to endure?

Tyr pulled back, watching as Hymir steadied himself on one leg. He was careful to stay just out of range, so when Hymir whipped his head around with narrowed eyes, searching for the god he sought to destroy, Tyr was nothing more than a blond blur.

"Are you too scared to face me?" Hymir taunted. Yellowed teeth peeked from between lips so dry they looked like they'd been dusted with baby powder. It was an unnaturally terrifying smile, and I shivered. *Poor Tyr.* Thank gods our parents had adopted him. I couldn't imagine growing up with a father like that.

Tyr kept himself just out of Hymir's line of vision, but I could see the calculations in his eyes. He was determining the optimal strike time. And because my brother hadn't lost a battle since taking his title, I knew he'd win this one, too.

I flexed my toes experimentally, and the tiny movement confirmed that my body was forcing the poison out again. But it still had a firm grip on my mobility, and even the slight motion sent a searing wave of pain through my leg. I wouldn't be going anywhere any time soon. A quick glance at Forse confirmed that he still had the upper hand, so I shifted my attention to Brynn.

Oh gods.

Brynn was in trouble. Runa had her pinned to the ground, and although Brynn struggled beneath Runa's muscular form, the giant-daughter stabbed her with a feather from one of the drones. The venom quickly penetrated Brynn's bloodstream, immobilizing her and giving Runa the upper hand. While Brynn lay helpless, Runa ripped Brynn's dagger out of its holster. As she raised it over Brynn's heart, my spirit let out a wail.

Stop! I shouted at Runa's spirit. *You can't do this!*

A dim light flickered inside Runa, but she continued to position the dagger for optimal damage.

I said stop. The command rang from my mind. The light flickered again, and Runa seemed to hesitate. That had to be a good sign. I pressed on. *Don't do this. You still have a choice—you* always *have a choice. You may have seen nothing but darkness in your existence, but my friend,*

Mia, recently reminded my brother about the power of faith. Her pastor preached that through agency and grace, we aren't destined to be what we observe. We can become what we believe. And I'm inclined to trust those words.

Runa grimaced as the flickering light grew stronger. She pushed the dagger at Brynn's heart, but it stopped an inch above the valkyrie's chest. "What the Hel is happening?" Runa shrieked.

I know you can overpower your host. You just have to believe it with me. I pleaded with Runa's spirit. It stayed silent, but I saw the light brighten. And though Runa fought frantically to drive the dagger into Brynn's chest, her hand pulled back, as if an invisible force guided her body.

Runa's spirit was taking over.

Thank you, Elsa. The spirit spoke at last. Runa shrieked as her body was wrenched backward off Brynn and into the trunk of a nearby tree. At the same time, Brynn leapt to her feet, the poison eradicated from her bloodstream.

"Oh, I don't think so." Brynn scowled. Then she dove for Runa, who was still being restrained by her spirit. Brynn ripped a set of handcuffs from her belt and Runa's wrists shot out, presenting themselves for imprisonment.

"What the Hel?" Runa shrieked again. If the situation weren't so serious, I would have laughed at the sight of the giantess, manipulated against her will by her own inner goodness. Unifying was seriously fantastic stuff.

Brynn slapped the cuffs on Runa's wrists and dragged her to her feet. "We've got a special pit in Asgard for monsters like you," she growled.

"Don't be too hard on her, Brynn," I urged. "There's hope for her yet."

Brynn snorted. "We'll see about that."

As Brynn pulled a second set of cuffs from her backpack, Runa's spirit pressed a thought into my consciousness. *You saved me.*

You saved yourself, I corrected. The spirit smiled.

And as Forse overpowered Tosk, and Tyr battled his father for the freedom to live in peace, Runa's spirit retreated to her body. Runa wailed at the ever-brightening light emanating from within, as her spirit sent me one final message. *Thank you.*

With that the spirit went quiet, and I settled my attention on the aftermath.

"He's dead." Forse's voice was hard. He spoke with one foot planted on Tosk's limp torso, giving the hilt of his sword a violent twist.

"Good riddance." Brynn didn't take her hands off Runa. In the endless minute it had taken Forse to finish off Tosk, Brynn had my captor doubly bound and gagged.

"Isn't the gag a bit excessive?" Tyr asked, as he crossed to my side. Since I was still curled in a ball, he bent low to remove my handcuffs with a flick of his sword. "*Hei*, Sis." He touched my shoulder lightly.

Ouch.

"Last time Runa was bound, she swallowed a magic rock and got superpowers. I'm not taking any chances." Brynn glared at our captive.

"Fair enough."

"What happened to Hymir?" Forse didn't take his hands off the sword, but his vigilance wasn't necessary. As he spoke, Tosk's spirit withdrew from his body. It was black and mangled; he'd been one of the rare truly dark souls. Without looking back, the spirit shot into the sky, no doubt journeying to Helheim, where it could live among kindred spirits.

Good riddance, indeed.

"Hymir got away," Tyr said.

"What? How? He was missing an arm; don't tell me he overpowered you." Disbelief colored Brynn's voice.

"He didn't overpower me. He opened a portal and jumped through. With everything going on here, I wasn't about to leave you vulnerable by following him. I have my agenda when it comes to Hymir, but you lot come first." Tyr nodded at me.

I nodded back, understanding. "We'll get him next time."

"Odin only knows how long he'll stay in hiding, but there's no doubt he'll be back," Tyr rumbled. "He'll need to rebuild, since we took down his officers. And he'll have to regroup—he lost a limb, and he doesn't have the brain trust we do to build him a Fred." Tyr flexed his prosthetic arm. He didn't sound sorry. He didn't sound anything. Everything about him, from his stance to his voice, screamed *impassive*. He'd shut down his emotional centers, something I knew he did when he fought, and it would be a while before he opened back up again. Seeing the lengths his father had gone to destroy the goodness in his spirit—again—had to hurt. But he'd get through this. He always did. The war god was one of the two strongest gods I knew.

The justice god was the other.

As Forse pulled the sword from Tosk's corpse and tossed it on the ground, the poison *finally* released its hold on my body. I jumped up and took off across the clearing. My feet sunk into the soot as I launched myself at the god I'd loved for centuries, no longer caring if I scared him off. Life, even an immortal life, was too short to tiptoe around the truth. And the truth was, I was head over heels, heartbreakingly devoted to, and overwhelmingly in love with Forse Styrke. And he could just deal with it.

"Oh my gods, he didn't kill you!" My sentence came on one hurried breath as I flew through the air, wrapping first my arms and then my legs around the god who'd owned my heart since Freya's spin-the-bottle party centuries ago. Forse caught me easily, tucking one arm around my waist and the other underneath my bottom. The movement brought me closer to him, and as I pressed my hips against his stomach, relief gave way to an entirely different sensation. One that was sure to send Forse running for the hills.

I didn't care.

I placed my hands on either side of his head and waited for his reaction. His eyebrows shot up in surprise. But his heart thudded against my chest, confirming that no matter what his overthinking justice-god brain was telling him, he wanted this every bit as much as I did.

Finally.

"Forse Styrke, don't you ever scare me like that again." I stroked the skin along his jaw. The days-old stubble felt rough against the pad of my thumb, while the adoration in his eyes was the very definition of gentle. As he'd always be, Forse was a study in contrasts.

"And if I do?" The corners of Forse's eyes crinkled. "Then what?'

"I'm...well, I'm..."

My words faded into silence. I was lost in a grass green vortex as Forse pressed his forehead to mine and let out a low chuckle. "Enough talking. There's something I need to do."

And before I could tell him to stop laughing at me, Forse hiked me higher on his waist and brought one hand to the back of my head. He laced his fingers through my hair and pulled my face to his. With a groan, he crushed his mouth against mine in a kiss that obliterated the artfully constructed image he was careful to maintain. To everyone else, he was cautious, rational, calm...the poster god for justice, and all that it represented. But as he moved his lips against mine in a maddening dance, he confirmed what I'd suspected all along: underneath Forse's calm façade was a passion that burned brighter than all the realms' suns combined.

And it was about to consume me.

A soft moan escaped my mouth, and Forse didn't miss the opportunity. He ran his tongue along my bottom lip and nipped softly at the sensitive skin. A warm sensation shot straight through me and I wrapped my legs tighter around him, moving slowly with each gentle sweep of his tongue. He tasted like spearmint and fresh air, and as his fingers tugged at my hair I let my head fall back. Forse's lips followed the trail along my jaw and down my neck. I arched my back as he neared the deep *V* of my neckline, but before my fantasy of being ravaged by the god of my dreams could come true, my darling brother intervened.

"Ahem." Tyr cleared his throat loudly. "We should probably take our prisoner and clear out before anyone else shows up. Also, that's my little sister. Knock it off."

Forse had the decency to remove his mouth from my neck. But when he placed his hands on my hips to help me down, I locked my legs in place.

"No way." I shook my head at Forse. "I've waited *forever* for this moment. Tyr can just deal."

Forse chuckled. "He's right. I need to take Runa into custody, and we need to get you back to the compound. After I sort through Runa's intake, I'll Bifrost straight to your place in Arcata. No pit stops."

My eyes narrowed. "Promise?"

Forse dropped his mouth to mine, and delivered a sweet kiss more in line with what I'd expected of the buttoned-up justice god. Then he raked his teeth along my bottom lip and sucked with a force that let me know that, when it suited him, he could be anything *but* sweet. *Oh my gods.*

"Promise?" I panted. Again.

Forse pulled back and brought his lips to my ear. "Have I ever broken my word?"

"No," I whispered, drawing my shoulders back as the shiver traversed my spine.

"Forse!" Tyr complained.

"Right." Forse gave me a wink and I reluctantly unwrapped my legs from his waist. He set me on the ground, careful to hold my hips as my knees wobbled unsteadily. Whatever intake involved, it better be quick. I wanted to be on the couch at my cottage with the god I adored, *not* watching a movie.

I wanted that *right now*.

"Come on." Brynn yanked Runa by her elbow and dragged her to Tyr's side. "Let's get you off to Odin. Oh, the things he will do to you."

"Brynn, wait." I laced my fingers through Forse's and walked to Brynn's side. Runa glared at me, but behind the anger was sadness. Her father had used her as a pawn before abandoning her—again. And the brother she'd fought to save was about to lock her up forever. As much as I wanted to see her imprisoned so she could never hurt anyone the way she and

Fenrir had hurt all of us, a part of me felt for her. She'd been born a good spirit—she'd just been overtaken by a series of unfortunate corporeal circumstances.

Brynn held up a hand. "Don't get too close, Elsa. Last time—"

"I know," I said softly. "Just give me a minute."

Then I closed my eyes and spoke to Runa's spirit.

You won today. I smiled.

Runa's spirit nodded in recognition. *Today, yes. What if the darkness wins next time?*

Keep shining your light in there, I pressed. *Runa doesn't want to hear it, but there's goodness in her. You're in her. You'll bring her around.*

Runa let out a high-pitched shriek, muffled by the gag tied tightly across her mouth. A series of wails followed, and garbled though they were, I clearly understood the words. "Get out of my head!"

Keep doing good, Elsa. Your mom would be so proud of you. Runa's spirit sent a wave of warmth at me. I imagined it was her way of giving me a hug.

I smiled, even as Runa's shrieking grew louder.

"Okay. I'm done. But there's one more thing we need to do before you go. Tyr?" I motioned for my brother. He approached cautiously, one hand on the hilt of his sword.

"What are you doing, Elsa?" he asked.

I drew a steady breath. "Tyr, I want to introduce you to your sister."

"Whatever she used to be, she is not my sister," he

hissed. "She's as responsible for our parents' deaths as Fenrir. And she tortured you."

I held up my hand. "Runa's made some awful choices. Some *horrific* choices," I emphasized. "But once upon a time, she loved you every bit as much as I do. Didn't you, Runa?"

Runa's eyes shot veritable fireballs at me.

"Okay, fine. I'll tell him." I turned back to Tyr. "Hymir's been a monster—"

"No kidding," Tyr muttered.

"Let me finish. Hymir's been a monster all your life. When you were little, he did terrible things to your birth mother. Truly heinous things you probably would have remembered and been deeply scarred by if Odin hadn't wiped your memory, and if your sister hadn't protected you."

"What do you mean?" Tyr didn't blink.

"When Hymir went on his rages, Runa kept you hidden away. She made sure Hymir never hurt you, and she tried to keep you from seeing all of the awful things he did to the people around you. But most importantly, she's the one who brought you to our parents. She risked her own life, and gave up her family, to make sure you had a chance at happiness."

Forse tightened his hand around mine and Brynn sucked in a breath.

"I know it seems impossible, but Runa gave up everything to save you, Tyr." I watched as my brother's gaze shifted to Runa.

"Is this true?" His voice was steady, but I noticed the

slight shift of his jaw as he bit the inside of his cheek. I hadn't seen the nervous tic in years, and Tyr's sudden vulnerability tugged at my heart.

Runa raised her chin in defiance. The fury radiating from her features made it clear that even if she wasn't gagged, she wouldn't be talking any time soon.

Tyr turned his eyes back to me. "This doesn't make any sense. If Runa brought me to our parents, why didn't they adopt her, too? And when she showed up in Asgard all those years later, why didn't she come to live with us? Mom had a heart the size of Vanaheim; there's no way she'd turn away someone who needed help."

Runa let out a low growl, and Forse shifted so he stood between her and me.

"Wrap it up, *hjärtat*," he murmured softly. I nodded. I was pressing my luck by keeping her here—there was a reason protocol dictated immediate custodial intake. There was no telling what she'd do if she overpowered us this time.

"From what I understand, Mom offered to adopt Runa at the same time she adopted you. Runa turned her down—she was afraid of what Hymir would do to her mom if she left her alone. And by the time she got herself to our realm, well…that's a longer story. We can talk more about it back in Arcata. Or maybe you and Runa can talk about it while you're checking her in up in Asgard."

Runa emitted a series of shrieks that suggested no such conversation would be happening any time soon.

I frowned. Runa's spirit had its work cut out for it.

But I had hope that one day, her seemingly lost good-ness would overpower her penchant for cruelty. Without the girl she'd once been, I wouldn't have my brother. Asgard wouldn't have its war god. And the tapestry of our unconventional little family would be devastatingly different. No matter what she'd become, I was grateful for Runa. I only hoped one day she would be open to seeing that.

I took a step back and nodded at my brother's sister. "Brynn, she's all yours. Just know I'm here for you if you ever want to make a change, Runa." I watched her carefully. Runa simply glared, but behind the cold look I sensed a flicker of recognition. And that split second of honesty filled me with joy.

Maybe someday her spirit would have a shot at her own happy ending. There was good in Runa yet.

"Come on, *hjärtat*. Let's get you home." Forse picked up his sword. He tugged my hand and I followed him to an open spot in the clearing. Tyr, Brynn, and our reluctant prisoner followed suit, and we huddled close together as we prepared to leave the dark realm. Although I felt a palpable relief to be going home, I took one final look at the realm where I'd learned I could live up to the gift my mother had given me, where I'd discovered a strength I hadn't known I possessed...and where I'd truly connected with the god I knew I'd love for all eternity. When my brother summoned the Bifrost, I squeezed Forse's hand. I left Svartalfheim with a joyful heart, looking forward to a future positively teeming with faith, with hope, and with all the love I'd waited a lifetime to give.

But more importantly, I left with the god who would *finally* cherish my heart every bit as much as I cherished his.

CHAPTER 18

"OH, *SÖTNOS. COME HERE.*" Henrik jogged the distance from the porch to the clearing, reaching Brynn's side before the Bifrost could fully retract. He held out his arm and stroked her back while she bent over, her face scrunched in concentration as she tried not to throw up on his shoes. He didn't mention her Bifrost sickness as she straightened up; he just pulled her into a hug and told her simply, "I missed you."

"I missed you, too." She rested her head on Henrik's chest, her eyes closed in blissful surrender as she wrapped her arms around his waist. The color returned to her cheeks, and when she opened her eyes I surmised the nausea had passed.

"Let me take that." Henrik gently removed Brynn's backpack and slung it over one shoulder. A quiet smile passed between them, and I couldn't help but grin.

When they weren't off killing things, they were just so sweet together.

"You're home!" Mia raced down the porch steps. The early afternoon light filtered through the trees that stood sentinel around the Arcata cabin, bathing the structure in a soft glow. The warm green foliage dusted with white snow was a stark contrast to the practically all-black landscape of Svartalfheim. As I caught a glimpse of the brilliant blue sky peeking down from the treetops, my chest filled with joy. I'd almost forgotten how peaceful our little corner of Midgard was. Even if it was only temporary, I was grateful to call Arcata home.

"Brynn and I are home," I corrected. Mia's grin disappeared, and she wrapped her arms around her stomach, her nails digging into her sides.

"Oh my god," she whispered. "No."

"Oh, I'm sorry, I didn't mean that." I reached out and held Mia's hands in mine. "Tyr's okay. Better than okay, actually, which is kind of a miracle considering his...we can talk later. He and Forse took Runa back to Asgard to book her into custody. After they check her in, they've got to meet with Odin's council so the big wigs can weigh in before Forse issues her sentence. But they should be home by morning. Lunchtime tomorrow at the latest."

"Thank god." Mia practically wilted with relief.

I wrapped my arms around her and squeezed gently. "I'm sorry you have to go through this every time he leaves. I know it's hard."

"I keep thinking it's going to get easier, but it doesn't. At least this time I had Henrik to distract me with baking wars." Mia offered Henrik a smile.

Henrik threw his arm around Brynn's shoulder and guided her back to the house. "May the best cake win. And by best, I mean mine."

"You wish. Red velvet *always* comes out on top. It's a no-brainer." Mia fell into step beside Henrik and I followed a meter behind, watching the easy banter between our human and the Asgardian assassin. Mia was adjusting so well. By all accounts, she should have run away from all of our craziness screaming. But, somehow, she'd managed to take not only our existence, but our sometimes hellish reality, in her stride, fitting herself into our world as if she'd been a part of it all along.

The Norns had been right about her. She'd already proven herself a tremendous use to Asgard, just keeping my brother grounded. I could only imagine what she could accomplish once I trained her.

The familiar trickle of anxiety nipped at my gut, but I shooed it away. I didn't have to be afraid anymore. Forse had shown me that unifying could come as naturally to me as healing, and now that I had the tools to access my gift, I was eager to pass it along to Mia. With monsters like Hymir lurking, Asgard needed all the help it could get.

"Are you coming, Elsa?" Brynn held the front door open. I walked up the porch steps and followed Henrik to the living room. Brynn nestled onto the couch and

Henrik settled in beside her. I tucked my legs beneath me as I settled into the armchair, and lay my head back on the cushion.

"Where's Mia?" I asked.

"Here!" She scurried into the living room, depositing a tray laden with snacks on the coffee table. "Sorry it's not fancier—if you give me a few minutes I can whip up sandwiches. But the tea's hot, and the cookies are only about twenty minutes out of the oven, so they should still be warm. Eat. Then fill us in." Mia picked up a teeming mug and sat on the far end of the L-shaped couch. She crossed her legs at the ankle and stared at me expectantly. "Well?"

"You said I could have a cookie!" I protested.

"I'm impatient. Henrik and I have been sitting here for *two days* with nothing to do but bake." Mia handed me a cookie, then resumed her anxious pose. "Now?"

"You win." I laughed. I bit into the treat. "Mmm, this is really good!"

"It's Meemaw's red velvet cookie recipe. One point for me." Mia stuck her tongue out at Henrik.

"Whatever. Brynn, try this one." Henrik leaned forward and removed a cookie from the plate. He handed it to his girlfriend, who took a bite. She closed her eyes and let out a moan as she chewed.

"Oh, wow. White chocolate macadamia?" she guessed. "*Perfekt.*"

"Point Henrik," Henrik taunted.

Mia rolled her eyes. "Obviously this can—and will —go on for days. But before we all agree I'm the superior baker, *would somebody please tell me what happened out there?* Elsa, you look like you've been through the ringer. I can see your skin's already healing itself, but some of those bruises look pretty bad. Did things not go as easily as you planned?"

I dusted the crumbs from my fingertips and shook my head. "Henrik didn't tell you? I thought Brynn was keeping him in the loop."

"I was." Brynn looked at Henrik quizzically.

"I might have glazed over some of the more... painful details," Henrik admitted. "I didn't want worry ruining Mia's baking game."

Mia shot Henrik a look. "You guys are going to have to stop protecting me at some point."

"And that point starts now." I nodded. "Mia's going to know *everything* now that she's starting her Unifier training."

Mia let out a small gasp. "You're going to train me? I thought you weren't ready. What changed?"

"A lot." I sighed. "When Runa had me locked in that tower—"

"What?" Mia's jaw dropped.

"Runa swallowed a piece of the crystal we brought as a trade and locked poor Elsa in a tower and tortured her to find out where we're hiding Fenrir. Of course she didn't break." Brynn shot me a grin. "We'll debrief you later, Mia."

"Oh, Elsa," Mia clucked. "I'm so sorry."

"It's fine. It's over." I waved my hand.

"But what does Runa want with Fenrir?" Mia looked confused.

"Fenrir's destined to play a role in the end of the world, and Hymir wants to make sure Tyr feels the onus of responsibility for Fenrir's crime…whenever he commits it. You know, because Tyr saved Fenrir way back when. And he's keeping him alive now." Brynn shrugged.

"He's keeping him locked away," I corrected. "Even the Norns say the ribbon that binds him is unbreakable."

"Yeah, well, if Hymir's this set on using Fenrir to destroy Tyr, maybe we'd be better off if Fenrir was out of the picture," Brynn mused.

"It's worth considering." Henrik ran his fingertips along Brynn's shoulder. "But we can talk about that tomorrow. You need to heal, Elsa. The cut on your forearm is still raw."

"I gave it a good dose of restorative energy, but it's still healing slower than the others," I agreed. "It came from Runa's lightning-hand power. Gods, if you two could harness that energy, just think of the arsenal you could build."

Henrik shook his head. "Too bad you weren't able to bring any of the crystal she swallowed home."

Brynn shot him a sly smile. "After we finished our first battle with Tosk—the one where Runa took Elsa— I scoured the soot until I found shards of the broken crystal. It's in the plastic baggie in the front pocket of my backpack. Looks like someone's having a hot date in the lab tonight. You. Me. Two pieces of Svar-talfheim's finest crystal, a microscope, and a mini blow torch."

"Gods, I love it when you talk nerdy to me." Henrik lowered his head to Brynn's ear and whispered something that made her cheeks turn red.

"Henrik!" She swatted his arm.

"Okay then, you can wear the—"

"Stop it!" Brynn shrieked.

I laughed. "If you two can hold it together another ten minutes, we can finish giving Mia the overview. And then you can get into all the science geeky hanky-panky you want."

Henrik let out a long-suffering sigh. "I guess."

Brynn grinned.

"Your coms worked, by the way." I tapped my fore-arm. "Runa never knew I had mine on, and Forse was able to send me pages of my mom's journals through it. The journals helped us figure out the key to unifying. I had it all wrong. I thought I was supposed to perform energy healings to bring people together, but all I needed to do was communicate directly with their spirits. Apparently spirits are much easier to work with than blocked energy. You'll see."

Mia blanched. "You're going to teach me how to talk to spirits? Like a human Ouija board? I'm not sure that's the best idea. Mama doesn't take that voodoo stuff lightly, and frankly I'm surprised—"

I shook my head. "It's not voodoo. It's actually a lot like science. There are clear steps to take, and since you're predisposed for it, it'll come naturally to you. Besides, most spirits are good—filled with light and love. And if you come across one that's not, well, then you'll call me in, and we'll deal with it together. But that's like, years ahead. We're going to take this slow and do it right." I smiled. "We're going to need you with us for the long haul. You in?"

Mia gripped her teacup. "You know I am. It's just… well, it sounds even crazier than I imagined."

"Things with us usually are." Henrik leaned back. "But you're a tough *flicka*. You can handle it."

Mia sucked in a breath and pulled back her shoulders. "When do we start?"

That's our human. "How about after your spring break? Let's give ourselves a few days to regroup. And eat more of your *delicious* cookies. Did you say there was another batch in the kitchen?"

Mia jumped to her feet. "There are seven dozen cookies, four cakes, and two pies. Y'all left us alone for two days, and we had to pass the time somehow."

"Plus Mia's parents and brother arrive soon," Henrik reminded me. "She wanted to make sure they didn't go hungry."

Brynn tilted her head. "Your parents and brother must *really* like dessert."

"They do," Mia blushed. "But really, I just needed to keep myself busy. Henrik knew how to help me do that. Thanks," she told him.

"What are friends for?" He stood up, pulling Brynn

along with him. "Come on, ladies. Let's do some damage in the kitchen."

"Ooh, are there more of those white chocolate ones?" Brynn skipped into the hallway, with Henrik close behind. As Mia stood, I gave her a gentle smile.

"You're going to be great at all of this," I reassured her. "Tyr wouldn't have let you get involved with us if he didn't believe he could keep you safe. And I wouldn't teach you if I didn't think you'd be a tremendous asset to Asgard. You know that."

Mia clutched her cup as she followed me into the hall. "I know. But it's scary."

"I know it is. And there's more scary to come. Tyr has some family stuff he'll want to talk over with you when he gets home. He went through a lot on this mission, but he'll be okay. He's tough." I nodded.

"He sure is." Mia paused. "What about you? You faced someone who helped kill your parents. Will you be okay?"

I scanned my feelings, but found no residual anger. Only sadness. "I'll never be okay with their being gone," I admitted. "But I was blessed to have parents who loved me and Tyr with every fiber of their hearts. I always knew how adored and cherished I was. Runa never knew that. And if she continues on this path, she never will. If anything, I feel bad for her." I meant it. "I hope she realizes the value she could bring to the realms, if only she could stop trying to destroy them."

Mia looked at me for a long moment. "You're something else, Elsa. You don't hold on to anything, do you?"

I tilted my head. "Only the things worth holding on to. Like friendships. And family." I squeezed her arm. "And love. Always love."

"Speaking of, how is our favorite stubborn justice god?"

"He's good. We're good. I think we're good," I corrected. "He kissed me."

"He kissed you?" Mia squealed. "Ohmygod, where? When? Why didn't you lead with that? That's huge!"

"It was just one kiss—I don't want to get my hopes too high, but I think...after everything he went through over the past few days...maybe he's ready to give us a shot."

"It's certainly taken him long enough." Mia grinned. "Now tell me everything!"

My cheeks warmed. "Didn't you say you had some cookies for me?"

Mia laughed as she walked toward the kitchen. "I'll get the sordid details out of you sooner or later!"

"I have no doubt you will. After all, we'll be spending lots of time together in the coming months. I hope you're ready, Miss Unifier."

Mia smiled over her shoulder. "Oh, I'm ready. The question is, are you?"

I didn't have to scan my feelings to know that I was ready to embrace my new role as Asgard's Unifier, Mia's teacher, and Forse's...well, whatever we were to each other, I was ready for that, too. I was more than ready to take on *whatever* the Fates had in store for me. And I couldn't wait to get started.

I joined Brynn at the counter as Mia and Henrik each held up a plate. With a joyful grin, I picked up a cookie and toasted our little group.

"To family. Even our impossibly unconventional, insanely weird, wholeheartedly devoted mash-up of one."

Mia, Brynn and Henrik held up their cookies. We tapped them together, and they echoed my toast.

"To family."

CHAPTER 19

"ELSA! YOU'RE HERE!" A raven-haired fairy waved joyfully from the top of Alfheim's tallest waterfall. She spread her wings and leapt from her perch, leaving a trail of golden dust in her wake as she descended. Lithe feet touched down in the grass beside the pond, and Lornara raced to my side in more of a glide than a run.

It was a universal truth that fairies got all the grace.

"Lornara!" I wrapped my arms around my friend, careful not to bump her wings. "How are you?"

"I'm well, but how are *you*?" Lornara held me at arm's length. She scrutinized me from head to toe, her mouth turning down as she took in the crimson scab on my forearm. "I heard about what happened in Svartalfheim. Do you need me to heal that arm for you?"

"It's mending itself, albeit slowly, *takk*. But I do need your help with something."

"Anything." Lornara tossed her long, black curls

over her shoulder, and pointed to a bench beside the water. "Shall we sit?"

"Please." I followed Lornara to the edge of the water. With each step, her fitted dress swished against the tops of her knees in an undulating movement. Even her clothing moved like a classically trained dancer.

"What brings you to Alfheim? Besides my fabulous company, of course." Lornara lowered herself onto the bench. I followed suit, crossing my ankles as I sat.

"I need to run something by you—one new-ish High Healer to another."

Lornara smiled. "I'm glad we took on our roles at around the same time—it would have been mortifying to have to learn all of this on my own."

"It's a lot easier testing out new remedies on you than on one of the Aesir," I agreed. "You wouldn't have gotten half as mad as Forse did when I accidentally made him think he was a cat."

Lornara giggled. "Have you been practicing your Unifying on Forse too? That god has the patience of a meadow elf, I swear."

"That's why I'm here." I stared at the waterfall. "Has Alfheim selected its new Unifier yet?" When the light elves had lost their Unifier, they hadn't appointed an interim like we had. For a seemingly Zen-like realm, Alfheim had a surprisingly intense selection process... and a *lot* of paranoid peacekeeping elves.

"Not yet." Lornara dropped her voice. "And between us, I don't know how much longer we can hold out. We've been detecting irregular surges of dark energy at one of our portals. And the weather's been really strange here all winter—some of the elders think it's one of the Ragnarok markers."

I knitted my fingers together. "Brynn and I are thinking the same thing. Midgard is having a bizarre winter, too—or at least, the quadrant I'm in is; I think the European quadrant is still holding up all right. But us...we're due for our third snowstorm in Arcata this month. Third! Arcata is at sea level. In *California*."

Lornara shook her head. "Two light realms without official Unifier Keys—no wonder the dark energy is closing in."

"We have to stop it. I know I don't have the authority to do this, and I'm in no way trying to step on Alfheim's political toes, so we should probably keep this between us, but we've got to go rogue or we're never going to survive this. As Asgard's interim, I'm enlisting you to act as Alfheim's until the rightful Keys step up—or in Alfheim's case, gets elected."

Lornara paled. "I don't know if I can hold down both jobs. If Ragnarok really is near, that would mean simultaneously shouldering two full-time, life or death positions."

"Please, Lornara. You have to help me. The attacks on Asgard, the hits surrounding Tyr, the dark surges at your portals, now the winters...it's too much. We can't let the darkness win."

"I don't know how to be a Unifier. But then I didn't know how to be High Healer when we got appointed, either." Lornara frowned, probably thinking of the untimely deaths of our healing predecessors. They were killed during a peacekeeping mission-turned-ambush in Jotunheim.

"Exactly. We figured that out together—we can crack this, too. I'm starting to get a handle on it—it turns out unifying's nothing like healing. The last time we brainstormed, we thought we should try removing energy blocks." I shifted my attention from the cascading water to the wide gold eyes of the fairy beside me. "But it turns out the key to unifying is to speak directly to spirits."

"Of course," Lornara said. "Why didn't we think of that before?"

"Why didn't I read my mom's journals before is the real question. Forse pointed me to them, and the answer was in there all along. I brought one with me." I reached into my bag and pulled out the bound notebook. "I've been poring over this one, and I think reading it will help you, too. It's the first one where Mom mentions talking to spirits." I sighed. Why couldn't Keys train their successors from birth, instead of when they came of age? Or at least write everything down in a step-by-step manual? It would have made all of this *so* much easier.

"I'll read it cover to cover, and treat it with all the love it deserves." Lornara gently removed my mom's journal from my hands, freeing me from my thoughts.

"So you'll be Alfheim's undercover interim? And we'll figure this out together?"

Lornara nodded. "I'll do my best."

"*Takk.*" I let out a heavy breath. "I'll feel a lot better knowing I'm not alone. It's you and me. And Mia."

"Your brother's mortal girlfriend?" Lornara's curls fell over her shoulder as she tilted her head.

"Yes." I ran my hands along the smooth grain of the wooden bench. "Mia will be Asgard's *true* Unifier. The Norns only need me to be her stand-in until I get her trained. But I hope the three of us can stave Ragnarok off for a little longer."

"Goddess willing." Lornara studied the sky, where a thick layer of clouds gathered. "I'm not ready for the end of days just yet."

"You're telling me. I've never been on a real *date*; I'm hardly ready to die."

As if on cue, my new phone rang—the one I'd picked up in Arcata the day after my return from Svar-talfheim. I freed the device from my bag, and my face broke into a grin at the name on the screen. "Forse Styrke," I said, as I tucked the phone to my ear. "Does this mean you're finally back from Asgard? We thought it was going to take a day—what's it been, a week?" Actually, it had been two days, twenty-one hours, and fourteen minutes since Forse had left my side. But I wasn't counting.

"Not just yet." Forse's deep voice carried across the realms, sending a flutter through my heart. "Odin's council is interrogating Runa pretty thoroughly, and I'm sitting in."

"Make sure they understand that there's some good left in her—but that she's extremely volatile, and might not recognize that part of herself for a long time." I studied the clouds. They'd shifted from off-white to menacing grey.

Tell him you miss him, Lornara mouthed. My cheeks warmed as I waved a hand at her.

"Hopefully they'll finish up sometime tonight. If so, I'll have Runa booked by tomorrow morning, and be back at your place mid-afternoon. I've got big plans for you." Forse's smile came through in his voice.

"Oh, do you?" I flirted. "Big plans like dress warm because it's cold inside the movie theatre, or big plans like pack a bag because we're heading to the southern hemisphere to get away from this irrational winter?"

At Forse's long pause, my heart skidded to a stop. *Stupid, Elsa. He kissed you one time. You don't even know if he's ready for a relationship. Don't scare him off!*

"Just…big plans," Forse answered cryptically.

"Oh." I filled my second energy center with soothing light, and dialed my enthusiasm down a notch. "That's fine." *No, it's not.*

"I've got to get back to the council room, but I am *really* looking forward to seeing you."

"Me too," I said with a forced calm.

"Oh, and Elsa?"

"Mmm?"

"I love you. Just thought you should know that." Forse lobbed my words from Svartalfheim back at me, and my heart warmed with joy. The brightness filled my entire body, so every one of my energy centers glowed with happiness.

"I love you, too," I murmured. "See you tomorrow."

"See you," Forse signed off, leaving me grinning like an adolescent school girl.

"Things going well with Forse?" Lornara teased.

"Something like that." I tucked my phone back into my bag and set it on the ground. "But it's early days, and I don't want to get my hopes too high."

Lornara raised an eyebrow. "Something tells me high hopes are *just* what the healer ordered. You two have been dancing around a relationship for way too long."

"We'll see." I kept my tone light.

"You know I'm a High Healer, too. I can literally see right through you."

I burst into nervous laughter. "Okay, fine. I'm so excited. And so scared. I don't want to mess this up."

"You won't." Lornara shook her head. "It's you and Forse. Justice and Inner Peace. How much more well suited could two Asgardians be?"

"Well when you put it like that, it does sound pretty *perfekt*." I grinned back at my friend.

"Let's go back to my house and have some lunch." Lornara glanced at the sky. "You'd better Bifrost out of here before that storm hits. You don't want to be stuck in Alfheim and miss your hot date."

I stood up and tucked my bag over my shoulder. "The Bifrost works in all weather."

"Okay. Then don't you want to hurry home to pull *all* of your clothes out of your closet and stare at them for hours before settling on your ideal first date outfit?" Lornara asked.

"You got me there." I linked my arm through hers as she stood, and followed her along the bank of the pond, back to her house. The wind picked up as we moved, bringing a cold chill through Alfheim. I shivered. "Let me know when you finish reading Mom's journal so we can meet up and strategize. I have a feeling things are going to get colder before they get better."

"Probably," Lornara agreed. "But they *will* get better. Our seers don't believe the Ragnarok prophesy is set in stone. They think there's someone out there—someone who hasn't revealed herself to us yet—who may be able to stop it. And they believe there's a second female who will be the force behind maintaining peace through the realms for centuries afterwards—maybe longer."

"Herself? Female? So two girls could save all the realms from the age-old foretelling of darkness, and keep the peace indefinitely?" I paused. "I'm going to run with that."

"Me, too." Lornara nodded. "Now, let's eat. No need to worry about the end of the world at the moment."

"Deal." I followed my friend across the grass. She was right—I didn't want to think about the end of the world today. Because *my* world would officially begin tomorrow afternoon—the minute Forse came home from Asgard.

Oh, gods, I hope I don't screw this up.

CHAPTER 20

THE NEXT AFTERNOON, A rainbow-colored beam shot down in the woods. I raced around my cabin, gathering food, drinks, and my favorite picnic blanket, and set everything up in the redwood-guarded meadow behind my house. The imminent snowfall had held off, and though a light dusting covered the grove, the sky looked like it would give us at least an hour outside. I pulled my thick sweater tighter around me while I waited in the woods. It felt like an eternity between the time the Bifrost retracted and I heard Forse's voice, but at long last a familiar figure emerged from the redwoods.

"There you are, *hjärtat*." Forse walked through the trees that separated my home from my brother's. He looked so different from the last time I saw him—he no longer wore the blood-caked, black T-shirt and cargo pants. Now he wore a crisp button-down and jeans that hugged his thighs just enough to showcase the impressive muscles beneath. The fierce Asgardian warrior had been usurped by the intellectual God of Justice. I wasn't sure which Forse was hotter.

"*Hei hei.*" I rose from my picnic, smoothing out the front of my ankle-length dress as I stood. I gestured to the sandwiches, bottled Cokes, and array of desserts on the blanket. "I saw the Bifrost, and I thought you might be hungry. But if I forgot anything, I can go back inside and—"

Forse swept to my side and tucked an arm around my waist, hiking me against his chest with a strength that stole my breath. My pulse spiked as he brought his lips to mine, claiming me in one singular, indisputable moment. I wrapped my arms around his neck and pushed my fingers through his hair, relishing the feel of his waves caressing my skin. I pulled him even closer, not wanting an inch of space to separate us. Forse shifted his weight, bringing his foot forward so his leg rested between mine. The sensation of being pressed against him in such an intimate way left me light-headed, and as my knees buckled, Forse tightened his grip around me.

"You all right, *hjärtat?*" He didn't remove his lips from mine.

"Better than all right," I whispered.

"Good." Forse resumed his heated kiss. As I strug-gled to regain my balance, he moved his hips lightly against mine.

Oh. My. Gods. This was *so* worth waiting an eternity for.

"Elsa," Forse murmured as my knees buckled again.

"Mmm?"

"I missed you." Forse ran his tongue along my bottom lip. He tasted like fresh air. And mint. And home.

"I missed you, too." I gazed up at him adoringly. "My heart feels like it's missing a piece when you're away."

"That could be because I still have our soulmate stone around my neck." Forse fingered the larimar necklace resting beneath his collar, and winked.

"You know what it is?" My eyes widened. "How?"

Forse kept one hand around my waist, holding me close, while he removed the necklace with the other. I tugged my hair to the side, taking the larimar from him and fastening the clasp behind my neck.

"It turns out"—Forse fingered the crystal as he spoke—"that Freya happens to have a stash of these back in Asgard. I bumped into her when I was home, and we got to talking."

"How is she feeling?" I asked.

"Okay." Forse looked thoughtful. "She still hasn't fully recovered from her stay in Helheim, and she's concerned because she feels like her love reserves are low. She's afraid it's going to start impacting her work."

"That's not good," I tutted. "What does she think is happening?"

"She's not sure. We spent some time discussing it, and to be honest, I'm concerned, too. She's not fully herself. Maybe she needs to take a break from Asgard and work, and come spend the summer or fall with us."

"That would be really nice." I smiled. I always enjoyed my time with Freya. "Maybe I can help heal whatever's happening with her."

"I'm sure you could." Forse winked at me. "But Freya and I talked about more than her health."

"Oh, did you now?"

"Mmm. When I mentioned your necklace to her, she became quite chatty. She explained what the stone was, and told me she was the one who put it in that jewelry store window, hoping I'd get it for you. That explains the clerk's confusion when I went in to buy it. He hadn't known he had one in stock."

"Figures." I smiled.

"*Ja*. Well, Freya and I had a very interesting talk. It turns out, what I was looking for was right in front of me all along."

"Is that so?" My lashes fluttered against my cheeks.

"I'm so sorry it's taken me this long to get here. I was afraid, Elsa. Afraid that after what I'd allowed to happen to you, you wouldn't be able to trust me. I've worked since the day Runa disappeared to bring her in, thinking that if I could capture her, I could make at least partial amends for my role in what she did. Some of my culpability has been alleviated now that Odin's sentenced her—he gave her a life term, with the possibility of parole in a few centuries, on account of what she did to save Tyr all those years ago. I doubt she'll qualify though; there's no way she'll be open to the healing stipulations Odin placed on the sentence."

I reached up to stroke Forse's jaw. It was clean-shaven now, the picture of respectability, just like the rest of him. "I'm glad she at least has a chance to redeem herself. I hope she sees the value in turning her path around. But Forse," I whispered, "you didn't have to make anything right. What Runa did wasn't your fault. I've never blamed you for her choices, and I've never needed you to do anything to earn my trust."

"Freya helped me see that," Forse admitted. "And she helped me see something else, too." He set me on my feet, so my shearling-lined boots rested on the blanket. Forse stepped back and reached in his back pocket. He pulled something out, and held it in a fist in front of his chest.

I tilted my head to the side, my blond waves falling over my shoulder. "What is that?"

"It's my version of a soulmate stone."

Time slowed to a standstill as Forse dropped to one knee on the edge of the blanket, kneeling lightly amidst a sea of snow-covered ground. A cathedral of redwoods circled the spot where Forse Styrke appeared to be preparing to do something I thought it would take him centuries to be ready for. *Oh my gods. Is this really happening?*

"I should preface this by saying that my brain knows it's too soon to ask this of you. You're probably way too young to want to get married, especially to someone you've only just 'officially' started seeing." *No,*

I'm not! My spirit sang with joy. "But my heart's telling me to throw reason out the window for once in my life and just go for it. Elsa Fredriksen, I'm in love with you. I've loved you all my existence, even when I was too stupid to do anything about it." Forse's gaze was steady as he spoke. "I'm far from *perfekt*—Odin knows I've been an idiot more times than not. But you are my *perfekt* balance. Where I act from my head, you act from your heart. And when we work together, we're a force to be reckoned with."

Forse's hand shook as he opened his palm to reveal a beautifully familiar piece of jewelry.

Moisture dampened my cheeks as I took in the sight of the god I loved, on bended knee, holding my mother's wedding ring. "I haven't seen that since…"

"I know. My mom removed it when she and my dad…well, she kept it safe. I think on some level, she knew I'd be the one to return it to you. But if you aren't ready to take this step, you can just hold on to it for a few years, or centuries, or however long it takes you to catch up to where I am. I'm not going anywhere. I've waited too long to let myself love you, and I intend to be at your side the minute you decide that you want—"

"I want you." I wiped a tear from my eye. "I love you."

"I love you, too." Forse held the ring between his fingers and stared at me with an intensity that left me breathless. "Elsa, I promise to spend the rest of our existence filling your heart with all of the love you deserve. I'll cherish you with every fiber of my being, from now until forever. You are my *hjärtat*—my heart's unique match. If you'll have me, I promise to give you every conceivable happiness."

The tears coursed down my cheeks, and my necklace warmed, absorbing the energy flowing between our hearts. Gods, I loved this god.

"Elsa Fredriksen"—Forse held up the ring—"will you marry me?"

I nodded, wiping my eyes so I could commit every detail of Forse's proposal to memory. "Yes," I declared, memorizing the way his lips pressed together nervously while he awaited my answer; the way a lock of hair fell adorably against his forehead; the way his eyes crinkled in a smile as I gave my consent; and, most importantly, the way his heart settled into a steady rhythm that pulsed in time with mine as he slid the ring over my fourth finger. In that moment, the crystal at my neck emitted a glow so bright, it rivaled the Midgardian sun. "Yes," I repeated with a laugh, as Forse jumped to his feet. He wrapped his arms around me and dipped me low, his kiss sealing the choice we'd waited lifetimes to make. When he righted me, his eyes twinkled with a palpable joy.

"Jeg elsker deg, hjärtat." He pressed his forehead to mine.

"I love you, too." I closed my eyes and breathed in his nearness, relishing the sensation of Forse's heart beating against mine. After an endless moment, I pulled my head back and rested my palm against his chest. My mother's diamond sparkled brightly against the crisp white of his shirt, reflecting the rays of the late afternoon sun. As I admired it, a thought flitted across my brain. "You know Tyr's going to be angry you gave this to me."

Forse looked surprised. "Why do you think that? I asked his permission for your hand—that's why it took me so long to get to you after the Bifrost dropped. He wanted to make sure I *really* understood that if I ever hurt you, he'd kill me. He had to take me on a long walk to impart that wisdom, thought, since I showed up while he was playing charades with Mia's family. He's trying to downplay his intimidation factor for her father."

"That sounds like him." I laughed. "But if I'm wearing Mom's ring, what is he going to give to Mia?"

Forse's eyebrows shot up. "He didn't say anything about proposing."

"He wouldn't have. He knows she's not ready yet." I tapped my temple. "But I spent a *lot* of time in his head while we were in Svartalfheim, and I saw things."

"Oh, did you?" Forse tilted his head back. "That should be interesting. Has he talked to Odin?"

I shook my head. "Odin's not receptive to lifting the ban on mortal admission to Asgard...or the one prohibiting inter-realm unions. But he's going to have to be open, on both counts. Henrik, Brynn, and I talked it over this week. And I visited Lornara in Alfheim. We all agree the recent attacks aren't coincidence. They're markers—signs leading to Ragnarok."

A low sound rumbled in Forse's chest. "Gods."

"I know." I nodded. "Tyr's heading to Asgard when the Ahlströms go home, to talk to Odin about increasing protection on your dad. He knows the prophesy surrounding Balder, and he's going to do everything he can to stop it."

Forse sucked in a breath. "What about you? Have there been any new prophesies about your safety?"

I reached up to cup his cheek, his skin smooth against my thumb. "I'm meant to train Asgard's true Unifier. And help Tyr find a way around the Odin situation so he can propose. But he's got time—the Norns haven't seen an imminent threat. They only know it's coming. And Lornara and I are going to do everything we can to hold it off until Mia becomes a Key."

Forse pressed his lips against my forehead. "Well, when it comes, we'll be ready. Between you and Mia, I have every confidence you'll convince prospective perps to turn away from the darkness. And once they defect to Asgard, we'll instill in them a sense of honor and decency that will prevent them from ever striking against us."

"Spoken like the true justice god. But for now, I've got an awful lot of food that needs attention." I tilted my head at the picnic blanket.

"Food's not the only thing." Forse stared meaningfully into my eyes. "There's a certain goddess that has consumed my every thought from the minute I left Svartalfheim. And if she's okay with leftovers, I'd much rather devote my full attention to *her*."

"Well you don't seem *terribly* hungry," I mused. "And I suppose we could always pack this up and—"

But I never got to finish my thought. Forse swept me up in his arms and raced us across the snowy meadow, barreling toward my cabin without a backward glance. As he opened the front door and carried me across the threshold, my heart soared. Whatever the future held, my present was beautifully *perfekt*. I was irrevocably tied to the love of my existence, standing at the starting line of an incredible journey. And I knew that between Forse's head and my heart, we could handle any challenge the Fates threw at us.

Together.

ACKNOWLEDGMENTS

An eternity of love to my handsome husband, for being my very own *perfekt* balance. *Jeg elsker deg. Tusen takk* to our biggest little blessings, who bring us laughter, joy, and so very much love. We thank God for you.

Takk to my editor, Lauren McKellar, for keeping the *Ære* crew in line; to Stacey Nash and Kristie Cook, for being all things awesome; and to my beta readers, technical advisors, production team, and the greatest street team in all the realms for keeping me on track.

To those who introduced me to the beauty of Elsa's gifts, *takk* for bringing a new layer of grace to my worlds—both real and imaginary. *Tusen takk* to every single reader who's taken a chance on these stories—you are the reason I get to keep on dreaming across the realms, and I am so very grateful for the privilege. Thank you for sharing your reading time with me.

And to MorMorMa, for everything. *Tusen takk*, from the bottom of my heart.

Before finding domestic bliss in suburbia, internationally bestselling author S.T. Bende lived in Manhattan Beach (became overly fond of Peet's Coffee) and Europe...where she became overly fond of McVitie's cookies. Her love of Scandinavian culture and a very patient Norwegian teacher inspired her YA Norse fantasy books. And her love of a galaxy far, far away inspired her to write children's books for Star Wars. She hopes her characters make you smile, and she dreams of skiing on Jotunheim and Hoth.

Learn more about the world of S.T. Bende at www.stbende.com.

mortal is the only thing keeping her in the light, but Freya's vow to the Norns prevents her from fully uniting with her *perfekt* match. When Hel returns to finish what she started, Freya must decide how much she's ready to sacrifice to save the family she loves… and whether she's willing to give up everything for the worlds she's sworn to protect.

With the forces of darkness aligning to destroy the realms, it's clear more than just Love hangs in the balance. Ragnarok has arrived. And it's shaping up to be the *perfekt* storm.

And now, a sneak peak at the final chapter in *The Ære Saga…*

FREYA

JASON AHLSTRÖM WAS CONSIDERABLY better looking than I'd expected. The strong planes of his cheeks gave way to an impressively square jaw, and his eyes held the timeless intelligence innate in older souls. Despite the frat-boy vibe radiating off his flannel shirt and strategically ripped jeans, it was clear that Jason was a man in command of both himself and his world. The easy way he settled into the room filled with some of the most alpha-gods in the Norse pantheon proved he had no problem holding his own—a trait mortal girls must have found highly attractive. Helheim, *I* found it highly attractive.

Not that I'd ever admit it.

And somewhere in Arcata, Jason's *perfekt* match was registering said attractive mortal's presence—a fact I knew because the quadrant of my brain dedicated to my duties as Goddess of Love now flashed like a homing beacon, indicating the proximity of a matched pair. I didn't usually oversee human relationships—I'd relegated that task to the subsidiaries who served under Verdandi, the primary Norn who'd bequeathed me my matchmaking title. But Jason must have been entitled to special treatment—either because his sister was matched with War, or his union with his *perfekt* match was somehow vital to the realms—because the cue that should have gone to a subsidiary was beaming straight to me.

The back of my brain was lit up like a Midgardian Christmas tree. And it was giving me a major headache.

I threw a mental redirect at the light, sending it to the Subsidiary Norn Compound in Asgard. Then I shifted my focus to the mortal in front of me. Jason now leaned forward, his forearms resting lightly on the island countertop. He'd cocked his head to the side, studying me with an affected calm that only barely betrayed his interest. I supposed it was fair—I was the only member of Mia's friend-family he hadn't met yet. He was no doubt sizing me up. And apparently, approving of what he saw.

Too bad I couldn't say the same.

Despite Jason's confident air and admittedly attractive appearance, the foremost detail in my consciousness was that he'd once left my valkyrie to fend for herself in a sea of drunken frat boys. Proper gentleman, he was not. And in spite of the appreciative glance he was shooting my way, or perhaps because of it, it served me well to remember the kind of guy Mia's brother really was.

"Jason! Are you listening to me?" Mia's irritation turned Jason's pale, pink lips up in a half smile. He offered me his hand in affable greeting.

"Hey," he drawled, a hint of a Southern accent in his erudite voice. "We haven't met. I'm Jason."

"Freya," I said primly. My hand shot out of its own accord, the pleasantry no doubt driven by the post-nap warmth that had ebbed back into heart. "Tyr and I grew up together."

"In Sweden?" Jason wrapped a large hand around mine and gave it a firm squeeze. A spark shot up my arm as I processed the energy. Jason's grip radiated confidence. He was clearly comfortable in his skin, a trait I respected...even if I couldn't respect the human who possessed it. "Freya? Freya?"

"Uh." I shook my head. "*Ja.* Tyr and I were neighbors. In Sweden." I hoped I was remembering our cover story correctly.

"And now you're here. Are you a student at Redwood State, too?" Jason still hadn't released my hand.

"Um..." The flashing in my head continued with a vengeance. *Wake up, Subsidiaries. I have one of yours.* "Uh..."

"Freya?" Brynn turned to Henrik. "She's swaying. Maybe she should lie down."

"No, I'm…uh…"

Gods, I wished I could turn off the light show. Somewhere in Asgard, a subsidiary norn was *not* doing her job.

The flashing intensified as Jason stepped right into my personal space. He lifted the hand not holding mine to my forehead, turning the inside of my head into a disco. "You're not warm, but you're white as a ghost. And Brynn's right, you're swaying. Lying down might not be a bad idea."

Him too?

Jason's words snapped me back from the ledge, and I wrenched my hand away. "I feel fine. *Fine.*" The second *fine* came out with more force than I'd meant it to, but I was so sick of being coddled. How was I supposed to heal if everyone insisted on treating me like I was on borrowed time?

Even the guy I'd known all of two minutes.

"*I'm fine,*" I said again, this time through gritted teeth.

Jason's eyes narrowed in concern. "Sorry, love. I didn't mean to upset you. I just want to make sure you're feeling all right."

"Love? Why did you call her Love?" Brynn blurted.

My own eyebrows shot up in surprise. Had the infinitely discreet Mia shared our secret?

"He calls all girls 'love.'" Tyr pegged Brynn with a look that clearly signaled *take it down a notch.*

Right. Because 'love' was a perfectly common human endearment.

"Well, he calls *special* girls 'love,'" Mia corrected. Her giggle earned her an eye roll from her brother. "Sorry. But it's true."

"Anyway." Henrik diffused the tension with a wave of his hand. "Mia and I have been baking like crazy, so we hope you're hungry. Welcome, *kille*."

"Thanks, man. Good to see you again." Jason crossed the kitchen, skirting carefully around me and proving he wasn't entirely daft. He high fived Henrik, and wrapped Brynn in a tight hug. She squealed as her feet left the ground. "Hey, Brynn."

"I missed you!" Brynn beamed up at Jason. "When's the pool tournament? I've *so* been looking forward to watching Tyr lose again."

"Hey," Tyr warned. "I've been practicing."

"Not nearly enough, I'm sure." Jason's laughter filled the kitchen. "If I recall, my record is undefeated."

"Which is why I call you for my team," Brynn declared. "Tyr, you can have Mia."

"What am I, chopped lutefisk?" Henrik frowned.

"You and Freya can be a team," Mia offered.

"Aw, man." Henrik groaned. "Freya's mean at pool."

"I am not mean," I countered. I ignored the flip in my stomach when Jason moved back to his spot at the island. It wasn't like I could *not* notice the way his jeans hugged his butt. Or his biceps flexed against his t-shirt.

I mean, I did have eyes.

"Freya, please. Did you, or did you not bench me the last time we were paired because I missed a shot?" Henrik raised an eyebrow. "And did you or did you not tell me I played pool like a little baby? In front of Brynn. I was trying to impress her!"

"I—"

"And didn't you tell my sister her 'magic rocks' made better partners than I did?" Tyr raised one eyebrow. "Because I cost us a point?"

"Well, if you'd have—"

"Now that I think about it, you did threaten to demote me a rank if I didn't carry my weight when we played boys versus girls last month." Brynn raised her shoulders in a shrug.

"You did," Mia agreed. She shot me a wink, and I realized in their weird way, my friends were trying to make me feel better. With my attention focused on self-defense, I'd stopped swaying...and my headache had nearly gone.

Bless.

Jason's gaze moved from Henrik to Brynn before settling on his sister. He raised one eyebrow, and at Mia's tight nod, his lips curled up in a grin. "Well, this I have to see. When's the first match?"

"After lunch...and dessert. Go unpack big brother. Tyr left your bag on your bed." Mia turned to me with an innocent smile. "Freya, why don't you show Jason to his room?"

"Me?" Wouldn't someone he'd met more than five minutes ago be a better choice?

"We put him in the downstairs guest room," Mia offered helpfully.

I looked to Tyr for help. My best friend gave me a helpless shrug. *Jerk.*

"Fine. It's this way." I motioned for Jason to follow me out of the kitchen and down the hall. When we were nearly to the front door, I pointed to the bedroom directly across from the living room—the one with the view of the front porch and the impressively sized *en suite* that Mia had occupied when Fenrir was on the loose; before my time in Helheim.

It felt like forever ago.

"You're staying here." I jabbed my thumb at the guest room.

"You don't like me, do you?" Jason crossed his arms and leaned against the doorjamb. "Don't worry, love. I'll bring you around."

I raised one perfectly groomed eyebrow. "You think awfully highly of yourself."

"And you think you've got me all figured out." Jason reached out a hand to tuck an errant strand behind my ear. "Careful, Freya. I might surprise you."

With a confident wink he slipped into the bedroom, shutting me out with a soft click. My jaw unhinged as I blinked at the glossy white door. I was not letting him get under my skin. Not when, for the first time in over a year, I *finally* felt like myself.

I was Freya Skönsten, Goddess of Love and High Commander of Odin's High Order of the Battle Goddesses, the Valkyries. And nothing, not even Midgard's most arrogant mortal, was going to bring me down.

Not when Ragnarok was upon us. And absolutely everything was on the line.

Meet the Vikings (including Henrik's Midgardian relative) in VIKING ACADEMY!

When seventeen-year-old Saga Skånstad discovers an antique dagger, she's sucked into a world where Vikings rule the seas and dragons roam the skies, and the only thing more dangerous than the chief who takes her captive is the rival who steals her away.

Learn more at www.stbende.com.

www.ingramcontent.com/pod-product-compliance
Lightning Source LLC
Chambersburg PA
CBHW032106180726
48284CB00002B/473